DISCARDED
from the Nashville Public Library

SIMON
THORN
AND THE
SHARK'S CAVE

Also by Aimée Carter

Simon Thorn and the Wolf's Den
Simon Thorn and the Viper's Pit

SIMON THORN AND THE SHARK'S CAVE

AIMÉE CARTER

BLOOMSBURY
NEW YORK LONDON OXFORD NEW DELHI SYDNEY

First published in the United States of America in February 2018
by Bloomsbury Children's Books
www.bloomsbury.com

Bloomsbury is a registered trademark of Bloomsbury Publishing Plc

For information about permission to reproduce selections from this book, write to Permissions, Bloomsbury Children's Books, 1385 Broadway, New York, New York 10018
Bloomsbury books may be purchased for business or promotional use. For information on bulk purchases please contact Macmillan Corporate and Premium Sales Department at specialmarkets@macmillan.com

Library of Congress Cataloging-in-Publication Data
Names: Carter, Aimée, author.
Title: Simon Thorn and the shark's cave / by Aimée Carter.
Description: New York : Bloomsbury, 2018.
Summary: Simon and his friends from Animalgam Academy race Bird Lord Orion to find a piece of a dangerous scepter in the underwater kingdom's headquarters outside of Los Angeles.
Identifiers: LCCN 2017022319 (print) | LCCN 2017037961 (e-book)
ISBN 978-1-61963-718-4 (hardcover) • ISBN 978-1-61963-719-1 (e-book)
Subjects: | CYAC: Human-animal communication—Fiction. | Shapeshifting—Fiction. | Animals—Fiction. | Adventure and adventurers—Fiction.
Classification: LCC PZ7.C24255 Sf 2018 (print) |LCC PZ7.C24255 (e-book) | DDC [Fic]—dc23
LC record available at https://lccn.loc.gov/2017022319

Book design by Donna Mark and John Candell
Typeset by Westchester Publishing Services
Printed and bound in the U.S.A. by Berryville Graphics Inc., Berryville, Virginia
2 4 6 8 10 9 7 5 3 1

All papers used by Bloomsbury Publishing, Inc., are natural, recyclable products made from wood grown in well-managed forests. The manufacturing processes conform to the environmental regulations of the country of origin.

For Amanda and Destin

1
TAILSPIN

As a general rule, Simon Thorn didn't brag.

He didn't like it when other people bragged, and he figured they wouldn't like it much if he tried, too. Besides, he usually didn't have much to brag about. He was an average twelve-year-old with average grades and average looks, except for his shorter than average height. He didn't stand out in a crowd, at least not for the right reasons—he *had* faced a greater than average number of bullies and thought there must have been some reason they picked on him, even if he wasn't sure what it was.

But as he flew a hundred feet above Central Park, the wings of a golden eagle stretched out on either side of his feathered body, he suddenly had something to brag about after all.

A red-tailed hawk clawed through the air nearly fifty feet behind him, struggling to keep itself in the sky. It was failing miserably, and anyone watching would have thought it was the hawk's first time flying. As it happened, it had flown at least three other times before, but had yet to get the hang of it. Simon had mostly managed the first time he'd flown, and considering the hawk had dragged Simon out of his warm bed so they could see the fresh blanket of snow that had fallen overnight, he was feeling decidedly smug about the whole thing right now.

"Simon, slow down! You're flying too fast!" shouted the hawk.

"And you're trying too hard," called Simon as he swooped over to it. "You don't have to flap your wings all the time. Just let the wind carry you and your instincts take over."

"Easy for you to say. You've been flying for months," grumbled the wobbling hawk. It dipped suddenly, and Simon could hear its frightened gasp. It would have been funny if Simon weren't worried the hawk would crash into the frozen ground below.

"We should take a break," said Simon. "See that tree down there? The tall one?"

"There are *dozens* of trees down there."

"Just follow my lead." Simon slowed so the hawk would be able to keep up, and he flew to a low branch, his wings fanning out to stop the rest of his body as his talons caught the icy wood.

The hawk wasn't so lucky. It didn't even make contact with the branch. Instead, as Simon watched helplessly, it plowed head-on into a snowbank below.

"Nolan!" Simon immediately flew to the hole the bird had created, his pulse racing as thoughts of the worst ran through his head. "Nolan, are you—"

A boy with blue eyes identical to Simon's stuck his head out of the snow, sputtering. "That was *awesome.*"

Simon let out a curse that would have made their uncle Malcolm thwap him over the head. Shifting into his human form, he slumped backward against the frozen ground, his arms stretched out on either side of him like they were still the wings of a golden eagle. "I thought you were *dead.*"

"Nah, can't kill me that easily." His twin brother brushed the snow from his light brown hair, which had been trimmed last weekend. That haircut was the only difference between the two boys: Simon's hair, also light brown, was shaggy after months of not seeing the sharp end of a pair of scissors. Malcolm had tried at first, but after Simon had refused three times in a row, he'd stopped pushing.

Simon sighed. The pink sky was beginning to brighten to gold as the sun rose over the Manhattan skyline. "We need to get back before the pack starts to howl."

"We have plenty of time," said Nolan, and he stood, rolling his shoulders in a stretch. "I want to fly some more."

"You want to crash some more, you mean," said Simon.

"You need to learn how to land first. There won't always be a pile of snow to soften your—*Nolan!*"

His brother had already begun to shift. His thin body shrank, and brown feathers sprouted from his skin and clothing as his arms turned into wings and his feet curled into yellow talons. In the space of a heartbeat, his human brother turned into a golden eagle, the same form Simon had taken earlier.

"Race you!" chirped the eagle, and before Simon could argue, he clumsily took off from the snow, teetering and unstable as he flapped his giant wings.

Frantically Simon looked around, hoping no one was close enough to see what had happened. Two boys appearing from the snow was one thing, but a boy turning into a bird wasn't as easily explained. Most of the people in New York City were normal humans, but Simon and his brother were Animalgams—a secret group of people born with the ability to shift into an animal. While the city wasn't exactly the most obvious place for them to live, it was the location of the most prestigious Animalgam academy in the country: the Leading Animalgam Institute for the Remarkable, or the L.A.I.R., which was hidden beneath the Central Park Zoo. Predators from all five kingdoms attended, and while they learned about history, zoology, and how to fight in their Animalgam form, they also learned about the laws of their world. And the most important was to make sure no human ever found out about them. If anyone had spotted Nolan shift, both boys would be in a world of trouble.

The few people who populated the park this early weren't anywhere near them, though, and Simon thanked his lucky stars. Shifting back into a golden eagle, he caught a frigid breeze, climbing into the sky until he caught up to his brother.

"Where are you going?" he called. They were headed straight for the Central Park Zoo, where he could make out several gray wolves prowling the empty pathways, but they were too high to land safely.

"Where do you think?" Nolan let out a peal of laughter and flew even higher, dangerously unsteady in the headwind. Simon could barely breathe as his brother flew over the edge of the park, away from any soft landings. Instead he soared toward a skyscraper a few blocks away. A glass-domed roof reflected the rays of the early-morning sun, and Simon's heart plummeted.

Sky Tower.

"Nolan, *no*," he shouted, but his cries were lost to the wind. His brother stretched out his talons and miraculously managed to grasp on to the edge of the roof, where he swayed for one terrifying moment before finally gaining his balance.

"See? I'm getting it," said Nolan proudly, walking toward the slope of the dome. Simon landed beside him, skidding on the icy glass.

"We can't be here," he panted, his eagle head twisting as a lump of fear rose in his throat. "Orion—"

"Orion isn't here." Nolan ruffled his feathers, but at least he had the good sense not to turn back into a human. Not when they were forty stories above the pavement. "And if he were, I'd kill him."

Simon shifted his weight nervously. Orion was the lord of the bird kingdom and, unfortunately, their maternal grandfather. Despite this familial connection, he had once thrown Simon off the roof of Sky Tower, and while Simon had managed to shift for the very first time midair, saving his life in the process, that wasn't the only awful thing that had happened on that roof.

For most of Simon's life, he had been raised in the Upper West Side of Manhattan, right across from Central Park, by his uncle Darryl. Darryl had been an Animalgam, too—a huge gray wolf—which Simon had only discovered when his mother was kidnapped by an army of rats, and Simon had been forced to run away to the Central Park Zoo to try to find her.

Ultimately his search had brought him here: to the roof of Sky Tower, where Orion had murdered Darryl in front of Simon. As he perched there shaking in the freezing wind, he could see the exact spot where his uncle had died. Almost four months of rain and snow had washed away any trace of blood, but Simon could still imagine his uncle's lifeless body.

"We need to go," he said, his voice catching as he turned away. Nolan began to protest, but he glanced in the same direction and seemed to deflate.

"Oh—I forgot. Your uncle."

"Your uncle, too," said Simon hollowly, though Nolan had never really met Darryl. Shortly after Orion had killed their father, their mother had separated the infant twins to keep them safe. While Darryl had raised Simon, Nolan had been raised by the Alpha of the mammal kingdom, Celeste, who was Darryl and Malcolm's mother and had adopted Simon's father. Their mother's choice had protected them, but it had also ensured he and Nolan had not only never met, but they hadn't known about the other until they'd come face-to-face twelve years later.

A shrill cry filled the air, and Simon snapped to attention. A pair of peregrine falcons circled above them, growing closer with each lap.

"Simon and Nolan Thorn!" cried the first in a voice too human to be a normal animal. "The Bird Lord commands your presence."

A shiver ran through Simon. "I *told* you so," he said to his brother. "Come on, if we can reach the zoo before—"

"I don't take orders from Orion," called Nolan, and he spread his wings. "If you want me, you're going to have to catch me!"

The falcon screeched—or maybe it was a laugh—and Simon groaned. "You're an idiot," he said as the brothers took off together, this time heading toward the zoo. "Peregrine falcons are the fastest in the sky."

"And you're . . ." Whatever Nolan said, it was lost in the wind. Or maybe he was focused so hard on flying that he hadn't finished at all.

The falcons dived through the crisp morning air, quickly closing the distance between them. "Stop, in the name of the Bird Lord!" one shouted. Simon mentally urged Nolan to fly faster, but despite his towering confidence, he hadn't gotten any better in the past thirty seconds.

As they approached Central Park, the golden eagle in front of Simon wobbled in the wind like a toddler taking his first steps, seemingly incapable of flying and dodging skyscrapers at the same time. Ahead of them loomed an old building called the Arsenal, which marked the entrance to the L.A.I.R. If Nolan could just make it that far . . .

But the falcons were closing in, and somehow, inexplicably, his brother was slowing down. He must have been flapping too much, or maybe he'd lost his wind. Either way, Simon's insides constricted, and he knew what he had to do.

"Hey, birdbrains!" he shouted, breaking from Nolan's trail and looping around to soar straight for the falcons instead. "Mind your own business."

For a split second, the falcons appeared startled, but it didn't last long. The slightly bigger bird adjusted its feathers to meet Simon head-on. An instant before they clashed, the falcon feinted, its talon catching Simon's wing.

Burning pain tore through his shoulder, and Simon cried out as his body spun wildly, careening toward a nearby window. Dimly he could hear the falcon's laughter, and it was only through sheer instinct that Simon managed to catch himself before he broke his delicate eagle bones on the glass.

"The Bird Lord wants them alive, you fool!" yelled the smaller falcon, who was getting closer and closer to Nolan. The larger one readjusted, heading for Simon once again, but this time Simon was ready.

He pushed his wing directly into the falcon's path, throwing his opponent off balance as it tried to avoid a direct collision. Simon caught the falcon by the tail feathers and, using the golden eagle's strength to his advantage, he spun the falcon toward the nearest roof as hard as he could.

The last thing he heard from the larger falcon was a piglike squeal, and had Simon been in a better mood, he would have laughed. As it was, Nolan was still in danger, and as soon as he was sure the falcon had landed on the roof hard enough to take him out of the fight, Simon dived toward the zoo.

The golden eagle had nearly reached the Arsenal now, but to Simon's horror, the second falcon was barely a feather's breadth from catching Nolan. With an outraged scream, Simon pushed himself as fast as he could go, his body tightening and elongating as he used his momentum to plunge toward the pair. If the remaining falcon pulled on Nolan's feathers, Nolan would undoubtedly spin out of control, and he didn't have the skills to recover. This time, when he crashed into the ground, Simon had no doubt his chances of survival would be slim.

As Nolan passed over the edge of the Central Park Zoo, the falcon's beak snapped at his tail feathers. Panic swept through Simon, and his lungs burned. "You'll kill him!" he shouted.

The falcon hesitated, and that was all Simon needed. In that fraction of a second, Simon caught up to it, and he grabbed it by the wings and pulled up with all his strength, throwing the smaller bird into the empty sky and away from the struggling golden eagle. For one awful moment, as Nolan once again jerked unsteadily, Simon was sure the falcon had yanked his brother with it. But amazingly, Nolan continued on a too-fast course directly for the seal exhibit in the middle of the zoo plaza.

"Watch out!" yelled Simon, but it was too late. His brother made a splash landing in the shallow pool, his wing catching one of the large boulders looming in the center, and before Simon could do a thing, he disappeared under the water until only ripples remained.

A CRASH OF SEALS

Cold with fear, Simon landed on the metal railing surrounding the seal exhibit and immediately shifted back into a human. There would be no tourists in the park this early, and even if someone did see him, he didn't care right now.

"Nolan!" He scanned the frigid pool, his weaker human vision unable to see into the dark water. "Nolan, where—"

His brother surfaced beside the boulder, his hair plastered to his face and his eyes squeezed shut in pain. Despite this, once he'd spit out a mouthful of water, he started to laugh.

"That was the coolest thing *ever.*"

Instantly Simon's fear dissolved, replaced with blinding fury. He wasn't usually the cautious one. When it came to the adventures he and his friends had been on recently,

Simon was almost always the first one to suggest making a reckless move. But he always had a reason for it, and it was always for a greater purpose. "Are you kidding? They could have *killed* you. They could have killed *us*."

As Nolan waded over, Simon gripped the metal railing and reached out to grab his arm, only for his brother to wince again. "Ow, ow, ow," cried Nolan. "Don't, please, I'm sorry—"

Simon let go. "You're not sorry," he snapped as he gently took his brother by the other elbow and helped him climb up to the edge of the railing. "You're never sorry. Why did you want to go to Sky Tower anyway? Do you have any idea what those falcons could have done to you?"

"I knew you could take them," said Nolan, his teeth chattering. "And if you couldn't, then I would have—"

"You would have what? Shifted in front of them?" growled a voice much deeper than theirs. Standing behind Simon at the edge of the exhibit, his massive arms crossed and his bulging muscles visible even underneath his winter coat, was Malcolm.

He was tall, with broad shoulders and the kind of obvious physical strength that made even the bravest of bullies keep their distance. Not only that, but the scars that riddled his body told everyone he met that he knew how to fight and win. The first time Simon had seen him, he had been terrified of him. Now, months later, he knew Malcolm was about as likely to use his advantages against the boys as he was to turn into a peacock and start strutting. Which, considering his uncle could only shift into a wolf, wasn't very likely at all.

"I—" Nolan shivered as he perched on the railing, still cradling his bad arm. "If I had to."

"Out in the open, where anyone could see you?" Despite the deadly look on Malcolm's face, he helped Nolan to the ground. "Do you understand what would happen if you shifted?"

"He didn't, though." Simon climbed over and landed on the cobblestones with a solid *thud*. Nolan was dripping wet, and his lips, which were no longer twisted into a self-satisfied smirk, were quickly turning blue. "And they didn't catch him. I would never let them," added Simon fiercely.

Most Animalgams could only turn into a single animal and belonged to one of the five kingdoms: mammals, birds, reptiles, insects, and underwater creatures. But Nolan was special. He had the supposedly unique ability to change into any animal he wanted, a gift he had inherited from the Beast King, a tyrannical ruler who had lorded over their world and absorbed the power of countless Animalgams hundreds of years ago. Eventually the five kingdoms had banded together to defeat him, but they hadn't known about his secret child who had inherited his powers. And so, for the countless generations that had followed, heir after heir had kept their talents secret, because if the five kingdoms found out the Beast King's abilities still existed, they would undoubtedly ensure that no Beast King could rise up again and threaten the Animalgam world.

Malcolm sighed and pulled off his coat, draping it over Nolan's shoulders. "No flying until after the holidays," he said at last. "And that means during vacation, too."

"But—" Nolan started to protest, but Malcolm cut him off, bending down so they were eye to eye.

"If you can't obey the rules I set out for you, then I'll just have to tell your teachers to give you extra homework each night. Is that what you want?"

Nolan's mouth dropped open. "That's not *fair*!"

"Neither is scaring me half to death and forcing your brother to risk his life to protect you." Malcolm checked his watch. "Breakfast starts in a few minutes. We need to—"

"Can I stay out longer?" said Simon suddenly, rubbing the fresh scratches on his shoulder. "I—I want to visit Darryl."

Malcolm's expression softened, and though he pursed his lips, he nodded. "Fifteen minutes. Not a second longer, understood?"

Simon nodded and watched as Malcolm helped Nolan toward the Arsenal, with a pair of hulking wolves trailing after them. The pack was always present in the zoo during closing hours, protecting the school entrance from intruders. While normally Simon was annoyed by their presence, today, as he glanced into the brightening sky, he was grateful.

He made his way to the secluded spot, where his uncle was buried under a stone statue of a howling wolf. Beside it stood a second wolf statue marking his father's grave, but

Simon didn't linger there today. Instead he patted the first wolf's muzzle, staring up at the scar running down the statue's face. Sometimes he talked to his uncle, and sometimes he didn't. Today, the silence said it all, and he sighed into the cold morning air.

Out of instinct, or habit, or maybe even a little hope, he glanced at the base of the statue, where a loose rock stuck out. Twice he'd discovered postcards from his mother there, but his heart sank as he saw that once again, there was nothing. When he'd lived with Darryl, she had sent him a postcard every single month while she supposedly traveled the country studying animals, and it was yet another thing missing from the life he'd known. He couldn't be mad at her for leaving, though, not now that he knew what she had really been doing: searching for the pieces of the Predator, the Beast King's weapon that had given him the power to absorb others' Animalgam abilities. The leaders of the five kingdoms had destroyed the weapon and each taken one of the five pieces to hide, and now, centuries later, both Celeste and Orion were trying to put the Predator back together. While Celeste had nearly succeeded, Simon had managed to stop her—but he hadn't been able to stop Orion from kidnapping his mother, who knew where each piece was hidden.

Between Darryl's death and losing his mother, the past four months had been the worst of Simon's life. He knew his mother was alive—thanks to her last postcard, he even knew she was in LA, where the General of the underwater kingdom lived. But he was stuck all the way across the country, under the careful watch of his uncle and a pack of wolf Animalgams who knew most of his tricks by now.

"Hey, Simon!" called a member of the pack, a wolf who was usually a curly-haired woman named Vanessa. "Your fifteen minutes are almost up. Aren't you cold?"

"A little," he admitted. He was already frozen through his thick down jacket, but he had been determined to visit. Each day he didn't see his uncle, he felt guilty, even if he knew Darryl wasn't really there anymore. If, somehow, Darryl did know, Simon never wanted him to think he'd forgotten him. He may not have had any memories of his father, but he had a lifetime of his uncle, and some days—most, if Simon was being honest with himself—he couldn't fully accept the fact that there would never be more.

Simon gave the statue one more pat before following the wolf back to the warmth of the Arsenal. A steep staircase led deep beneath the building, and he ran his fingers over the wall to keep his balance. The secret door at the bottom of the stairs opened up to a massive cavern that was as big as the entire zoo, and the pentagon-shaped school stood on the opposite side of a moat filled with piranhas, jellyfish, and Simon's least favorite—sharks.

Thankfully it seemed mostly empty now, save for a few schools of fish doing morning drills, and Simon hurried across, his stomach rumbling. His friends would be at breakfast by now, and maybe telling them about the trip to Sky Tower would ease the knot of anxiety in his chest. Nolan's stupidity still rankled at him, and it was the only thing keeping him from mentally berating himself for his own idiocy. It had been a close call—too close. Simon knew better than anyone that Orion was trying to put the pieces of the weapon together for one reason and one reason only: to kill Nolan and steal the Beast King's powers.

Unbeknownst to Orion, though, Nolan wasn't the only one who had inherited those abilities. Simon had them, too—a secret no one but his mother and closest friends knew, not even his uncle and brother. For now, all he could do was use them to hunt down the pieces and protect his brother. But if the five kingdoms ever discovered that there were two living Beast King heirs, they would tear the entire Animalgam world apart until Simon and Nolan were both dead.

To Simon's relief, as soon as he entered the noisy dining hall, he spotted a familiar shock of blond hair. Jam's head was bowed as he buried his nose in a novel, and Simon grabbed some breakfast before hurrying over.

"You won't believe what Nolan did this time," he said, setting his tray down with a clatter and nearly upsetting his juice. "We were flying, and—"

"Say that a little louder. I don't think the mammals heard you." Ariana dropped her own tray onto the table. Her hair was a freshly dyed shade of royal blue, and she flipped it over her shoulder as she slid into a chair beside Jam, who still didn't look up.

Simon frowned. She was right—they may have known

his and Nolan's secret, but the other students had no idea, not even Nolan's close friends in the mammal kingdom. And Simon had to make sure it stayed that way. Just because he was angry didn't mean he could be careless, and he dropped his voice so only his friends could hear him. "We were flying—"

"Did you not see me in the hall, Simon?" A girl with long dark hair sat beside him. Winter only had a glass of juice, and without asking, she stole a pancake off Simon's plate and dipped it in his syrup. "You walked right by me."

"I—sorry," he said, sheepish. In his defense, Winter was very short. "It's been a long morning. You won't believe—"

Ariana elbowed Jam in the ribs. "We're here."

"What?" Jam snapped his head up, clearly startled to see them. "I—oh. Hi."

Simon exhaled slowly. "Hi, Jam. Good book?"

"Great," he said, though his tone was anything but enthusiastic. Closing the cover, he added, "Have they posted it yet?"

"Five minutes ago," said Ariana. "You're fifth round. Winter's fourth. I'm going in the first round, naturally, and of course Simon advances straight to the finals—"

"What?" Giving up any hope of telling his friends what had happened that morning, Simon sat down. "Finals of what?"

All three of them stared at him, and if Simon hadn't been used to having no idea what was going on, he would have been embarrassed.

"Haven't you been paying attention?" said Winter. She reached for another pancake, and Simon didn't bother stopping her. "The midwinter tournament. They posted the order today."

It was Simon's turn to look at her blankly, and she rolled her eyes. "You know what a tournament is, right?"

"We all fight the other members of our kingdom in the pit one by one," cut in Ariana, who was somehow already halfway through her breakfast of fruit and toast. "Whoever wins the last round in their kingdom advances to the finals, where they fight until only one's left standing. It's a huge deal, especially if your kingdom wins."

Simon blinked. Fighting in the pit was the school's version of sport—where students battled in their Animalgam form to not only learn their own strengths, but also to learn other kingdoms' weaknesses. And he hated it. He wasn't very strong in his eagle form, not against predators from the other kingdoms, and he was always worried he would accidentally shift into another animal and give his secret away. "What do you mean, I advance straight to the finals?"

"You're the only member of the bird kingdom in the L.A.I.R.," said Winter as if it were obvious. Simon supposed it was.

"But—I don't want to," he protested.

"Then lose your first round and you won't have to anymore," said Ariana with a shrug. Before Simon could come up with a response, she focused on Jam. "You're awfully quiet. They'll probably let you guys fight in the water, you know."

Jam shrugged. He was a dolphin and a member of the underwater kingdom, which always had a disadvantage in the sand-filled pit. "None of us have ever won the tournament. I'm not worried."

"Then what's wrong?" she said. "Were they out of your favorite sushi again?"

With his expression pinched, Jam pulled out a sealed envelope from between the pages of his book. "The General wrote me."

"Your dad?" said Winter. "What's so bad about that?"

"He hasn't written since we got back from Paradise Valley," said Simon, instantly understanding the anxiety on Jam's face. While Simon had never met the General of the underwater kingdom, he'd heard all about him from Jam, and he was strict—far stricter than any parent Simon had ever encountered, and his silence over the past six weeks had become painful for Jam. "Have you opened it?"

Jam shook his head. "Couldn't. What if he pulls me out of school? What if he makes me attend one of the academies at home? What if—"

Ariana plucked the envelope from his fingers. Without preamble, she ripped it open and began to read.

"Hey!" cried Simon, trying to snatch it away from her, but Jam just stared at the table.

Ariana had to stand up in order to keep it out of Simon's reach, but she scanned the letter, her eyes widening. "It's an official summons."

Jam groaned and buried his face in his hands. "I knew it."

Winter stood and peered over Ariana's shoulder. "Stop complaining. He just wants you home for the holidays."

"He'll find an excuse to keep me there, and you'll never see me again," said Jam miserably. "Goodbye, friends. Goodbye, free time. Goodbye, everything I've ever loved—"

"You're more dramatic than I am," said Winter, sitting back down.

Jam shook his head. "You don't understand what it's like there. Everything's scheduled down to the last second. Exactly five minutes to get dressed. Two minutes to brush my teeth. Five minutes to use the toilet—"

"We get it," said Ariana. As she sat back down, she handed Simon the letter. "But winter break is only two weeks. You'll survive."

"Without you guys? I'll be shark chum within the hour," mumbled Jam.

Simon scanned the letter. It was typed up, and there was a very official-looking header declaring it from the desk of the General of the underwater kingdom of North America. Part of him expected a long message, but it was only a couple of lines long.

> OFFICIAL SUMMONS for Benjamin Fluke to return to Avalon. Report to General Fluke at 1800 hours on 21 Dec. Expected to remain through 1100 hours on 04 Jan.

It wasn't even signed. Simon set the letter down on Jam's open book. "Where is Avalon?"

"Near Los Angeles," said Jam, eyeing the letter like it was about to bite him. "Off the coast."

An idea began to form in Simon's mind. It couldn't have been more perfect if he'd planned it himself, and he looked between his friends, leaning in. "Are you thinking what I'm thinking?"

Jam blinked behind his thick glasses as it dawned on him. "Simon—*no*."

"We have to go there eventually," insisted Simon. "This is exactly the excuse we've been waiting for."

"The General's already mad enough. He'll never let me bring friends."

"He's right, Simon," said Ariana grimly, drumming her fingers against the table. "The underwater kingdom is notorious for being closed to members of the other kingdoms. It even takes a special request for my mom to visit."

While Jam's father was the head of the underwater kingdom, Ariana's mother, the Black Widow Queen, was head of the insect and spider kingdom. Even Celeste, who had been the Alpha of the mammal kingdom up until September, was afraid of her. And as far as Simon knew, no one ever told her no.

"They especially hate reptiles and birds," said Winter, who was still disgruntled about inheriting the ability to shift into a cottonmouth snake rather than a bird. "Even if the General did let Jam bring friends, you and I would never be allowed in."

"So—I'll hide," said Simon. "We have to go. Orion's

been there for over a month now. Sooner or later, he'll figure out where the General hid the underwater kingdom's piece, and then—"

He stopped short. What felt like a brilliant idea was quickly crumbling, but he needed to get to LA. His mother had tasked him with finding the hidden pieces before anyone else could get their hands on them, and the Bird Lord was close—too close. And he was sneaky. If he had the right ally working for him, they could already be too late.

"I'm sorry, Simon," said Jam, and he really did sound it. "There's nothing I can do."

"Please, just ask him," he said. "If he says no, then—okay. But this might be our only shot. You know how important this is, Jam. You all do. It isn't only about my mom anymore. It's about the entire Animalgam world."

"I know," mumbled Jam, staring at his plate of untouched breakfast. Finally, with a heavy sigh, he said, "Okay, I'll ask. But if he says no—"

"It's not like you can get into any more trouble," said Winter, stealing the last of Simon's pancakes. He was so relieved that he didn't even mind.

"Thanks, Jam," he said. "I owe you big-time."

"You don't owe me anything," said Jam. "We're friends. But I *will* expect you to write me if the General keeps me under house arrest until I'm an adult."

"Every day," promised Simon. But as frightened as Jam was of his father, they both knew they had bigger things to worry about. Whatever it took, they had to find the underwater kingdom's piece of the Predator. The Beast King's weapon could only be destroyed when it was assembled, and in order to do that, they couldn't let a single piece fall into Orion's hands. Even if it meant facing the wrath of a very angry General and the entire underwater army, Simon had to take that chance. They all did.

3

WINGING IT

Nolan reappeared in their History of the Animalgam World class later that morning, sporting a sling and a story about falling down a staircase as he and Simon had raced to the bottom. Simon had started to protest, especially when he saw the way Nolan's friends were glaring at him, but he supposed it was a step in the right direction. Only a few months ago, Nolan would have told everyone that Simon had pushed him.

Finally, once wheezy Mr. Barnes had finished his lecture on the seventeenth-century feuds between the many divided factions of the insect kingdom—which, as Ariana liked to point out, also included arachnids and other creatures most people would just call *bugs*—Simon followed

Jam toward the underwater kingdom's section of the L.A.I.R. That narrow corridor was, as far as Simon was concerned, the coolest part of the school. The glass hallway was surrounded by water, and everything from schools of fish to the sharks that guarded the moat swam past, going through the daily training drills the members of the underwater kingdom had to endure. It was no secret how much Jam hated the regimented life of his kingdom, but Simon thought the views might have made up for it.

They ducked down the trapdoor that led underneath the tunnel, into the section where the students slept. Rather than head to the dormitory, Jam led Simon to an office that smelled of sardines. A hulking man with a neatly trimmed moustache sat behind a desk, his size giving the impression it was meant for a child rather than a full-grown man.

"Sir," said Jam at the threshold, saluting the man—a great white shark Simon only knew as the captain. "Apologies for the intrusion, sir. Permission requested to make a phone call, sir."

The captain didn't bother looking up. "Is it an emergency, soldier?"

"I—" Jam glanced at Simon and swallowed. "I received an official summons from the General, sir, and—yes, sir. It's an emergency, sir."

The captain exhaled and grudgingly said, "Very well, soldier. Permission granted."

Jam saluted once more and backed out of the doorway.

"Come on," he said quietly to Simon. "The phone booth is this way."

Jam showed him a cramped booth with a stainless steel phone hanging from the wall. It had barely enough room for a single person to sit down, so while Jam dialed, Simon stayed outside to make sure no one was around to overhear. He wanted to go to LA so badly that he felt nauseated, and the possibility that the General would say no ate away at him. Worst case, he supposed he could sneak away during winter break and fly to California. It wouldn't be fun living off whatever golden eagles liked to feast on—rats and small animals, more than likely, and he probably would have known if he'd bothered paying attention in zoology—but he could do it if he had to.

"Ma'am, this is Private Benjamin Fluke, ma'am," said Jam into the receiver. He didn't sound like the quiet but confident bookworm he was at school; instead his voice quavered, and as Simon watched, he paled. "I'm calling for General Fluke. Yes, ma'am. I'll hold, ma'am."

Simon caught his eye, and he flashed Jam a thumbs-up. He knew it was completely unhelpful, but he didn't know what else to do. It was his fault Jam was in so much trouble to begin with, and now he was practically forcing his friend into digging the hole even deeper.

"Sir!" Jam's voice rose an octave, giving him the impression of a squeaking mouse. "Yes, sir, I received your—yes, sir, I'll be—yes, sir, eighteen hundred hours—yes, sir, I know what I did was—"

Jam grimaced and held the phone an inch from his ear. In the quiet hallway, Simon could hear a booming voice yell what sounded like a well-rehearsed lecture, though Simon couldn't make out what he was saying. Not that he needed to. No doubt he was ranting about the impromptu trip they'd taken to Arizona to find the reptiles' piece of the Predator. They'd succeeded, and it was currently hidden underneath a fake bottom Simon had created in his sock drawer, but while Ariana's mother hadn't seemed to mind, clearly Jam's father did.

At last Jam said in a meek voice, "Yes, sir. I won't do it again, sir. May I—" He swallowed hard and glanced at Simon. "May I make a request, sir? May I bring friends home to celebrate the holidays with us, sir?"

A moment passed, and Jam pressed his lips together, inhaling slowly. "Simon Thorn, sir. The Alpha's nephew. And Ariana Webster, sir, the Black Widow Queen's daughter. And Winter Rivera, the—" He winced and pulled the phone away from his ear again. "Yes, sir. The Bird Lord's adopted—yes, sir. But—but she doesn't have any contact with him anymore, and—"

Another beat, and Simon inched closer to the opening of the booth, knowing better than to hope, but he wasn't willing to give up yet. The General had to say yes. If he didn't . . .

"I thought it would be a good idea, sir. Future leaders of the five kingdoms, sir. The more time we spend together—"

Jam's expression fell, and another long silence passed.

"Yes, sir. I understand, sir. No foreigners inside the city, sir. I apologize for asking you to break protocol, sir."

Simon's heart plummeted. The answer was no. He tried to keep his expression as neutral as possible, not wanting Jam to feel bad when Simon was the one who'd pushed him into this, but it didn't matter. Jam refused to look at him.

"Yes, sir. I won't be late, sir. Eighteen hundred hours, sir." With that, Jam slowly hung up the phone, gaze still focused on his shoes. "I'm sorry, Simon."

"It's all right," he said, even though it wasn't. Jam had done his best, and he couldn't be mad at him for that. "We'll find another way. Maybe I can hitch a ride in your suitcase. Or maybe—"

"You don't understand. Security is too heavy, and the General has entire armies at his command, including at least seven different battalions of sharks. You'll never sneak in, Simon. It's impossible. Believe me, I've spent my whole life trying to sneak out. It just won't work."

Jam sounded so utterly defeated that Simon stopped himself before he blurted out something painfully optimistic. Jam knew Avalon better than any of them. If he said there was no way, then there was no way.

While he did his best to cheer Jam up, Simon spent the rest of the day in a fog. He had to do *something* to stop Orion from getting the underwater piece. Even if it was dangerous, even if Jam thought it was impossible, he still had to try. Sometime in the middle of Tracking and Survival, he found himself deeply upset at the universe for ever putting him in this position. He didn't usually complain, not really, but it was all becoming too much. How was he supposed to keep these secrets, save the world, *and* do his homework on time?

After his final class of the day ended, Simon trudged toward the Alpha's section, but before he could reach it, a breathless boy named Tomas ran up to him. "The Alpha wants to see you right away," he panted, readjusting the black armband that had slipped down to his elbow. On it was the silhouette of a grizzly bear.

"He does?" said Simon, panic edging toward him. "Is everything okay?"

Tomas nodded. "He's in the pit."

Simon all but ran down the hallways, his mind whirling with possibilities. Had the General called and told him what Jam had suggested? Had something happened to Nolan or his mother?

By the time he reached the sandy pit, he was so tense that his muscles ached from the strain, and he burst in on two dozen students from the mammal kingdom as they took turns throwing each other. They all turned to stare at him, and Simon's face grew hot.

"Pay attention!" called Vanessa, who must have been overseeing the training. Most of the students returned to their drills, and Simon spotted Malcolm at the top of the spiral staircase that led to the upper floor. His uncle leaned against the railing, watching them with a strange look on his face. But he didn't look frightened or upset, the way Simon would have expected if it were anything bad. The fist around his stomach loosened its grip as he began to climb up the bleachers.

"Hey, birdbrain!" called Garrett, who was a year older than Simon and much, much bigger. While he was one of Nolan's best friends, he'd never forgiven Simon for humiliating him multiple times, and he always had an insult to throw. "Spying on us before the tournament? You know that's illegal, right?"

"I'm not spying," called Simon halfheartedly. "I already know what you can do, and it's not exactly something to brag about."

The other students laughed, but Simon didn't dare turn around to see the hateful look that was inevitably on Garrett's face. With immense reluctance, Simon trudged up the steps, ignoring the jeers from the students below.

"I don't really have to fight, do I?" he said miserably. "They'll eat me alive."

"You have to learn how to survive a fight with the other kingdoms, Simon," said his uncle without so much as glancing at him.

"I already know how," he said. "Fly away."

Malcolm chuckled, even though Simon hadn't meant to be funny. "Your mother would be proud to see you in the pit. She was an excellent fighter."

"Is," corrected Simon. "She *is* an excellent fighter."

His uncle's smile fell. "I meant that she was an excellent

fighter when we all attended the L.A.I.R. But yes, you're right. No doubt she's only gotten better since then."

An uncomfortable silence settled between them. While Simon loved his uncle, they didn't know each other very well, and the subject of his mother was a touchy one. "Tomas said you needed to see me," he said cautiously. His uncle finally looked at him and frowned.

"I received an interesting call this afternoon."

"Oh?" he said, his voice breaking. Self-conscious, he cleared his throat. "I bet you get a lot of interesting calls."

"Not as interesting as this one," he said. "General Fluke informed me that his son apparently wanted to bring you and your friends home with him for the holidays."

His mind raced. "Yeah. Jam's really worried about going home after the whole Arizona trip, and—and we thought it'd be good for us to go with him. Moral support and all."

"Mm. I see. Moral support." Malcolm raised an eyebrow. "It wouldn't have anything to do with Orion being spotted nearby, would it?"

Simon exhaled sharply. "He was? How close is he? Is he still there?" The moment he spoke, he regretted it, but he couldn't take it back. Instead he watched his uncle, not bothering to disguise his hope. Every day he worried Orion might have found the piece and moved on, but if the General himself said he was still there . . .

His uncle slouched. "I know you want to find your mother, Simon. I want to find her, too. But running across the country on a wild-goose chase isn't going to help bring her home."

"It might," said Simon. "It's worth a shot, isn't it?" But even as he said it, the words felt sticky in his mouth. Sending the packs after Orion meant sending his uncle after Orion, too, and Simon had promised himself he would never put another member of his family in danger again. Besides, his mother didn't actually *want* to be rescued. When he had tried in Arizona, she had gone back to the Bird Lord, insisting she was better off leading him away from the real pieces. That had hurt more than Simon wanted to admit, and part of him still ached at the memory of her flying away from him to return to Orion. But as much as he hated it, she was right. Her misdirection was the only thing that would likely buy Simon the time he needed to find all five pieces.

Malcolm let out a low growl. "You know it's too dangerous—"

"I know," he mumbled. "I don't want anyone else to get hurt. I just—I want to see her, that's all. I want to make sure she's okay."

"It isn't safe for you to go anywhere without me," said Malcolm. "You and Nolan learned that the hard way this morning. He won't be flying again any time soon. At least not using his wings." He grimaced, the lines in his face deepening for a moment. "The General has called an emergency summit with the leaders of the remaining kingdoms to discuss the situation with Orion. Apparently something your friend said to him struck a chord."

A tiny ember of hope sparked inside Simon, and he looked up at his uncle, hardly daring to believe it. "An emergency summit? You mean—"

"You, me, and Nolan will be spending our Christmas in the generous hospitality of the Fluke family."

Malcolm's expression soured, but it took everything Simon had not to whoop with excitement. It had worked. They were really going to Avalon.

Except—

Simon's enthusiasm faded. "Nolan's coming, too?" he said.

"Of course. We're not leaving him behind."

That would be a problem, though Simon wasn't entirely sure how much of one yet. Maybe Nolan would be miserable about spending Christmas in California and sulk the whole time. Or maybe he would insist on following Simon everywhere. Hard to say.

"Your friends have been invited, too," added his uncle. "The General wants Jam present for the summit, and the Black Widow Queen has apparently requested the same of Ariana."

"What about Winter?" said Simon. "She doesn't have anywhere to go for the holidays."

"I know. I explained the situation to General Fluke, and while he's . . . reluctant, he did agree to let her come along."

He straightened to his full height. "The General wants to meet as soon as possible, so we'll be leaving tomorrow."

Tomorrow. That meant they would miss the tournament. "Good," said Simon with a touch too much ferocity. Malcolm chuckled and started down the spiral staircase.

"I'm postponing finals until January. Sorry, Simon," he added. "One way or the other, you're going to have to fight."

As Simon watched his uncle join the mammal students, a heavy weight settled over him. Malcolm had no idea how true that was, but Simon was the one who was clueless about what Avalon and the underwater kingdom would bring—or where in the vast Pacific Ocean the General might have hidden his piece.

4
MOUSETRAP

"What do you mean, I'm not coming?" squeaked Felix after dinner that evening. The little brown mouse perched on the edge of the bed while Simon threw some clothes into a suitcase he'd borrowed from Nolan.

"It's too dangerous," said Simon. "Jam said if you get caught—"

"I don't care. I want to come with you."

"Why?" said Simon. "You hated flying the last time, remember? I had to clean up mouse vomit from my socks. So why do you want to take two flights this time?"

"Because—" Felix sniffed, and he pulled indignantly on his tail. "You're going to LA. Do you have any idea how many television shows they film out there?"

Simon sighed. Though Felix was a normal mouse—if

not a little smarter and sassier than Simon would have preferred sometimes—he had a penchant for watching television, a luxury he couldn't indulge in while at the L.A.I.R. Simon didn't know what he did all day to amuse himself while Simon was in training and his classes, but he did know that almost every evening, Felix made sure Simon knew exactly how bored he was. And how many episodes of his favorite series he had missed.

"We're going to Avalon, not LA," said Simon. "It's not the same place."

"Close enough." Felix sat back on his haunches. "Like it or not, I'm coming with you. Now, what's the plan?"

There was no use arguing with him when he got like this. The last time Simon had refused to let him come, he'd sneaked into his backpack, and Simon still shuddered every time he thought about how easy it would have been to accidentally crush him without ever knowing he was there. At least this way, Simon would have time to come up with an excuse if the underwater kingdom caught him. "I'm going to look for their piece while everyone else is busy with the summit. Malcolm will expect me to try to find Orion, not go underwater. If he asks, I'll tell him I wanted to go swimming."

"What if that's what Orion's waiting for?" said Felix. "You to show up and lead him right to the piece?"

Simon hesitated. He hadn't thought of that. "Orion doesn't know I can shift into anything I want. He'll be looking for a golden eagle, not a shark."

"Unless he figures out that you *are* the shark. Then your secret's out, and everything gets a million times worse than it already is."

Felix was right, as much as Simon hated to admit it. He frowned. "Maybe he'll think I'm Nolan."

"Not when any idiot can tell the difference between you two," said Felix. "You have a perfectly good identical twin, yet you insist on keeping your hair longer than his. How is anyone supposed to mistake you for each other if you look different?"

Simon touched the ends of his shaggy hair. "You think I should let Malcolm cut my hair?"

"I think if you're banking on anyone mistaking you for Nolan, you're gonna have to." Felix stood on his hind legs, nose sniffing the air. "I smell food. You're holding out on me."

Simon pulled a napkin from his pocket and opened it, producing a few crumbling crackers. "If you keep eating like this, you're never going to find out how your shows end."

Felix shrugged, his mouth already too full to reply. Simon pulled open his sock drawer and, after emptying his socks onto his bed and shoving several pairs into his suitcase, he gingerly undid a nearly invisible latch and lifted the false bottom. Hidden beneath the wooden panel was a notebook full of his mother's scribbles on the Beast King, research she and his father had done together, as far as Simon could tell. He had also tucked away the pocket watch she had given him the night she had been kidnapped, which boasted the Beast King's crest. Simon wasn't sure why she'd insisted on him having it, but it had been his father's, and he had discovered a strange thing in Arizona: it grew warm whenever it was around a piece of the Predator.

As a result, Simon had wrapped the reptiles' piece in an old sock on the opposite side of the drawer, though that foot or so didn't seem to make much difference. Both were hot to the touch. Reluctantly, though Simon slipped his father's pocket watch into his jeans, he left the piece where it was. It wasn't the most ingenious hiding spot ever, but he couldn't risk taking it to Avalon with him, either. The fake bottom in the drawer would have to do.

As soon as Simon finished packing, he went to find Malcolm. Despite the evening hour, he was in his office on the upper level of the school, and he waved Simon inside while he completed a phone call, a deep line furrowed between his brows.

". . . not even a teenager. How—" He paused and glanced at Simon. "We'll speak when I arrive. But this discussion isn't over. It would be a burden for anyone, let alone—" He stopped again and sighed. "Fine. I'll see you tomorrow, Colonel. Give the General my regards."

As soon as he hung up, Simon said, "What's going on?"

"Nothing you need to worry about," said Malcolm, even though he looked worried enough for the both of them. "What can I do for you, kid?"

Simon hesitated. Now that he was here, he was reluctant

to go through with it, but he knew it was necessary, especially now that Nolan was tagging along with him. "I was wondering . . ." Simon paused and touched the ends of his hair. The last person who had given him a haircut was Darryl. This felt wrong, but logically he knew his hair had nothing to do with remembering his uncle. He could let it grow out as much as he wanted, but Darryl would still be dead. "Do you have time to cut my hair before we leave?"

Malcolm's expression softened. "Sure," he said, pushing his chair back. "Just let me get a pair of scissors."

Simon nodded and sat still, trying not to let guilt eat away at him. It was just a haircut. And if it meant that Orion wouldn't be able to tell which twin he was, then it would be worth it.

The next morning, Simon tucked Felix into a box in the corner of his borrowed luggage, making sure the mouse had plenty of food for the trip and that clothes weren't covering the air holes before he zipped up the bag. With his suitcase in one hand and his backpack slung over the opposite shoulder, he headed down the spiral staircase and into the atrium of the Alpha section, which was carpeted with real grass and full of trees that reached toward the high ceiling. It was originally supposed to be the bird kingdom's section, but after Orion had attacked and nearly destroyed the original location of the L.A.I.R., the Academy had not only moved to their backup school beneath Central Park, affectionately called the Den by staff and students, but the mammal kingdom had taken charge and banned all birds from attending. Simon was the lone exception, and even then, he wasn't really a member of the bird kingdom. He, like Nolan, was a member of every kingdom and no kingdom at the same time.

The door to the rest of the school opened, and Winter walked inside, pulling a fancy roller suitcase behind her. The wheels got stuck in the grass, and she huffed, leaving it where it was. "Is Simon down yet?" she said curtly, looking him straight in the eye.

"What?" said Simon, confused. "I'm right here."

She did a double take. "Oh. *Oh*. You finally got your hair cut." Leaning toward him, she squinted. "The resemblance is uncanny."

"We *are* identical," he said. "Where are Jam and Ariana?"

"Jam said he had to do extra drills before we left, since we're missing some school, and Ariana's probably hanging from a rafter somewhere listening to a conversation she isn't supposed to hear. I'm sure they'll be here soon. You know this is a terrible idea, right?"

"What's a terrible idea?" said Simon, running his hand through his shortened hair. The back of his neck was cold, and his ears felt strangely exposed.

"Going to Avalon. I know why you want to," she added quickly as Simon opened his mouth to object. "But this is way more dangerous than infiltrating the reptile council. The underwater kingdom is a military society, and they take punishment for breaking their laws very, *very* seriously. They don't care if you're an adult or not. If you're old enough to shift, then you're old enough to be held accountable for your actions. And considering how many laws they have, I assume we'll be breaking at least a dozen before this is over."

"I won't let anyone else get into trouble because of this," said Simon. "I promise."

Winter shook her head. "You can't keep making promises like that, Simon. We're going to help you any way we can. You know that, we know that, and there's no point pretending we're not all risking something by doing this. You're risking a lot just by showing up, you know, considering how much the General hates Orion."

"So we both hate my grandfather. That's a good thing," said Simon.

"It doesn't matter. Everyone thinks you're a bird," she pointed out, lowering her voice. "At least Nolan's pretending to be a mammal, so they'll be decent to him. But birds are about as welcome in Avalon as the plague. Reptiles, too," she added. "The reptile kingdom and the underwater kingdom have been fighting over amphibians for as long as they've both existed."

Simon stared at her. "Amphibians?"

"You know. Frogs, toads, salamanders, other gross, slimy things that look like reptiles but live part-time in the water—"

"I know what amphibians are. Why are they fighting over them?"

Winter shrugged. "It's stupid, but both kingdoms keep claiming them, and they've fought countless wars over it. Just—be prepared for them not to like both of us, all right?"

Still baffled, Simon nodded. "Guess it won't be that much different from school, will it?"

Winter snorted. "At this rate, nothing ever will be."

A few minutes later, Jam and Ariana arrived. Jam's face was pale, and Ariana had dark circles under her eyes. While Simon knew what Jam was worried about, he couldn't figure out what might have made Ariana lose sleep.

"Are you okay?" he said.

"I'm fine. Just tired," she muttered, refusing to meet his curious gaze. Simon glanced at Jam and Winter, but neither of them seemed to be paying attention.

"Here, let me carry your bag," he said, reaching for it, but Ariana's grip tightened on the handle.

"I'm tired, not helpless," she snapped. Simon dropped his hand sheepishly.

"Sorry, I just—I want to help."

Her expression softened. "Sorry," she mumbled, tucking a lock of blue hair behind her ear. "I called my mom really late. About going, I mean. She seems to think this is a good idea, but . . ."

Ariana trailed off, her forehead wrinkling. It took Simon a moment to realize why she might be worried about visiting the underwater kingdom, but once he did, he felt like an idiot.

"It won't be that bad," he said. "You won't have to go near the ocean if you don't want to."

Ariana gave him a strange look. "Don't you remember what Jam said?"

"When?" said Simon, puzzled.

Before Ariana could reply, Nolan bounded down the staircase, with Malcolm trailing after him looking worse for wear. Apparently Ariana wasn't the only one who hadn't gotten much sleep last night.

"I can't *believe* we're spending Christmas in California," said Nolan, practically buzzing with excitement. His arm was still in a sling, and Malcolm carried his suitcase for him. "This is going to be the best Christmas *ever*."

At least someone was happy about it. Simon offered him a wan smile. "First one we get to spend together, too."

Nolan's grin faded, and he eyed Simon up and down. "You look different."

"I look like you," he said. "Haircut."

"A good one, too, if you ask me," said Malcolm, patting Simon on the back. "Everyone ready?"

"As ready as we'll ever be," mumbled Jam. "Let's get this over with."

The ride to the airport was a long one in the early-morning city traffic, and by the time they reached their gate, the plane was boarding. The flight to Los Angeles was six hours long, and during those six hours, none of them spoke much. Even Nolan seemed to sense the tension between them, and he spent most of the flight with his nose in a stack of comic books he'd brought along.

Simon, on the other hand, alternated between trying to read his book, watching his friends anxiously, and doing his best not to worry about how they would get the underwater kingdom's piece of the Predator. He couldn't shake the feeling that they had gotten incredibly, impossibly lucky in Arizona. This time, the piece could be anywhere in the Pacific Ocean, if it was anywhere near Avalon to begin with.

California was much warmer than snowy New York, and Simon peeled off his coat inside the SUV the General had sent for them. They passed rows and rows of palm trees, pink and yellow buildings that reminded Simon of Arizona, and at last, miles of white sand beaches where the sun shone so brightly that he had to squint as he peered out the window.

"This is where you grew up?" said Simon to Jam, who had his eyes closed as if he were pretending they were anywhere but here.

"Sort of," he mumbled, cracking open an eye. "We're almost to the harbor."

"How are you so pale?" said Winter. "If I lived here, I'd be out in the sun every day."

"And you claim you're nothing like the other reptiles," said Ariana with a smirk. That made Winter's expression sour, and she turned to face her.

"You know Avalon's on an island, right?" she said nastily.

"And you know what that means, right? We're gonna have to go on a *boat*."

Oh. That's what Ariana had been talking about, Simon realized—Jam had said that Avalon was off the coast of California, not on it. No wonder she was so anxious.

Nolan, who sat on the other side of Jam, laughed. "That's right. You're afraid of water, aren't you?"

Now it was Ariana's turn to pale, and she crossed her arms. "I'll be fine," she muttered, even though she didn't sound it.

"Uh-huh. How many times do you think she'll puke?" said Nolan to Simon. "I bet you it'll be at least twice—"

"Let it go, okay?" said Simon. "Unless you want me to tell them what happened when you jumped into the polar bear enclosure."

Nolan gave him a nasty look, but at least he shut up, and they spent the rest of the drive in relative silence. By the time they reached the harbor, Ariana looked like she would be proving Nolan right, and this time she didn't protest when Simon carried her suitcase to the speedboat that was waiting for them.

A man who looked eerily similar to a pirate with his stringy black hair and leathery skin stood on the stern, and he helped them over the gap between the dock and the edge of the vessel. "Benjamin," he said with a curt nod as Jam hopped aboard without any help.

"Dampier," said Jam dully. "These are my friends. Simon,

Nolan, Winter, and Ariana, and the Alpha of the mammal kingdom, Malcolm Thorn."

Rather than greet them, Dampier merely sniffed and pulled up the anchor effortlessly. "Best be on our way. The General's in a foul mood today."

"How long until we get to Avalon?" said Malcolm, following Dampier to the controls.

"Forty minutes, with this weather," he said, eyeing the waves. "Best hold on."

"Forty *minutes*?" said Ariana, turning a sickening shade of green. Dampier took one look at her and tossed her an empty bucket.

"If you get my deck dirty, you're cleaning it up, missy."

Ariana clutched the bucket and didn't say another word throughout the trip. She was, however, sick in it twice and once overboard, and Simon felt so sorry for her that he held her hair back every time. It was his fault she was here, after all, even if they'd all known they would have to get the underwater piece of the Predator eventually.

It was the longest forty minutes of Simon's life—and probably Ariana's, too. By the time the silhouette of an island came into view, he was fairly sure she was minutes away from passing out. Still, he couldn't stop himself from staring as the boat neared a circular harbor and the little town of Avalon.

It looked like something out of one of his mother's postcards. Dozens upon dozens of boats floated in the sparkling blue water, and green mountains loomed above the town, as if sheltering it from whatever lay beyond. Avalon itself was tiny compared to the cities Simon was used to, and he couldn't help wondering where the rest of it was.

"This is where the General of the underwater kingdom lives?" he said, skeptical. As stunning as it was, especially in the bright California sunshine that had made the back of his neck grow hot, it didn't look much different from any number of seaside towns Simon had seen in movies. He couldn't imagine this being the center of one of the five Animalgam kingdoms.

"The General?" Dampier snorted as he navigated the boat to a pier near the edge of the harbor. "He only comes here when he has to. Don't know much about us, do you?"

"Not really," said Simon. But considering he'd only discovered Animalgams existed four months ago, he thought he was doing pretty okay so far.

Ariana was the first off the boat, practically taking a flying leap onto the marina. Simon followed, watching the colony of seagulls that was beginning to circle them. Maybe that was normal seagull behavior, but considering Orion was close, Simon doubted it. A shiver ran through him. How long would it be before the Bird Lord knew they were in Avalon?

"Might want to keep that bucket, missy," said Dampier as he helped Malcolm with their luggage. "This was the easy part."

"What's he talking about?" said Ariana to Jam, who pursed his lips and averted his gaze.

"I'm sorry," he said. "It's against the law to tell anyone. It's how we keep outsiders away."

"Away from what?" she demanded. He shuffled his feet. "Away from *what*, Jam?"

Just then, a huge swell rose up not ten feet from the dock. At first, Simon had no idea what it was, but as they all stared, the water slid away, leaving a submarine bobbing on the surface.

"My family doesn't really live in Avalon," said Jam. "We live in Atlantis."

"Atlantis?" she said, her voice trembling. "Like—like the underwater city?"

Jam nodded, and before anyone else could say a thing, Ariana fainted.

5

ATLANTIS

Ariana wasn't unconscious long, but once she came to, it took another twenty minutes for Malcolm to coax her into the submarine. By the time she shakily climbed aboard, tears streaming down her cheeks, Dampier was grumbling about schedules, and Simon was struggling to resist the overwhelming urge to sock him in the nose.

"It's not that bad," said Jam desperately as the submarine descended underneath the surface. Ariana clung to Malcolm, hiding her face in his chest as her shoulders shook with silent sobs. "It's all enclosed. You can walk around and breathe like normal."

"Except it's surrounded by water," said Winter, who, despite their bickering in the car, was suddenly on Ariana's side. "We could have let her stay in Avalon, you know."

"I'm sorry," said Simon, feeling about as guilty as Jam looked. "I didn't know. I wouldn't have—"

He stopped short. He couldn't say he wouldn't have asked them to come if he'd known, not in front of Malcolm and Nolan. Besides, he knew Ariana. Despite her phobia, she would have come anyway. It was the surprise, he thought, that probably affected her most—the lack of time to prepare herself for facing her greatest fear.

It didn't matter what he said, anyway. It wouldn't make a difference. Simon sat nearby as she continued to hide in Malcolm's protective embrace for the entire trip below the surface, which lasted nearly as long as the boat ride had. And when he looked out the porthole and his heart fluttered with excitement at the dark water around them, he somehow felt even worse. He had no right to be enjoying this when it scared Ariana so badly.

The tension broke abruptly, however, when Nolan shouted from the other end of the submarine, where he hovered near a porthole. "Guys, come check this out!"

Winter was the only one who darted over, and her jaw dropped as she looked through the glass. "Simon, you have *got* to see this."

Reluctantly Simon slid off the bench and joined them. "What am I supposed to be—" he began, but as soon as he peered through the porthole, he stopped.

Though they were deep enough now that very little sunlight penetrated the dark waters, the submarine approached a dome that shone with glittering silver light. It looked like a giant snow globe, thought Simon, but instead of a cottage or polar bear inside, there was an entire underwater city.

Atlantis.

Silver buildings rose high from the ocean floor, and several tubes ran through the giant enclosure that let out into the open ocean, acting like highways, judging by the array of underwater animals swimming through them. Though he couldn't make out much decoration, everything was uniform in color and seemed to be organized into columns and rows. Outside the city in the glowing waters that surrounded it, entire brigades of sea creatures swam drills in unison, including jellyfish, dolphins, stingrays, swordfish, and—Simon gulped—great white sharks.

The submarine slowly navigated one of the wider tunnels at the bottom of the dome, and soon enough it stopped completely, a loud sucking sound echoing through the metal body. The door opened in the ceiling, and one by one they climbed onto the air-locked dock, where a squad of soldiers stood at attention to greet them.

Standing in front of them was a woman who looked like she might've been in her early twenties. She was dressed in a blue military uniform, her brown hair pulled back in a bun, and Simon spotted a horizontal scar on her cheek. As they approached, she didn't smile. "Alpha," she said to Malcolm. "Welcome to Atlantis. I am Colonel Rhode. We spoke yesterday."

"Colonel," said Malcolm with a terse nod. "I remember. I take it the General is waiting for us."

"He is. I'm afraid we're already running late, so if you would come with me. Soldier," she added by way of greeting, barely glancing at Jam.

"Colonel," he squeaked. Simon wondered what that was about, but he didn't have time to ask before they began to hurry into the city at a brisk pace. All Simon could see at the edge of the dome were the tops of several towering gray buildings hovering above the wall that separated this area from the city, as well as one of the wide passageways full of water that let out fifty feet above their heads. It was oddly colorless and not at all what he might have expected from an underwater city, and he would have been disappointed if he'd let himself think about it.

As they followed Colonel Rhode, the squad of soldiers surrounded them. An uneasy feeling settled in the pit of Simon's stomach, and he leaned in toward Jam. "Is this normal?" he whispered, and Jam shrugged.

"Not really, but it isn't normal for strangers to be invited, either." Jam frowned. "Just go along with it, all right? Don't upset them."

Right. Don't upset the soldiers with guns holstered to their hips. Simon's apprehension grew as they moved beyond the wall and into the city proper. It was gray building after gray building, with no pictures or art or advertisements anywhere. The only color came from the blue street signs, and Simon noted they were on Pacific Way.

At last they entered a wide silver tower. It seemed bigger than the rest somehow, looming over them with spectacular foreboding, and as Simon stepped inside the large foyer, the temperature seemed to drop. The walls were mirrored, giving the impression that the room was somehow endlessly replicated over and over again, stretching out into infinite darkness. And to make matters worse, inside the otherwise empty foyer stood another group of soldiers, each more intimidating than the last.

"You'll all have to go through a security inspection to earn entry," said Rhode. Malcolm raised an eyebrow, and she added, "Standard protocol, I assure you."

In pairs, they stepped up to the guards, who searched their luggage and waved a metal detector wand over them. Malcolm and Nolan went first. Even though Malcolm was the Alpha of the entire mammal kingdom, by the time he'd finished, he'd lost his belt, boots, and the contents of his pockets. His duffel bag was searched thoroughly as well, and only grudgingly did the soldier hand it back to him. Even Nolan didn't escape scrutiny, though it turned out he had nothing they deemed dangerous. If they only knew, Simon thought to himself.

Jam passed through easily, but security proceeded to remove several small blades, lock picks, and other metal devices from Ariana's pockets and luggage, making Simon wonder exactly how she'd gotten it all through airport security. By the time she was done, they had even forced her to remove her necklace, which turned out to be a secret penknife.

"I know exactly what's there," warned Ariana. Her face was still blotchy and puffy from all the crying, but otherwise she seemed to have pulled herself together now that they were inside the city.

"Your belongings will be returned to you at the end of your visit," said Rhode in a no-nonsense voice, but even she was eyeing Ariana's contraband warily.

Simon and Winter were last. While the others lingered near the door, waiting for them, the soldiers gave Simon an embarrassingly thorough pat down. As Simon reluctantly handed over his pocket watch for inspection, he found himself relieved he hadn't brought the reptiles' piece of the Predator with him. Even if they hadn't known what it was, Malcolm surely would have recognized it.

"Colonel," said the soldier rummaging through Simon's suitcase. "We have a stowaway."

"What?" said Simon, and he tried to see around the soldier. "You mean—"

"Unhand me this instant!" shouted a shrill voice. Simon's insides turned to ice.

"Wait—that's Felix. He's my friend, and he's harmless, I swear—"

"He's unauthorized," said Rhode coolly. "Detain him."

A soldier pulled out a metal cage seemingly from nowhere and deposited a squirming Felix inside. "You can't do that!" said Simon, horrified. "He's not going to hurt anyone."

"He's unauthorized," repeated Rhode, as if that explained everything. "If you'll follow me. We can't keep the General waiting."

Simon tried to stand his ground and remain in the foyer with Felix, but the other soldiers surrounded them, forcing him through the door. "Felix!" he shouted. "Do what they tell you!"

"Quiet," said one of the guards in a deep voice. Simon looked to Malcolm, desperate for him to help, but his uncle shook his head. Logically Simon knew that underwater, there wasn't much Malcolm could do, but still. He could have at least tried.

"What are you going to do with him?" demanded Simon, trotting to catch up with Rhode. "He's just a mouse. He won't hurt anyone."

"He will be interrogated and either arrested or returned to you," said Rhode without looking at him. "I would recommend you not press the issue and make it more difficult for him. This is standard protocol."

Gritting his teeth, Simon glared at her, but if she noticed, she didn't react. Simon had a feeling that even if the dome were caving in, she wouldn't do anything unless it was *standard protocol.*

"This is the General's compound," said Rhode as she led them through a maze of mirrored hallways, clearly designed to confuse anyone trying to infiltrate. There were no decorations or signs to mark their location, making it impossible to tell one hallway from the next. By the third turn, Simon was well and truly lost, but he was too upset to care. "You are to be escorted by a representative of our kingdom at all times. At no point will any of you be authorized to wander on your own. Your schedules will be delivered each morning at precisely six o'clock, and you will follow them to the letter. Any deviation will be met with the highest level of scrutiny, and should you make a habit of it, you will be removed from Atlantis. Is that understood?"

"Do you intend on treating my family like enemies the entire time we're here?" said Malcolm. "Or is this the underwater kingdom's idea of hospitality?"

"I apologize for any perceived slight, Alpha, but this is how we run things down here," said Rhode, stopping at a mirrored double door with yet another pair of soldiers guarding the entrance. "The General is a very busy man, so introductions will be brief."

The soldiers pushed open the door, revealing a conference room with deep red walls and a long mahogany table down the middle, giving it a much homier feel than the rest of the compound. A man with neatly trimmed salt-and-pepper hair stood with his back to them as he studied a map on the wall—the California coast, from what Simon could tell.

Jam and Rhode both snapped to attention, their backs rigid, heels clicked together, and their arms glued to their sides. "General," said Rhode. "The visitors are here to greet you."

"You're late," said the General in a booming voice that filled the room. He turned around, and Simon immediately understood why Jam was so afraid of him. His expression held no warmth, not even to greet his son, and he wore his military uniform like armor. Simon knew his Animalgam form was a dolphin, but looking at him, he would have guessed something deeply unfriendly—a barracuda, or maybe an anglerfish. But even the latter had a dangling light to lure in prey. There was nothing welcoming about the General at all.

Malcolm bristled, his shoulders straightening like he was about to start a fight. "General—"

"It's my fault," said Ariana, stepping forward. If she was afraid of him, she didn't show it. "I didn't know we would be coming to Atlantis. I thought we would be above the water, and I'm not exactly a fan of the ocean. *You* should have warned us," she added, admonishing him. "It was incredibly rude of you not to, and I'm sure the Black Widow Queen won't be happy to hear about it."

Rather than throw Ariana out of the room, like Simon half expected, the General studied her. "You must be Princess Ariana," he said in a shockingly even tone. "Lord Anthony informed me earlier today that he will be advising you while you represent the insect and arachnid kingdom on behalf of your mother at the security summit. It's a shame she couldn't join us."

Simon glanced at Jam, stunned. Ariana was here to represent her mother at the summit? Jam was focused on his father, though, looking vaguely like he was going to keel over. And if anyone else was as surprised by this as Simon was, they didn't show it.

"You should be glad she didn't, if this is how you treat all your ambassadors and dignitaries," snapped Ariana. "Have you been down here so long that you've forgotten the basics of common decency? Or have you decided we're hostages instead of honored guests?"

"No one here is a hostage, Your Highness," said the General slowly. "And you will all be treated with the respect your positions deserve."

"Then why was one of our friends detained?" she said.

The General's gaze fixed on Rhode. "Colonel?"

"He was unauthorized. A member of the mammal kingdom," said Rhode. "A mouse found in one of the twins' suitcases. Clearly a stowaway, sir."

"He's my friend," said Simon, his palms sweaty. "He isn't a stowaway. That's how he travels with me. His name's Felix—"

"And he is an unauthorized member of the mammal kingdom," said the General, peering at Simon. "Which one is this?"

"I—" Rhode glanced back and forth between Simon and Nolan. "I'm not sure, sir."

"If I may," said Malcolm in a tone that implied he didn't care if the General was all right with it or not. "My nephew didn't realize he was doing anything wrong. The mouse has been living in the Den since September. I've had several conversations with him myself, and despite a tendency to mouth off, he's harmless. Considering he is a member of my kingdom, I must insist you release him into my nephew's care, or I will be forced to leave before the security summit begins. And I will be taking Ariana with me."

The General didn't respond. Instead, he moved toward them one slow step at a time, his hands clasped behind his back. His gaze was fixed on Simon, and though every bone in Simon's body screamed at him to look away, he refused.

"We haven't been properly introduced," said the General, stopping in front of Simon. "I am Isaiah Fluke, General of the Seas and the underwater kingdom. And you are?"

He considered lying, but what good would that do him? It would only put a target on Nolan's back instead. "Simon Thorn," he said, biting back a "sir."

"Ah. Grandson and heir to the Bird Lord." The General stooped down so they were eye level with each other. "Tell me, when was the last time you saw your grandfather?"

"I only met him a few months ago," said Simon heatedly. "He killed my uncle—"

"My brother, Darryl," interrupted Malcolm quietly. "I don't know if you've heard or not, General."

"I have," he said slowly, his gaze still focused on Simon. "Which makes me all the more curious as to why you have allowed Orion's heir to continue at your school, even if he is your nephew."

"Because I don't judge others based solely on who they're related to or what animal they shift into," said Malcolm, a challenge in his voice. "Simon has proven himself and his loyalty to our family again and again, and I also don't believe in isolating others simply because they're different." It may have been Simon's imagination, but he could have sworn Malcolm glanced at Jam. "Simon may shift into a golden eagle, but he is still my blood."

"He is not mine," said the General. "And I have no intention of allowing a member of the bird kingdom to remain in Atlantis. He will be on the next submarine back to Avalon, where he may wait with the rest of the birds that have invaded the beaches of Santa Catalina Island."

Simon's heart skipped a beat. Orion was undoubtedly among them, and if Orion was there, then that meant his mother would be, too.

Malcolm crossed his arms over his broad chest, giving him the impression of being even bigger than he already was. "If you insist. Come on, kids. We'll leave General Fluke to fight off the bird kingdom on his own."

He started to walk toward the door, and the General grumbled something that sounded like a curse. "Stop," he muttered. "If you vouch for him, then I will allow him to stay—under the condition that he is never left alone."

Malcolm turned back around slowly. "And the mouse?"

The General scoffed, but when Malcolm made to leave again, he sighed. "The pet is unauthorized—"

"He's not a pet," said Simon. "He's my friend."

"I did not think a member of the bird kingdom, let alone Orion's heir, could possibly befriend a member of another kingdom," said the General. "Are you sure you're not simply keeping him as a snack for later on?"

Simon's stomach turned, but before he could say anything, Malcolm cut in. "Enough of this, Fluke. You assured me that every member of my party would be granted access to the city. Was that a lie?"

"It was not a lie," said the General, his lined face slowly turning red. "Do not insult me in my own home, Alpha—"

"It was a question, General, not an insult. And if it wasn't a lie, then will you let him go, or will we be leaving now?"

The corner of the General's mouth twitched, and for a moment Simon thought he might actually punch Malcolm. Not that he could do much damage against the towering Alpha, but it would almost be worth it to watch. "Colonel," he said, seething, and Rhode snapped to attention once more. "Alert security that unless this mouse poses an immediate tangible threat, he is to be released into Mr. Thorn's care."

"His Highness's care," corrected Malcolm in a frigid voice. Simon squirmed.

"We do not recognize the bird kingdom here," said the General with equal coldness.

"But you recognize my kingdom," said Malcolm. "And as you yourself observed, he is my nephew."

The General's jaw clenched, and Simon could practically feel the anger rolling off him. He opened his mouth to insist he was fine being just Simon, and that he didn't want to be prince of anything, when Ariana spoke up instead.

"Is this how the summit's going to go? You two bickering all the time while we get nothing done?"

She sounded so authoritative that, despite her small size, both fully grown men instantly looked chagrined. At last the General muttered, "Your mammal friend will be released, and your nephew will be allowed to stay. They will not, however, be granted the diplomatic immunity promised to the rest of your party. Both will follow the laws of our kingdom and be held accountable for their actions, along with your little reptile friend."

Winter, who lingered beside Simon, bristled. "My name is Winter," she said in a voice that could have sliced through diamond. "We've met twice, General."

"And as I recall, when we did, you were a member of Orion's party," he said. "Familiarity will get you nowhere, I'm afraid. A member of my family will be tasked with escorting you both at all times, and any unlawfulness will see you detained. Is that fair, Alpha?"

Malcolm gave Simon a long look. "That's fair," he said gruffly. "If you would excuse us, General, we've had a long trip."

He nodded once. "Colonel Rhode, see our guests to their quarters. Soldier," he added to Jam, the first time he'd acknowledged him. "You and I are overdue for a very long discussion."

Jam gulped, and Simon gave him an apologetic look as Rhode led them back into the maze of mirrored hallways. No doubt *discussion* really meant *lecture that would make Jam's ears bleed*, and Simon swallowed his guilt, focusing on following the colonel instead. He did his best to remember where they turned, but as soon as they stepped into an elevator, he was lost.

Rhode showed them to a set of guest rooms several floors up. "Someone will be by to escort you to dinner at nineteen hundred hours," she said before turning on her heel and disappearing. Briefly Simon wondered why she'd left them unattended, but of course she must have known they wouldn't try to go anywhere, not in the mirrored hallways.

As soon as she left, Malcolm ushered them all into the bedroom meant for Simon and Nolan to share. Though the walls were painted a deep and inviting sapphire, it was sparsely furnished, with only the bare necessities that included two beds, a small dresser to share, and a lamp that flickered. Simon had seen nicer cells in prison films.

"Why didn't you tell me you brought Felix?" said his uncle, sounding more frustrated than disappointed. "You nearly started an international incident."

"I'm sorry," he said, staring at the cream carpet. At least that was soft. "I didn't think—"

"That much was obvious." Malcolm sighed. "Simon, Winter—the General *will* have you arrested the first chance he gets, so I need you to promise me you won't give him that chance. There's nothing I can do to help you down here, so it's up to you both to protect yourselves."

Winter mumbled her reassurance, while Simon nodded numbly. He'd faced bigger threats than being arrested before, but something about this place made imprisonment sound like a punishment worse than death. There was nothing welcoming about it—the entire compound felt like it had been designed to keep everyone out, and even without the security measures, the soldiers' dour expressions and the General's booming voice would have been enough to make anyone with an ounce of common sense stay away. No wonder Jam was miserable here. Simon didn't know how he would get through winter break, let alone spend his entire life in this place.

Malcolm patted Simon on the shoulder. "Good. I'm counting on you both. We have some time before dinner, so everyone unpack, and try not to get into any trouble, all right?"

They left for the other guest rooms—Winter and Ariana were sharing one across the hall, while Malcolm had his own next door—and once they were gone, Simon collapsed on the stiff mattress. "So much for a vacation on the beach."

"Great job talking Malcolm into this," muttered Nolan, who was struggling to lift his suitcase onto his bed with his good arm. "Best Christmas ever, right?"

"It isn't my fault," said Simon, and that wasn't technically a lie. He hadn't expected Nolan to come, after all. "Do you need—"

"I'm fine," said Nolan, managing with a grunt. "Leave me alone."

Simon closed his eyes, the hopelessness of his situation settling over him like a suffocating blanket he couldn't push away. With the bird army stationed on Santa Catalina Island, Orion was already close—too close. But Simon couldn't fathom the General hiding his piece of the Predator in Atlantis, not when he had the entire underwater kingdom at his disposal. And no matter how determined Simon might have been, no matter how many friends wanted to help, he had no idea how he could possibly search the entire ocean for a crystal no bigger than his palm.

6

A FAMILY OF FLUKES

A knock on the door startled Simon out of his unexpected nap, and his eyes snapped open, taking in the blue walls. For a split second, he forgot where he was, until Nolan groaned from the bed across from his.

"Simon?" said Jam through the door. "It's me."

"And me," squeaked a tiny voice indignantly.

Simon leaped out of bed and pulled open the door. "Felix! You're all right," he said, scooping up the mouse from Jam's shoulder. "They didn't hurt you, did they?"

Felix tugged on the end of his tail. "Interrogated me within an inch of my life, but don't worry, I didn't squeal."

"Didn't squeal on what?" said Nolan, who was suddenly hovering directly behind them.

"I thought you weren't speaking to me," said Simon.

"I was talking to Felix, not you," grumbled Nolan, but he pushed past them without another word. Once he disappeared into their uncle's room, Simon's shoulders sagged with relief.

"Thanks," he said to Jam. "Are you okay?"

"I'm fine. This is how it always is," he said miserably. "The General ordered me to tell you it's time for dinner, but the—the rat isn't invited."

"I am *not* a rat!" squeaked Felix, but Simon ignored him. "I'll be right out."

Jam nodded and turned away, heading to the nearby doors to gather the others for dinner. Simon hated the look of defeat in his eyes, but there wasn't much he could do. Slipping back into the room, Simon returned Felix to his suitcase.

"Don't go anywhere," he warned. "I mean it. They'll arrest you again, and this time they won't let you go."

Felix smoothed his whiskers and huddled against a pair of socks. "Brutes," he muttered. "Think they're better than me just because they can swim. Smell like fish, all of them. Probably taste like fish, too."

Figuring that was all the agreement he would get out of Felix right now, Simon joined the others in the hallway. Everyone had gathered except one.

"Where's Ariana?" he said, trying to peek into the girls' room.

"She wanted to nap, but her mother's adviser showed up and dragged her away," said Winter sourly.

"She's here as a representative of the insect and arachnid

kingdom," warned Malcolm. "She won't get to spend much time with you."

"But she still needs to sleep," protested Simon.

"And I'll make sure she does," said his uncle. "Come on, we can't be late for dinner."

Ariana rejoined them right as they reached the dining room, along with a thin older man Simon could only assume was her mother's adviser. The dark circles underneath Ariana's eyes seemed deeper than before, and she barely looked at them before shuffling into the dining room behind Malcolm.

Simon expected more utilitarian décor inside, but instead he stepped into a warm, cheerful room with paintings hanging from the golden walls. Around the wide oak dining table laden with food sat nine other people, including the General and Rhode.

"Alpha, Princess, Lord Anthony," said the General, not bothering to stand. The others followed his lead and remained seated. "Come sit by me. We have much to discuss."

Ariana stared at the ground as she followed Malcolm and the adviser to the head of the table, where the General had reserved three seats. Simon trailed after Jam toward the opposite end of the dining room, hoping that Ariana didn't mind being left on her own up there, stuck between the General and Rhode. Another woman sat beside Malcolm, and she looked too much like Jam not to be his mother.

The rest of the table was occupied by girls—Jam's

sisters, Simon assumed. Most of them whispered to one another as they passed, but a couple looked about as pleased to see them as they were to be there.

"The prodigal son returns," said one of the older sisters nastily. She would have been one of the prettiest girls Simon had ever seen if her face hadn't been pinched in a sneer. "Just in time to save the kingdom, too."

"I don't know *what* we would've done without the patience and guidance of our little brother," said the girl beside her with a laugh.

Jam turned red. "Hi, Ondine. Good to see you, too, Halie," he mumbled before hurrying to his seat. Simon wanted to retort, but the way Jam slumped in his chair stopped him. He would only make things worse if he tried. Instead he made his way to the end of the table and sat down beside him.

"How many sisters *do* you have?" said Winter as she also took her place.

"Seven," said Jam in that same gloomy tone he'd been using since they'd arrived in California. "Rhode is the oldest—"

"Rhode? Colonel Rhode?" said Simon, chancing a glance up the table at her. "She's your sister?" Judging by how she'd greeted him, he would have never guessed.

"Unfortunately," muttered Jam, but it was so quiet that Simon wasn't sure he'd heard him right. "She's the General's favorite. None of the others serve on his private council like she does."

"If she were really the General's favorite, he wouldn't

still insist on you being his heir," said the pretty sister—Ondine—from the middle of the table. Jam fell silent and stared at his plate.

"Who's that?" said Nolan, nodding to the youngest, who was on the other side of Winter. The sister caught Nolan's eye and quickly looked away.

"That's Pearl, who's only pretending to be shy," said Jam. "She's a year older than me. Then there's Lorelei, Nixie, Halie, Ondine, and Coralia."

"They don't attend the L.A.I.R., too, do they?" said Simon, studying their faces. Several of them stared back, and he lowered his gaze. He couldn't remember ever seeing them before. Besides, none of the sisters had traveled back with them, and school was still in session.

Jam shook his head. "Rhode attended years ago, when it was still on the Beast King's island, but that's it. She was there during the bird attacks and everything, inside one of the wings that was destroyed."

"Is that how she got the scar on her cheek?" said Winter, who could usually be relied on to ask those kinds of questions. Jam nodded.

"Apparently she almost died, and Mom refused to let everyone else go. The General put his foot down for me, though," continued Jam. "Said I had to go to the L.A.I.R. since I'm going to rule someday."

"Unfortunately," said another one of the sisters as she stabbed her crab salad. Lorelei, thought Simon, but he couldn't be sure.

"Girls," said their mother in a gentle voice, but there was a hint of sharpness underneath. "We all know it's unfair, but the decision's been made. If you want to do something about it, bother your father, not your brother. It isn't his fault the General is biased against sharks."

"I am not biased," said the General abruptly, looking up from his quiet conversation with Malcolm. "Dolphins have ruled our kingdom for over a thousand years. I won't end an unbroken line simply because the girls aren't mature enough to understand the importance of tradition."

As the rest of the table broke out into a loud argument, with several of the sisters all talking at once, Simon studied Rhode, who remained quiet. He had visited the Beast King's island on his first full day at the Academy, for Unity Day—the anniversary of the day the five kingdoms had overthrown the Beast King hundreds of years before. He had been overwhelmed, having learned only the day before that Animalgams existed and he had an entire family he'd never known about, but he could vividly remember the devastated wings of the castle, with a mountain of broken stone where great halls had once stood. He couldn't imagine anyone surviving that, not if they'd been inside.

"Your sisters are all sharks?" said Nolan, his voice squeaking despite his attempt to hide it.

"Yes, but we don't bite, I promise," said a new, playful voice. The youngest sister—Pearl, who hadn't jumped in on the argument happening at the rest of the table—smiled shyly. "What's your name?"

Nolan immediately sat up straighter and puffed out his chest a little, as if to prove he wasn't scared. "I'm Nolan Thorn," he said. "The Alpha is my uncle."

"Do you turn into a wolf, too?" said Pearl, leaning toward him and practically into Winter's lap.

"Yes, he does," said Winter tersely. "I'm Winter, by the way, in case you're interested. Since you're getting so close and all."

Pearl settled back into her seat and studied her, barely batting an eye. "You must be the cottonmouth. I'm surprised the General let you into the city."

"She's my friend," said Jam with more force than Simon had heard from him since they'd left New York that morning. "And she isn't going to report back to anyone."

"What about your other friend?" said Pearl, and this time her gaze shifted over to Simon. "The General said—"

Suddenly a loud, anguished cry came from near the head of the table, where one of the older sisters—Coralia, Simon thought—stood up, her chair scraping against the floor. "I'm nineteen years old. You can't tell me what to do anymore!"

Dead silence. Even the General looked startled by her outburst, and at last he said, with more dignity than should have been possible, "Sit down, Coralia. We'll discuss this another time—"

"You always say that, and it's never a good time." Her voice caught in her throat. "I love him. I'm marrying him. I don't care what you say. I don't need your permission to live my life."

"She's *still* dating him?" whispered Jam to Pearl, who seemed to have forgotten what she was going to say about Simon in favor of whatever was going on with her older sister.

Pearl nodded as the argument down the table continued. "He proposed last month." With an impish little smile, she added, "We might have a human as a brother-in-law."

"He'd still be more capable of running the kingdom than Benjamin," said a dour voice—another one of the sisters sitting a few spots down. Nixie. Simon's skin prickled.

"You have no idea what he's capable of," he said, and she raised a single eyebrow. Her brown hair was tied back in a knot of braids, and her fingernails were painted black. There was nothing messy about her appearance, but Simon had a feeling it toed the General's strict line.

"Don't I?" she said. "And how long have you known him, exactly? Because I'm pretty sure he's my little brother, not yours."

Jam had gone red again. "It's fine, Simon. In case you can't tell, they're always like this. The General doesn't care. He thinks it's character building."

"Speaking of building character, you should have heard him when he found out you ditched school and went to Arizona," said Nixie with undisguised relish. "He nearly had an aneurysm."

"He did it to help me," said Winter, who looked less and less impressed with Nixie as the conversation went on.

"Sometimes being a good person means breaking the rules. Not that I'd expect you to know anything about that."

Nixie sniffed and looked Winter up and down. "The General was asking for volunteers to babysit you for the next two weeks. Maybe my homework can wait after all."

"What a rebel," said Winter with a roll of her eyes. She stabbed a piece of sushi on her plate. "Hope you enjoy wasting your time."

Simon was quiet for the rest of the meal. As Jam bickered with his sisters and Pearl flirted with Nolan, who didn't seem to mind, Simon strained to hear snatches of conversation from the head of the table, where the General was back to having a low debate with Malcolm and Ariana. At first Simon wondered what they were talking about, but every so often, one of them would glance down the table and meet his eye.

They were discussing him. Or—if not *him*, exactly, then the bird kingdom. Orion.

By the time Jam led them back to their guest rooms, he was anxious to talk to Ariana. He waited until Nolan was brushing his teeth, humming happily to himself as he did so, before sneaking out of the room and knocking on the door straight across the hall.

"I hate them," said Winter as she ushered him inside. "All of them. Especially Nixie."

Simon looked around their room, which was as bare as

his and Nolan's, though the walls in here were purple. "I'm pretty sure she feels the same way."

"If she's following me the whole time, then how am I supposed to help you?" said Winter with a huff.

"I don't like them, either, but we can't make waves, not down here." Ariana perched on the edge of her bed in a pair of pajamas, looking like she was seconds from passing out. "You heard Malcolm. You can't sneak around."

Simon blinked. Ariana was the last person he ever expected to tell him that he couldn't break a rule or two in order to find the piece, but there was something different about her—ever since she'd met with her mother's adviser, she'd looked . . . wilted. It was almost as if someone had doused the fire inside her with a bucket of water, and all she could do now was limp along.

Maybe it was Atlantis, he thought. He found it easy enough to forget they were underwater, but no doubt Ariana had a much more difficult time doing so. He didn't think that was it, though, not entirely. Something else was going on, and it worried him.

He knew her well enough to know that asking her outright wouldn't help—if anything, it would only make her even more closed off and distant, so he didn't bother. If she wanted to talk, she would eventually. "What did you and Malcolm and the General talk about the whole time?" he said instead.

"Mostly about Orion," said Ariana. "The General sees the bird army's invasion of the Santa Catalina beaches as an act of war, but he doesn't have the numbers to mobilize for an aboveground strike. That's why he asked everyone here. It isn't just about keeping the piece of the Predator safe. He wants to go to war with Orion."

"Sounds like a good idea to me," said Winter bitterly. Simon shouldn't have been surprised, but he was. Orion had raised Winter as his own granddaughter, but had abandoned her when he'd discovered she was a cottonmouth snake instead of a bird. Outside of Simon, she had the most reason to hate him.

"If the kingdoms go to war, innocent people will die," he said. "We can't let that happen. We need to make sure they keep circling each other until we find the pieces and destroy the Predator."

"Easier said than done," said Ariana wearily. "Malcolm isn't for it, either, but if the reptiles agree—"

"But the reptiles hate the underwater kingdom," said Winter. "They'll never side with them."

Ariana grimaced. "Maybe. But if they think Orion's on the verge of putting the weapon together, that might be the one thing that would unite the kingdoms."

The three of them fell quiet. At last, with his heart pounding, Simon said in a voice so low that he almost couldn't hear himself, "I could tell them what we're doing."

"No," said Winter immediately. "Don't you dare."

"He might not have a choice," said Ariana tiredly. "If we really want to avoid war—"

"Telling them what we're really doing will only start one, and this time, they'll all be after Simon," said Winter, exasperated. "You're on the inside, Ariana. Convince them to hold off. Or distract them. Anything, I don't care—just do *something* instead of acting like a spineless jellyfish."

Ariana clawed her fingers through her blue hair. "I'm trying, okay? There's only so much I can do. They won't listen to me—"

"Then make them listen," said Winter vehemently. "Or have you given up already?"

"I haven't given up," said Ariana. Her eyes grew watery. "This is a lot harder than we thought it'd be, okay? It isn't just us anymore. Real lives are on the line—"

"I don't want anyone else dying because of me," said Simon suddenly. "You need to stop them, Ariana, all right? Whatever you have to do, buy us as much time as you can."

She closed her eyes, looking worn down and defeated. "I'll do my best."

Winter flopped down on her bed. "Let's hope it's good enough."

"It will be," said Simon, but even he couldn't be sure anymore. There were too many people and too many kingdoms closing in on them, and sooner or later, time would run out.

7

A GALAXY OF STARFISH

Rhode hadn't been kidding about handing out schedules.

Pearl, the youngest sister, arrived at their door at exactly 0600—six o'clock in the morning—to deliver a minute-by-minute breakdown of their days. To Simon's dread, he saw that other than meals, he was only supposed to do one thing: *remain with chaperon.*

"Who's my chaperon?" he said as Pearl led them to breakfast. Malcolm and Ariana had already disappeared with Rhode, and neither had looked happy about it.

"Me, of course," she said cheerfully, trying to loop her arm through his. Simon immediately stepped away.

"I'm Simon," he said, and her expression dropped.

"Oh. Then I don't know." She moved toward Nolan instead, who had taken extra care to style his hair that morning and had left his sling on the bed. "We are going to have so much *fun* today!"

Winter made a gagging motion behind their backs, and Simon had to bite his cheek to stop himself from laughing.

While Pearl cooed over Nolan during breakfast—6:20 to 6:45—Simon choked down a reasonable amount of sushi and kelp to stop the growling in his stomach. By the end of this trip, he had a sneaking suspicion he would either learn to love raw fish or starve to death. Apparently there would be no in between.

"I'd kill for some bacon right now," muttered Winter as she pushed away her untouched tuna. "Do you think they're doing this on purpose?"

"Probably," said Simon. "Bet Ariana and Malcolm are getting pancakes."

"With chocolate chips and blueberries. And scrambled eggs and toast and—"

"Stop it," he groaned. "You're making me hungry."

The dining room door burst open, and a red-faced and breathless Jam appeared, his blond hair wild. Now that he was home, he wore a blue uniform like Rhode, but it was rumpled and buttoned up the wrong way. "Yes! Made it."

He flopped into the seat beside Simon's and began to wolf down the food he hadn't touched. Simon and Winter exchanged a look.

"Did you sleep in?" said Simon, who hadn't had any trouble getting up early thanks to the time difference between New York and California.

Jam shook his head. "Did drills early," he said through a mouthful of fish. "The General said I could spend the morning with you if I did, since Coralia's still upset and refused to help out."

Winter let out a sigh of relief. "I was sure Nixie would be our chaperon."

"Don't worry, you're not slithering away that easily." Nixie sauntered up behind her and snatched a tuna roll off her plate. "Jam is Simon's chaperon. I'm yours."

Winter blanched. "Delightful."

"I thought so." Nixie grinned. "I've got some mussels waiting to be harvested in the coral gardens. It shouldn't take more than five or six hours."

Winter turned a dangerous shade of purple, but before she could explode, Jam interjected. "The General said we were supposed to show them around and keep them out of trouble. I'm pretty sure slave labor isn't included in that."

"He didn't specify how," argued Nixie. "And she's my hostage, not yours."

"We're not hostages," said Simon. "And do you really want to be alone in a garden with someone who turns into a venomous snake?"

"Yeah," said Jam. "You know cottonmouths and water moccasins are the same thing, right?"

Judging by the look of unease on Nixie's face, she hadn't known that. Neither, apparently, had Winter, who seemed strangely pleased by the revelation. Considering she usually wanted nothing to do with her Animalgam form, Simon thought this was a step in the right direction.

"We can garden if you'd like," she said sweetly to Nixie. "I haven't bitten anyone in months."

Narrowing her eyes, Nixie snatched Winter's plate and stormed to the other end of the table, staying there for the rest of breakfast.

They stopped in their rooms long enough to get their things, and Simon tucked Felix safely into the pocket of his sweatshirt. As dangerous as it was to risk Felix being seen by other members of the underwater kingdom, Simon thought it would be worse keeping him in the guest room all day, tempting him to sneak out and take a look around for himself. At least this way, Simon knew where he was at all times.

While leaving the mirrored compound, they were all subjected to the same security search, and Jam triple-checked that all of their names, including Felix's, were on the list to get back in. As soon as they stepped outside into the giant dome that was Atlantis, Simon let out a heavy sigh.

"I don't know how you stand it here," he said to Jam as they headed down a concrete sidewalk with tall gray buildings on either side. The city was still colorless and dreary, but anything was better than the compound. "It constantly feels like the walls are closing in."

"Just used to it, I guess," said Jam with a shrug. "The whole city was built for security, so no one can break in—"

"Has anyone ever tried?" said Winter. Nixie hovered nearby, her heavily made-up eyes focused solely on Winter.

"Not yet," she said. "No need, when we're letting them in and treating them like guests now."

"I don't know why anyone ever would," said Winter, making a face. "It's the kind of place you escape from, not escape to."

"Good. Hate it all you want, if that means you'll stay away."

"It's not that bad," said Jam quickly. "You're only seeing the parts of it that strangers are supposed to see. It isn't supposed to look inviting on the outside. That's the whole point. But you saw the rooms in the compound—they're full of art and color."

"Your rooms, maybe," muttered Winter under her breath. Jam either didn't hear her or ignored her.

"Most of the other kingdoms think we're cold or heartless or—or soulless," he continued. "But that's because they never look long enough to see who we are beyond the military. Like—here."

He moved toward a door that blended in seamlessly with the gray building beside them. There was a small unadorned sign beside it reading WHITE SHARK CAFÉ. Just as he reached for the handle, Simon hesitated.

"Are you sure we can go in there?" he said.

"Trust me," said Jam, and he pushed open the door.

Inside was nothing like the sterile eating hall Simon expected. Instead, the small café was crammed with worn armchairs, sofas, and rickety tables shoved into every nook and cranny, with a colorful chalkboard displaying the day's specials—along with a handful of shark jokes—hanging behind the counter. A woman in a blue apron greeted them warmly, and as Jam ordered them all hot cocoas, Simon lingered in the background.

Every inch of wall space was covered in art. Not the kind of fancy, expensive art the reptiles might have hung, but rather homemade drawings, cartoons, even some graffiti. There was a small stage, and Simon spotted a schedule advertising open mic night, a poetry slam, and an acoustic singer.

"This is incredible," he said, gratefully accepting the hot cocoa Jam handed him. The ceiling was dominated by a large painting of the Pacific Ocean, and he spotted various sea creatures—real and mythical—among the waves. "Are you sure this isn't part of the reptile kingdom?" he joked.

"We've got some color, too," said Jam proudly, looking around. "No one's on duty all the time."

"Except maybe the General," said Nixie, glaring at them from over the rim of her drink.

Jam cleared his throat. "The point is, our kingdom is like the ocean. You don't really see us unless you look beneath the surface. We're not robots. Not everyone here likes art or music or reading, but there's other stuff hidden away that they like. The gardens, the planetarium—"

"You have a planetarium underwater?" said Simon as half a dozen uniformed men and women strode into the café. At first he felt a pang of fear at the possibility that they were after him and Winter, but they all headed to the counter to order.

"Something like that," said Jam with a surprising grin. "Want to see it?"

Seeing the sights was the last thing they should have been doing, but Simon couldn't very well bring up their real mission in front of Nixie, Nolan, and Pearl. So, with more reluctance than he should've been showing when faced with the prospect of an underwater planetarium, Simon nodded while Pearl squealed and hugged Nolan's arm.

"You'll love it there. It's the best place in the whole city."

Nixie rolled her eyes. "You really think it's better than the gardens?"

"Just because *you're* weird and like gardening rocks doesn't mean the rest of us do," said Pearl nastily. But when she turned back to Nolan, any trace of agitation was gone. "And maybe after, we can come back here and share a cupcake."

How Nolan managed not to burst out laughing baffled Simon, but he was careful not to look Jam's way, lest he accidentally lose it.

The planetarium wasn't far from the café, and as they headed toward the center of the city, Simon looked around at the buildings surrounding them. Maybe it wasn't so bad here after all. As dull and gloomy as it might have seemed inside the dome, they were still underwater—*actually* underwater—and as Simon looked up, he saw a gray whale lazily making its way through one of the tubes that served as highways through the dome.

"Look," he said, nudging Winter. She glanced upward, and while he thought he saw a flicker of interest in her eyes, it disappeared almost immediately, replaced by the bored look he'd seen her wear so often.

"Let me know when you see a narwhal," she muttered.

Simon didn't let her bad mood sour his. He still would have rather been on the surface, but as they walked down the street, he asked Jam what each building held. Most were offices or places where members of the underwater kingdom lived, but Jam also pointed out his favorite bookshop and an art studio one of his sisters frequented.

Finally they reached the squat stone planetarium. At this early hour, it was practically empty, and as Jam paid the entrance fee for them all, Felix poked his head out of Simon's pocket. "*This* is your big tourist attraction?"

"It gets busy after morning drills are done," said Jam as he handed out their tickets. "Lots of people come here to eat lunch, or to relax during their free hour."

"You get a *whole* free hour?" said Winter.

"Every day," said Pearl, apparently oblivious to her sarcasm. She and Nolan led the way down a sloping passageway that seemed to lead under the city itself, while Winter followed, looking about as disgusted with their handholding as Simon felt. Behind her trailed Nixie, and while Simon's interest was now piqued, he joined Jam at the rear and let their pace slow as they fell farther and farther behind, until at last the others had disappeared around a corner.

"We need to look for the piece," whispered Simon as soon as he was sure he and Jam were alone. "Do you think your father would have hidden it in Atlantis?"

"I don't know," said Jam. "It's possible, but I don't think so. The compound is too obvious, and it wouldn't be secure anywhere else in the city. At least in the ocean, there wouldn't be much of a chance of anyone accidentally finding it."

"Do you think he would have left some kind of record of where he put it?" said Simon.

"I—" Jam squirmed. "I don't know."

"If you'd left me behind, I could have looked for you," said Felix casually, cleaning his whiskers. "But no, you couldn't trust me not to get into trouble."

"It's not that I don't trust you. It's that I don't trust everyone else not to eat you," said Simon, glancing around the narrow corridor. "Is there any way out of here?"

Jam hesitated. "There's a tunnel that leads out past the edge of Atlantis. It'll get us into open water far away enough that none of the patrols will catch us. But what are we going to do out there, Simon? Scour the whole ocean?"

"I don't know," he admitted. "We have to at least look. Maybe my mother left a clue in her postcards, and something we see triggers it. Or maybe there's a trail we have to follow. We won't know until we get out there."

Jam grimaced. "If you go missing even for a minute, the General will—"

"What? Throw me out of Atlantis?" said Simon. "I've been in trouble before. If we get caught, we'll figure something out, but we have to at least try. This might be the only shot we have."

Gripping a handful of his blond hair, Jam began to pace. "Okay, all right. We'll look. But what about Winter?"

"We have to ditch her," said Simon. Jam's eyes widened behind his glasses, and as he started to protest, Simon hastily added, "I don't like it, either, but we don't have a choice."

"But—she'll murder us if we leave her behind."

"No, she won't. Your sister won't let her out of her sight, and she knows how important this is—"

"How important what is?"

Nixie appeared from around the corner, a devious look in her eyes. Simon clammed up.

"How important it is for this summit to happen," lied Jam smoothly—so smoothly, in fact, that Simon nearly did a double take. "And with the way you're treating Winter, we're worried she's going to throw a fit and leave, taking Malcolm and Ariana with her."

His sister stared at them, and Simon couldn't decide if she believed Jam or not. "It's not my fault she's delicate," she finally said.

"After the summit falls through, make sure to phrase it exactly like that when the General asks why you were torturing her," said Jam.

Nixie's expression darkened. "I'm not torturing her—"

"You're being rude and bullying her for being a reptile. She gets enough of that at the L.A.I.R., and if you keep this up, they'll all be gone before dinner."

She took a threatening step toward them. "You're not the boss of me."

Jam squared his shoulders, rising to his full height—which was still several inches shorter than Nixie. "I will be one day," he said, his voice trembling slightly. "And I don't care if you're my sister. If you treat my friends badly now, you'll regret it later."

Nixie hesitated, and although she rolled her eyes a split second later, Simon thought she didn't look as certain as she had before. "Fine. I'll try to remember she can't take a joke."

That was, as far as Simon could tell, the best they would get from her, and Jam nodded. The boys exchanged a look as the three of them headed down the dim hallway. The tunnel would have to wait until no one was watching. But how long would that take? They couldn't count on luck. Even if they managed to scour the ocean floor every waking hour for the next two weeks, their chances of finding the piece were practically zero.

He would have to examine the postcard his mother had sent him as soon as they returned, Simon decided. Maybe there was a clue he'd missed. Maybe—

Lost in his thoughts, Simon almost didn't notice when they entered the planetarium. It was only the change in temperature that alerted him, and as soon as he realized where he was, he stopped dead in his tracks.

They'd stepped inside a cool, damp cavern that was at least two stories high. There was no artificial light, as far as Simon could tell—instead, the walls and soaring ceiling emitted a soft blue luminescent light that seemed to come from the rock itself. Dumbfounded, Simon craned his neck to get a good look and walked toward the center of the cavern. "What *is* that?" he said. "It looks like someone opened a giant glow stick and—"

"Stop!" cried Pearl, and Simon froze at the edge of a shallow pool of crystal-clear water. Looking down at where he'd been about to step, he gulped and carefully he set his foot back down on the shore. He'd come within half an inch of crushing a starfish.

It wasn't the only starfish, either. Hundreds of them lounged in the pool, clinging to rocks and submerged in the water. While Simon couldn't see their eyes—wasn't even sure they had them—he could practically feel them all giving him dirty looks.

"Oh." He blinked. "Starfish. Planetarium. I get it now."

Jam cleared his throat. "They prefer 'sea stars,' actually. Get a little touchy about not being fish."

"Right," said Simon, and to the shallow pool he added, "Sorry. Sea stars."

"The General created this sanctuary for them after the population started to dwindle around Atlantis," chimed in Pearl. "They're free to go whenever they want, but most of them spend their days here, safe from predators, and we feed them."

"They can push their stomachs out of their bodies," added Nixie, nudging one of the five-legged creatures with her toe. "It's really cool to watch."

Winter made a face while Nolan said, "Why is the ceiling glowing?"

"Bioluminescent bacteria," said Pearl cheerfully. "Isn't it beautiful?"

"Pretty sure that's the first time anyone's ever called bacteria beautiful," said Winter, plopping down on a long, flat rock that served as a bench, but her eyes were focused on the blue glow. Even she couldn't hide her awe.

Simon sat beside her and waited until the others had gone over to the other side of the cavern to inspect a particularly colorful sea star. Once they were out of earshot, he wrapped his arm around her, figuring she needed it about as much as he did right now.

"Jam and I are going to look for the piece," he said quietly. "We'd take you with us, but—"

"I can't breathe underwater, and Nixie won't let me out of her sight," muttered Winter, slumping her shoulders.

He bit his lip. "Jam told Nixie to lay off. If she tries to bully you again, act like you're going to take the first submarine back to the surface, okay?"

She nodded warily. "Do you know where it is?"

"Not yet. Do you think you could distract them long enough for us to sneak out?"

They bent their heads together and whispered until the others returned to their side of the cave. Simon's arm was still around Winter, and Nixie stopped a foot in front of them, snorting.

"Figures. You two are perfect for each other."

Simon dropped his arm, and Winter stood, going toe to toe with Nixie, who was a good six inches taller than her. "What's your problem? Are you so miserable you can't stand to see anyone else happy?"

Nixie's eyes widened for a split second, but her scowl snapped back into place as quickly as it'd disappeared. "You're my problem, snake breath. Your grandfather's done nothing but make our lives miserable. I'm one of the deadliest predators in the ocean, but I can't leave Atlantis without an escort because there are birds on the beaches and reptiles like *you* in the ocean. If anything happens with another Animalgam, the General swears it will be enough to start a war, and—"

"And you think that's my fault?" said Winter, standing on her tiptoes and shoving her face in Nixie's. "You think that somehow, I can wave my magic wand and fix it for you? Maybe if your *General* weren't such a jerk, your relationships with the other kingdoms would be better, and you wouldn't have to worry about starting a war just because you're an idiot who snacked on the wrong turtle, *chum breath*."

Nixie let out a shriek that echoed throughout the cavern, and she shoved Winter backward. Simon caught her before she could fall, and rather than thank him, Winter screeched and charged straight for Nixie, tackling her.

With a splash, the pair fell into the shallow water, and Simon heard the murmur of angry voices as the sea stars scattered, moving faster than he knew they could. From the edge, Nolan and Pearl gaped at the wrestling pair, and Simon couldn't blame them. Winter was definitely prickly, but considering her small stature, she usually had the good sense to stay away from physical arguments. He'd never seen her get *this* confrontational before.

But in the middle of the fight, their eyes met, and Winter jutted her chin toward the door. Then it dawned on him. This wasn't for her benefit. It was for his.

He inched toward Jam. "Come on, while she's distracting them," he whispered, and as Winter let out another enraged scream, he and Jam slipped out through the exit and back into the hallway.

They ran only a few dozen feet before Jam stopped and shoved open a door that blended into the walls. "Through here," he said, and Simon ducked inside. They stumbled into a low-lit storage room that reeked of fish, and while Felix made gagging sounds in the pocket of his sweatshirt, Simon covered his mouth with his sleeve and followed Jam.

"The exit's right over here, I think." Jam bent down and felt around a dark wall. At last a small square door popped open. "It's a tight fit, but it connects to the tunnel the sea stars use to come and go."

Simon pulled off his sweatshirt. "Felix, you should stay here."

"What?" Despite the putrid smell in the feeding room, the little mouse launched himself out of Simon's pocket and onto his shoulder. "First you make me come with you, and now you're going to abandon me in a room that smells like rotting shark excrement?"

"Can you breathe underwater?" said Simon patiently. Felix sputtered.

"What's that got to do with anything?"

"Because we're going into the ocean," he pointed out. "And if you can't breathe underwater, then you'll drown."

Felix huffed. "That still doesn't mean you have a right to abandon me here."

"Go hang out with the sea stars for a while," said Jam. "They probably won't eat you. We'll be back by eleven hundred hours anyway. We're on a schedule."

"See?" said Simon. "It won't be long."

Felix sulked, but Simon didn't feel the least bit bad for him, not this time. Felix could complain all he wanted, but he had been the one who'd wanted to come to Atlantis with him in the first place.

Jam went first into the narrow opening, which expanded into a wet and slippery cave that angled sharply downward. The only light along the steep path was that same bioluminescent glow splashed across the walls, and Simon shivered. Without his sweatshirt, it felt much cooler.

"Watch your step," said Jam as he deftly navigated the slope. Simon followed at a much slower pace, gingerly testing each step before he put his full weight down. Even though they had no time to spare, Jam didn't complain, and after what felt like an hour, they finally reached the point in the tunnel where the ocean had seeped in, flooding the last hundred feet.

"Ready to go?" said Jam, grinning. "This is the first time you've swum, isn't it?"

"In an ocean," said Simon, eyeing the dark water. "I've swum in pools before. And the moat at the L.A.I.R." But all of those times had been as a human.

"Take a deep breath and follow my lead. And don't say anything to Al and Floyd. I'll handle them."

"Al and Floyd?" said Simon. "Who are they?"

But Jam was already shifting. His skin turned smooth and gray, his arms shrank into flippers, and his feet fused together to form a tail. A dorsal fin sprouted from his back, and his face elongated into a snout, until finally Simon wasn't looking at his human friend anymore, but a dolphin.

"Come on!" said Jam, splashing his fins. "The water's warm."

Simon somehow doubted that, given how cold the cave was, but he closed his eyes and focused. His body began to shift, painlessly turning from human into dolphin, and as he took a breath and dived into the water, the transformation was complete.

"Whoa." He gave an experimental kick with his tail and nearly barreled headfirst into the wall. The water *was* warm. "This is awesome."

"Just wait until we get into open ocean," said Jam, and with that, he swam into the depths of the tunnel. Simon followed.

He could see underwater—that was surprising, though he figured he probably should have guessed it. In front of him, Jam made a curious clicking noise, and Simon tried to imitate him.

Immediately something happened, though Simon wasn't exactly sure what. He seemed to grow aware of the shape of the cave around them, and that the exit was no more than fifty feet ahead. Beyond that was ocean floor, and—

"Is this echolocation?" he said, stunned. "Is this how you always know where things are?"

"I guess," said Jam as they approached the opening. "I don't think about it too much. Technically I'm not allowed out on my own, and the General's always too busy to swim with me, so I've never had the chance to ask if I'm doing it right."

"But don't you leave for drills?" said Simon.

"Sure, but we stick close to the city. You saw the platoons when we were approaching. Only the most experienced go very far."

"Then how are you ever supposed to learn how to protect your kingdom if you don't even know what's in it?"

"Beats me," said Jam as they swam through the cave

exit. "The General keeps promising he'll give me the grand tour, but—"

"'Lo there."

Without warning, a huge great white shark appeared inches in front of Simon and Jam, cutting off their path to open water. The shark grinned, baring hundreds of sharp teeth as it circled them.

"Going somewhere?"

8

CHUM BAY

Simon had never been face-to-face with a shark before, not like this. The captain, who drilled the students of the underwater kingdom at the L.A.I.R, had usually remained a safe distance away while in shark form, although there had been one memorable occasion Simon had been underwater with him at the same time. Still, he'd known the captain wouldn't eat him. This shark, he wasn't so sure.

He was ready to beg forgiveness and swim back into the cave as fast as he could when beside him, Jam spoke. "Do you really have to do this every single time, Al? You know who I am."

"Don't know who that one is," said a second great white shark, circling above Simon and Jam.

"He's my friend, Floyd, so does it matter?" said Jam. "You're going to let him through anyway."

"Are we now?" The first shark—Al—tightened his circle. "And who says we gotta?"

"I do. And I'm going to be your General someday, so unless you want to be ground into chum first chance I get—"

"Yeah, yeah, we got it," said the second shark, Floyd, from above. "Big talk for a couple of little dolphins. We ain't had a decent meal all morning, but you'd barely make up an appetizer, the both of you."

Simon kept his mouth shut, but he gave Jam a look that made it clear how much he wasn't enjoying this. Jam shook his head irritably.

"You have five seconds to decide whether you want to fight me and have the entire underwater army come after you and your little gangs," he threatened, "or if you're going to look the other way like you always do and let us both go. Choose wisely."

Al looked to Floyd, who seemed to be considering the offer. "Fine," he muttered. "But next time, he's ours."

They stopped circling long enough for Simon and Jam to swim past, and it wasn't until they were well out of earshot that Simon swore. "I thought Animalgams weren't allowed to eat other Animalgams."

"They aren't Animalgams," said Jam. "They're real sharks."

If Simon could've gone pale, he would have. As it was, he suddenly had a difficult time keeping his breakfast down. "We almost got eaten by *real sharks*?"

"Nah. Al and Floyd like to pretend to be all big and tough, but they're mostly harmless," said Jam. "I mean, don't get me wrong, most real sharks don't like us. They're supposed to be kings of the ocean, and here we are, telling them we're in charge. But the General mostly keeps the peace. And traditionally, the ruler of the underwater kingdom marries a shark Animalgam," he added. "So that helps."

Simon looked at him, startled. "You're supposed to marry a shark?"

"A girl that can turn into a shark, yeah. There are a few families on the island." Though Simon couldn't see Jam's face—and wasn't even sure dolphins had expressions the way humans did—he didn't sound very happy about it. "It doesn't matter."

"Yeah, it does," said Simon, glancing around the open water. They were far enough away now that he couldn't see the cave entrance, or its guards, but he still felt an almost undeniable urge to swim as fast as he could. "How can you stand this? The way your family treats you, all the rules and traditions—"

"I don't," said Jam, a flicker of something dark in his voice. "Sometimes I think it'd be easier if I ran away. Then the General would have to make Rhode his heir, and no one would bother me or bark orders at me, and we could all be happy. But then I wouldn't have my family anymore.

And they're not all bad," he added as Simon opened his mouth to protest. "I know how it looks, and I'm not saying it isn't awful. But there are good moments, too."

No amount of good moments could make up for the things they'd said to Jam at dinner, as far as Simon was concerned. "Family shouldn't treat each other the way they treat you."

"Mom sticks up for me most of the time. I mean, don't get me wrong, she wants Rhode to be General, too—everyone does—but she doesn't let them be too nasty." Jam sighed. "It's only for two weeks. Then we'll go back to the L.A.I.R., and I won't have to think about it for another six months."

"What happens after school lets out?" said Simon. "You're just going to let them keep this up?"

"I—" Jam faltered, his fins growing still. "I don't know. Maybe it'll be better by then."

Simon knew it wouldn't be, and Jam must have known, too. But if he wanted to stay, then there wasn't much Simon could do to change his mind. "The things they say—you know they aren't true, right?"

"They are," said Jam in a resigned, matter-of-fact way that made Simon feel awful for him. "I'll make a terrible General. I don't like rules or traditions, and the thought of yelling at everyone all day makes me sick."

"So be a different kind of General," he said. "Be the kind of General people can look up to, not the kind they're afraid of."

"Maybe," mumbled Jam in a way that made it clear he was done talking about it. "Where are we going?"

Simon hesitated, but pressing the issue wouldn't help, not if Jam didn't want to talk anymore. "I don't know," he said, letting the subject drop. "My mom's old postcard didn't say much. There were some facts about great white sharks, and she said that they were a 'greatly misunderstood and feared breed,' but she wouldn't recommend befriending one no matter how *chummy* it seemed. Does that mean anything to you?"

"Maybe," mused Jam. "There's a place on Santa Catalina Island that the local sharks call Chum Bay. Lots of them hang out there, inside the bones of an old shipwreck."

Simon wasn't exactly excited about the prospect of facing even more sharks after dealing with Al and Floyd, but he didn't have much of a choice. "Maybe we can swim by," he said nervously. "See what it's like."

"They'll never let us anywhere near the ship, but we can see if there are any more clues," agreed Jam, and though Simon's heart was pounding, he followed him toward Chum Bay.

He tried to remind himself again and again that he was an Animalgam, and there was no reason to be afraid of great white sharks when he could turn into one, but that didn't help much. Instead, as the water grew a brighter blue and they approached the coast of Santa Catalina, Simon was so jittery with nerves that he almost couldn't contain them. He wasn't used to being this afraid, but now, out in the ocean, surrounded by nothing but water and animals he'd never seen before, he felt completely out of his element.

As they surfaced, Simon sucked in a giant breath, relieved to see the sky again. "What's the plan?"

"Follow my lead," said Jam. "The shipwreck's in that cove over there."

Simon looked at the picturesque beach with glittering blue water, and his stomach turned to lava. "Are there any animals sharks are afraid of?"

Jam thought for a moment. "Killer whales, I guess. They aren't actually whales, you know. They're more like us—like dolphins, I mean. But they're huge, and they eat sharks."

"Got it," said Simon. "If any of the sharks come after us, turn into Shamu."

"Or flip them on their backs," said Jam. "If you do that, they won't be able to attack."

Tucking that nugget of information away, Simon took another deep breath and ducked back under the water. He mustered up his courage and followed Jam, and before long, a shipwreck began to take shape in the blue water.

It must have been a magnificent ship a hundred years ago, but now what was left of the wooden hull was covered in coral, algae, and barnacles, giving it the look of a thriving underwater neighborhood rather than the bones of a man-made vessel. From a distance, Simon couldn't make out details, but almost immediately he spotted silhouettes so large they could only be sharks.

He and Jam took cover behind a large rock. "How many

are usually here?" said Simon quietly, afraid of drawing the sharks' attention.

"A dozen, usually," said Jam. "Depends on the time of day. And you don't have to worry about them hearing you. They've been able to smell us for the past ten minutes."

That didn't help ease Simon's anxiety at all, and he peeked around the corner. "Then why are we hiding?"

"Because they've probably just eaten, and chasing us is too much effort. Unless we give them a reason."

Simon's fins twitched. "And I'm guessing trying to look for the piece would be the perfect reason."

"Unfortunately."

They watched the sharks lazily circle through the shipwreck, scaring off the other fish, and Simon tried to spot a pattern—any kind of pattern that might give him and Jam an opening. But even that was too risky, especially when they didn't have much to go on. His mother could have meant anything with that *chum* comment.

With a sigh, Simon finally resigned himself to the fact that, for now, he wasn't getting in there alone. Even if he shifted into a great white shark, they might ask questions he couldn't answer, and as soon as they grew suspicious, Simon was sure he'd be a goner. And shifting into a killer whale might have chased them away, but he would be too big to look around, and they might decide to attack him anyway, since they would have the advantages in numbers.

Instead, he surfaced once more and looked toward the

nearest beach on Santa Catalina Island. They were much closer now, and Simon could see dozens of people gathered on the sandy shore. At first glance, they could have easily been sunbathers and swimmers, but it didn't take Simon long to notice that none of them were wearing swimsuits or wading out into the water. Even more chilling were the hundreds of birds perched in the trees around the cove.

"I think we found Orion," he muttered, glancing nervously into the sky. Above them flew countless birds—hawks, eagles, falcons, and even seagulls joined in, honking noisily to one another. "They weren't there before, were they?"

"No, they weren't," said Jam, gulping. "Come on, before they spot us."

"I think they already have," said Simon as a few hawks dived for a closer look. A screech echoed through the air, and he and Jam both ducked back into the water, swimming as fast as their fins could manage.

A pang of regret shot through him as they put distance between themselves and the cove, and it took him several long seconds before he realized why he felt like he was leaving something behind. His mother was on that beach with the birds, held captive by Orion.

No. Not held captive. She was choosing to stay with him, and Simon had to remember that. No matter how much he missed her, no matter how much he wanted to reassure himself that she was all right, there was no point in taking the risk to see her. It was too dangerous. Besides, he didn't trust himself not to try convincing her to come with him, and right now, they didn't have any time to waste.

"They don't know we're Animalgams, right?" said Simon as they swam deep enough into the water that the birds wouldn't be able to spot them. "Maybe they weren't suspicious."

"Orion's always suspicious," said Jam. "If this gets back to the General—"

"He has no way of knowing it was us," said Simon. "They think I'm an eagle, remember?"

Still, Jam continued to fret, until at last Simon had no choice but to try to distract him. "There must be other really cool stuff down here," he said. It all looked turquoise and hazy to him, but Jam did perk up.

"My favorite spot isn't far," he said. "We still have time if you want to see it."

After surfacing far from shore to take another breath, they headed deeper into the water. It was darker down here, with little sunlight reaching the ocean floor, and Simon shivered. With all its different creatures and glowing walls in caverns full of starfish, the underwater kingdom was spectacular, but he still couldn't shake the feeling that he didn't belong down here.

"This is it," said Jam proudly as they approached a gaping entrance. "It's a huge maze of caves, and there are so many that I still haven't explored every one. Pearl told me about it when I shifted for the first time last winter. I don't think she was supposed to," he added. "She told me I had to be careful not to come when my sisters were here. I think it's their secret clubhouse or something."

Simon looked around the murky ocean floor warily, half expecting another shark to pop up. Considering their morning so far, he wasn't sure his nerves could take another unexpected visit from something with that many teeth. "Are you sure they aren't here right now?"

"Probably not," said Jam. "They all have drills."

"*Probably* not?"

But Jam was already swimming through the mouth of the cave. Cursing to himself, Simon hurried to catch up, not liking this one bit.

"Which way do you want to go?" Jam had stopped at a fork twenty feet inside, waiting for him. Simon glanced between the two options.

"Right," he decided. It looked lighter that way. And, he figured, if he only chose the right option, it would be easier to find their way out. So, again and again, whenever they came across a new choice, Simon went right.

"Are you doing this on purpose?" said Jam, but instead of sounding disappointed, he seemed almost giddy with excitement.

"Doing what?" said Simon, not wanting to explain that he simply didn't want to get lost. Usually it was Jam who was the nervous one, not him.

"You'll see. Choose right again," said Jam, and obediently Simon did as told.

This tunnel was shorter and darker than the others, and as the walls began to close in, Simon wished he'd chosen left instead. But as soon as the tunnel seemed like it would never end, it opened up into a large cavern.

It wasn't just any cavern, though. Like the planetarium, the ceiling was covered with bioluminescent liquid that cast enough light for them to see what was inside. This time, instead of sea stars, the floor of the cavern was covered in sparkling rocks and shells that reflected the blue glow. Some were small, no bigger than pebbles, but amid the quartz and corroding coins, Simon spotted what looked like real gems that were the size of his fist. His mouth dropped open.

"What is this place?"

"It's an octopus garden," said Jam. "You know, like the song."

"What song?"

Jam stared at him. "You've never—" He hummed a few notes in his squeaky dolphin voice, as if that would jolt Simon's memory.

"Sorry," he said. "Uncle Darryl didn't listen to much music."

Jam shook his head, seemingly dismayed. "Never mind. Octopuses collect rocks and other shiny things, and they make these gardens. I mean, mostly they're just hoarding stuff, but they're cool to look at. The one that lives here is really old and cranky, but he's almost always out in the morning. Isn't it awesome?"

It *was* pretty great. Slowly the knot in the pit of Simon's stomach loosened, and he relaxed as he and Jam looked around the garden. There were, as Simon suspected, real gemstones, though a small glittering stone in particular caught his attention. In the blue light, it looked like the starry night sky.

"Winter would love this place," he said, picking up the rock with his mouth. "Gonna bring this to her."

His words were garbled, but Jam seemed to understand. "We have to get back anyway," he said. "It's almost lunchtime, and if we're late, the General won't let me be your chaperon again."

The last thing Simon wanted was one of Jam's sisters breathing down his neck all day, so he followed Jam out of the caves without complaint. Now that they knew where they were going, it was quick swimming back to the entrance beneath Atlantis, and after Jam greeted Al and Floyd like they hadn't threatened to eat them earlier, they headed up through the tunnel and into the open air. Simon spit the rock onto the ground and shifted back into a human, stretching.

"That was fun," he said as he tucked the stone into his pocket. "I mean, except for the part where we almost got eaten multiple times."

"I'm telling you, they wouldn't have eaten us," said Jam, who seemed to be in a much better mood now, and they continued their friendly argument as they climbed back up the slippery rocks. Somehow, through whatever magic gave them the ability to shift in the first place, their clothes remained dry.

Still, Simon was happy to pull his sweatshirt back on when they reached the storage room. With any luck, it wouldn't smell like fish guts for too long. As he stuck his hands in his pockets, however, he remembered one very important thing he'd left behind.

"Felix?" he called as loudly as he dared. "Felix, are you in here?"

"Probably waiting for us outside," said Jam, checking his watch. "We're a little early."

They hurried into the planetarium, which was now full of people eating their lunch as they gazed at the pool of sea stars. Simon and Jam checked under seats, behind rocks, and even the edge of the pool to make sure Felix hadn't decided to go for a dip. He was nowhere to be found.

By now, their meeting time had come and gone, and Simon was beginning to worry. "What if someone caught him and thought he was a spy?" he said after they'd checked the storage room again.

"They would have reported him to the General," said Jam. "Come on, I'm sure he's around here somewhere."

Reluctantly Simon let Jam lead him out of the planetarium and back onto the streets of Atlantis. They passed the White Shark Café once more, and Simon checked inside to make sure Felix hadn't tried to steal a croissant. No luck.

"He's probably back at the compound, right?" said Simon, hurrying down the sidewalk.

"Probably went back for a nap," agreed Jam, but there was a note of worry in his voice now, too. Simon walked faster, and even though Jam was taller, he had to trot to keep up.

They burst into the foyer, and after a terse conversation with one of the guards, Jam reviewed the list. "If he's back, security didn't check him in," he said. "But he's small. Maybe they didn't see him."

Considering the last time Felix had interacted with the guards, when they'd put him in a cage, Simon wouldn't have blamed him for sneaking in. Forcing himself to relax, he submitted to a pat-down while a security guard inspected the pocket watch and the small rock he'd brought back for Winter. After the guard had decided neither were weapons, Simon was allowed to enter the compound, and he and Jam rushed back to the guest rooms.

"Felix?" said Simon, bursting into the room. "Felix, are you—"

"You're late," said Rhode, appearing behind them in the doorway. How they'd missed her in the hallway, Simon had no idea. "By three minutes."

"We were here on time," said Jam testily. "Security took forever. Have you seen Felix?"

"Who?"

"Felix. My mouse," said Simon as panic began to consume

his common sense. His suitcase was empty, and so was the rest of his side of the room. He ducked into the bathroom, but Felix wasn't there, either. "You know, the one you arrested yesterday."

"The General ordered his release," said Rhode. "If he's wandered off, that's hardly my fault."

Simon rounded on her. "You're the one who thinks he's a spy. You never wanted him here to begin with—"

"I don't want you in the city, either, but here we are," she said crisply. "I follow the General's orders. No one else's."

"She wouldn't have done anything to him unless the General ordered it," said Jam, though he shot his sister a sharp look. "Come on, maybe someone else has seen him."

"Before you go to the dining room, the General needs to speak to you, soldier," said Rhode. "Immediately. I'll escort Simon to lunch."

"But—" Simon began to protest.

"This doesn't concern you, Mr. Thorn," said Rhode, cutting him off. And when he turned to Jam for help, all his friend could do was give him an apologetic look.

"I'll help you look later," promised Jam, and he hurried off, leaving Simon alone with Rhode.

Terrific. Simon had no idea what to say, and the pair of them stared at each other for a long moment, her blue eyes studying him as if he were something disgusting, but not revolting enough to give her an excuse to run.

"You have no idea what your influence is doing to him, do you?" she said quietly, and for the first time, Simon thought he was talking to Jam's sister, not his superior officer. "He's going to be the next General of our kingdom. He can't afford to keep getting into trouble and defying orders."

"I'm not—" started Simon, but she cut him off.

"I read all of the Alpha's dispatches to the General. I know what you two have been up to, and I've done my best to shield my brother from the worst of the General's wrath, but you're not helping." She crossed her arms. "If you're really his friend, you'll stop getting him into trouble, and you'll start supporting his successes."

"I am supporting his successes," said Simon, although he wasn't entirely sure what she meant by that. "I'm not trying to get anyone into trouble—"

"You just can't help it if you always get caught," Rhode sneered. "I don't like you, Simon Thorn."

"Really? I couldn't tell," he muttered. She ignored him.

"I'll like you even less if you continue endangering my baby brother and placing him at odds with the General and our family. So I'll only tell you this once, and you'd better listen." She took a step closer, leaning down so she was looming over him. "Whatever it is you're doing, leave him out of it. If you don't, you'll force me to get involved, and I can promise you won't like that one bit."

With that, she marched out of the room and headed toward the dining room. Simon gritted his teeth. Maybe she was right—maybe Jam was getting into all kinds of trouble because of him, and he already felt guilty enough for putting his friends at risk during their search for the pieces of the Predator. But Simon knew without question that the General and the rest of Jam's family hadn't thought much of him long before Simon ever showed up. That wasn't his fault.

"If you don't want to lose Jam, maybe you should think about not being such a jerk to him all the time," he retorted as he followed her down the mirrored hallway. "That hurts him more than anything we ever do."

Rhode glared at him over her shoulder, and for a split second, he thought he saw a flash of pain in her eyes. "Our family doesn't concern you."

"Yes, it does. Jam's my best friend, and you're making him miserable."

"He's making himself miserable. There's nothing I can do to help him as long as he refuses to help himself."

She increased her stride, but Simon didn't bother keeping up with her. Instead, mostly out of concern for Felix, but also a little out of spite, he took his time searching every corridor they passed for the little brown mouse. At first he thought she might leave him behind to get lost in the compound, but she stuck with him, even if she made it a point to huff loudly. He didn't care. She could be as frustrated as she wanted—she had no idea what she was talking about, not when it came to Jam. And he wouldn't risk leaving Felix behind just because she wanted to get to lunch.

When they finally reached the dining room, it was packed with soldiers and civilians helping themselves to a buffet-style lunch. To Simon's surprise, the General and Jam had already arrived, and they stood in the middle of the crowded room while the General lectured Jam on something that, judging from the few snippets Simon could hear, sounded suspiciously like the timetable for the tides. After slipping away from Rhode, Simon tried to weave through the crowd to reach the corner where Winter was sulking, but before he could go more than a few steps, a familiar old man with sparse white hair and tortoiseshell glasses stepped in front of him, blocking his way.

"Ah, Simon, my boy," said Crocker, leaning heavily on his cane as a woman Simon recognized as another member of the reptile council pulled out a chair for him. "You look like you've seen better days."

"My friend is missing," said Simon, automatically glancing at the floor to check. "You remember Felix?"

"The mouse? Yes, yes," murmured Crocker. "Pity. No doubt he'll turn up. Malcolm, your nephew has finally arrived."

Malcolm was on the other side of Crocker, talking to a redheaded woman wearing a baggy sweater and ripped black jeans. Her back was turned to Simon, but they both glanced over, and Simon felt a jolt run through him.

Zia Stone, the leader of a mammal community he and his friends had come across on their trip to Arizona. What was she doing here?

"There you are, Simon," said Malcolm. He looked like he'd aged ten years in a day. "Your brother said you ran off."

"We went exploring," he said. It wasn't exactly a lie. "Felix is missing. I've looked everywhere for him—"

"Are you sure he didn't get bored and wander off?" said Malcolm.

"I—no," admitted Simon. "But what if he didn't? What if someone sees him and thinks he's a spy?"

"Why did you let him get lost in the first place?" said his uncle. "You're supposed to be keeping an eye on him."

"You know he doesn't listen to me," said Simon, anguished. "I'm sorry, I—please, Malcolm. He could be hurt. Or—or worse."

Malcolm grimaced. "That mouse is going to be the death of me and all five kingdoms." He gave Zia an apologetic look. "If you'll excuse me, I need to speak to the General."

He left to join the General, who was now talking to Rhode—and, Simon noticed, glancing his way. He tried to slip out of view, but Zia stepped in front of him and caught his arm in a friendly squeeze.

"Fancy seeing you here, Simon," she said in an amused voice that made him itch. There was something about her he didn't trust. "With Orion camped out on the island, I thought the General would rather eat his own fins than let birds into the city."

"Malcolm made him," said Simon, trying to move around her, but Coralia was blocking his way now. "Aren't you supposed to be watching over Stonehaven?"

"Your uncle asked me to come," she said with a shrug.

The shoulder of her oversize sweater slipped, and he saw the scars she'd gotten protecting him from Celeste while in Arizona. Even if Simon wasn't sure he could trust her, she *had* gone to a lot of trouble to stop others from getting in his way. "Enjoying your time in Atlantis?"

"Not really," he said. "Felix—"

"Is missing. Right." Zia tilted her head, considering him. "Have you asked if there are any televisions anywhere?"

"Doubt they get any channels down here." But he hadn't thought of that. It was another place to look, at least. "Did Bonnie, Billy, and Butch ever turn up?" He and his friends had met the orphaned raccoon family in Chicago, and as a favor to him, Zia had promised to take them in if they'd decided to join her at Stonehaven.

"They did," she said cheerfully. "They're getting an education, hot meals, beds to sleep in, friends, family, the works. And they're causing more trouble than a pack of wild coyotes, so naturally I adore them."

"Simon!" barked Malcolm from the other side of the room. He gestured for Simon to join him, and Simon muttered an apology before hurrying through the crowd, grateful to get away from Zia's piercing stare.

"I'll issue a city-wide alert," grumbled the General after Simon explained the situation, leaving out the part where he and Jam had left him alone while they'd gone swimming. "Make sure the citizens know he's a guest, not an enemy combatant."

"Thanks," said Simon, not sure whether to feel relieved or more concerned. "They would report to you if they found him, right? I mean, no one would—"

"No one will hurt him," promised Malcolm before the General could answer. "He'll be back before you know it. Now do me a favor and make sure Ariana is all right. She seemed a little off during the meeting."

Simon was too worried about Felix to focus much on anything else, but he also wanted to know what was going on with the security summit. So, without arguing, he searched the crowd for Ariana's telltale blue hair, quickly spotting her in the corner with Jam and Winter. Her face was drawn, and she looked vaguely sick, though whether that was due to the nearby tray of sushi or something else, Simon couldn't say.

"Are you okay?" he said once he'd made his way over to them. She shook her head.

"We have a problem," said Jam. "A big one."

Fear trickled through him as images of Felix underneath a heavy soldier's boot flashed through his mind. "What's going on?" he said, bracing himself for the worst. The three of them glanced at one another.

"The General decided to move the piece," said Ariana.

"And he wants me to come with him," added Jam. "We're going tonight."

9

BLOOD IN THE WATER

"But—*why*?" repeated Simon for what felt like the hundredth time as he paced across the worn patterned carpet. They'd sneaked out of the dining room and into a nearby parlor that looked like it hadn't been touched in a decade, but at least no one would overhear their conversation. "Why move it now, when that's almost definitely what Orion's waiting for?"

"Because he's convinced the location is compromised," said Ariana, slumped in a stiff maroon armchair. "I guess the bird army is too close for comfort."

"Maybe it is at Chum Bay after all," said Jam, who was seated on a matching velvet sofa. "That would explain why Orion's camped out so close. But there's no way he would be able to get past the sharks."

"Are they always there?" said Simon. "Or do they move around?"

"They hunt at night," said Jam. "But that probably just means there will be more of them at the shipwreck."

"Shipwreck?" said Winter from her spot beside Jam. "What shipwreck?"

Simon hastily explained where they'd gone. "If that's where the General hid the piece, then the bird army doesn't stand a chance of getting it as long as it's there, but if the General moves it . . ." He scowled at the unoffending carpet. "He's taking security with him, right?"

"No," admitted Jam. "He doesn't want anyone else to find out where he's hiding the piece. It's just him and me."

Simon muttered something deeply unflattering about the General. "Do the other summit members at least know what's happening?"

"He wasn't specific," said Ariana. "He only said he'd make sure Orion wouldn't be able to find it."

"So what do we do now?" said Jam, wringing his hands.

"Do you think you can convince him not to move it?" said Simon.

"I can try. The General doesn't really listen to me, though. He sort of just . . . lectures and barks orders."

"But he has to when it's this important," insisted Winter. "What if we go back and find it first?"

"With that many sharks around, it'd be impossible," said Jam glumly, pushing his glasses up his nose. "I'm sorry, Simon. I don't know what to do."

Simon shook his head and continued to pace across the parlor. "It's not your fault. We'll figure something out. Go with him, all right? And I'll try to follow. Maybe I can grab the piece before anything happens to it."

Winter rolled her eyes. "Did the salt water turn your brain into stew? If the General catches you—"

"And what if Orion gets it instead? What happens then?"

"Winter's right," said Ariana tiredly, slumping forward in her chair. "It's too much of a risk. You'd be tried for treason at best, and at worst, you'll be tried for treason *and* everyone will know you have the Beast King's powers."

"So I won't let him catch me," said Simon firmly, focusing on Jam. "He'll never know I'm following you. I'll stay a safe distance behind, I'll shift into different creatures—I'll be careful."

Jam pressed his lips together. "What if Orion attacks?"

"He only has the flock. He can't get underwater."

"But what if—"

"I swear you guys are no better than the people at the summit," said Ariana, rubbing her temples. "We'll know where the piece is in the morning, Simon. You and Jam can go after it then."

"But—" began Simon.

"And," she continued, drowning him out, "if you absolutely insist on going after them to make sure no one else intercepts it, then fine. But only as long as you don't take any unnecessary risks. If you get caught, we'll lose more than just the underwater kingdom's piece."

Simon opened and shut his mouth. "And if Orion attacks?"

"Then you shift into the biggest, baddest shark you can think of and eat him," said Ariana, as if the answer were obvious. "I hear eagle tastes like chicken."

Simon made a face. "Great."

"Jam, you carry Simon in your pocket," she said. "Once you reach the water, stay out of sight. It shouldn't be too hard at night."

Jam buried his face in his hands and groaned. "This is crazy. The General is smart. He'll be looking for tricks like this, and if he sees Simon crawl out of my pocket, or if he somehow spots him in the ocean—"

"This whole mission is crazy," agreed Simon. "But if we don't do it, who will? We can't save the world without taking some risks. Otherwise someone else would have done it by now."

"Inspiring," said Winter flatly, hopping off the sofa. "I'll make sure to put it on your tombstone. Now, if you don't mind, I need to get back to the dining room before Nixie discovers I'm missing. Unless there's something I can do to help."

Simon, Ariana, and Jam exchanged looks, and Winter sighed.

"Didn't think so. See you all later. Try not to die."

She left, closing the door behind her and leaving the three of them to stare at one another. Maybe this was stupid, maybe it was reckless, but the only other choice Simon had was to do nothing. And right now, *nothing* could mean losing the underwater piece—and the war.

A little risk, he decided, was worth it.

The rest of the day went by at a snail's pace. Jam had afternoon drills, leaving Simon in the less-than-attentive hands of Coralia, who was so upset about the General disapproving of her boyfriend that she didn't seem to care what Simon did. She followed him around the compound as he looked for Felix, and while she did make him listen to a speech meant to convince her father that marrying a human was better than her leaving and him never seeing her again—though mostly it wound up being a lot of ranting about how miserable she was in Atlantis—Simon didn't mind. Even though he'd only been underwater a day, he could empathize.

After the afternoon ended with no sign of Felix, Simon barely touched his dinner, both worried sick and sick of sushi. His friends may not have been as concerned about Felix as he was, but they were nervous about the piece being moved, and none of them were in the mood for laughing, not even at Nolan's mushy story about how Pearl had tripped in the coral gardens earlier that day, leaving it to Nolan to catch her.

That evening, Simon had no choice but to shove his fears for Felix aside and focus on the bigger problem instead. While his brother was brushing his teeth, Simon slipped into the mirrored hallway. Jam had drawn him a map on the back of a napkin at dinner, and while Simon wasn't sure about a few turns, at last he arrived at a room he was pretty confident belonged to Jam.

Knocking so softly that his knuckles barely brushed the door, he waited, glancing around nervously. This floor was where the family lived, and if someone came out and saw him—

"It's about time!" Jam opened the door and yanked him inside his bedroom. "The General's due any minute."

"Nolan distracted me," said Simon. Unlike the bare décor of the guest rooms, Jam's walls were hidden by bookshelves crammed full of everything from novels to comic books to movies, and any section that wasn't covered in shelves was adorned with pictures of different parts of the world. The Sahara Desert, the Swiss Alps, the Great Wall of China—all places that were far from Los Angeles. "And this room is really hard to find. How do you know where everything is in this place?"

"I know where things are, remember?" said Jam. "My sisters are the ones who get lost sometimes. Come on—I figure you'll be safe if you pretend you're Felix."

"What?" said Simon, freezing in place as he bent over to inspect Jam's comic book collection.

"If the General realizes you're in my pocket, at least we can pretend you're Felix," said Jam. "It's not perfect, but it's better than me trying to explain why I'm carrying around a cockroach or something."

"A cockroach? You think I'd shift into a cockroach?"

"Ariana says they're misunderstood," said Jam defensively. "It doesn't matter, all right? I just think it'd be a good idea—"

"All right, fine, I'm shifting," said Simon, because it *was* a good idea, even if the thought of taking advantage of Felix's disappearance made Simon feel sticky with unease. Closing his eyes, he pictured Felix in his head. He'd only ever shifted into a gray mouse before and wasn't sure if the Beast King had absorbed the powers of any others all those years ago. But as his body began to shrink, brown fur sprouted from his skin, and he breathed a sigh of relief. At least this part of the plan would work. He hoped.

He wriggled into Jam's pocket two seconds before a knock sounded on the door. "Soldier," said the General, his voice still booming despite his apparent attempt to whisper.

Jam threw open the door. "Ready for duty, sir," he said, and while Simon couldn't see through the fabric, he thought he felt Jam salute.

The pair walked through the mirrored compound, and Simon discovered a newfound respect for Felix, who'd spent all that time in his pocket and had never once complained. Well, not much, anyway. It was comfortable, but cramped, and he swayed with every step Jam took, which gave him a strange sense of motion sickness. Maybe Felix was used to it. Or maybe he'd stuck his head out to be sick, and Simon had never noticed.

He was so focused on not tossing his tiny mouse cookies that he almost forgot what he was doing. It wasn't until a chill in the air permeated Jam's pocket that he realized they were no longer in the compound.

"You're never to use this exit without my direct authorization, is that understood?" said the General. Simon tried to peek out of Jam's pocket to see where they were, but it was dark now.

"Yes, sir," said Jam, his voice shaking. "Sir, if I may—"

"Hold that thought, soldier. The water at night is treacherous, and I need you to stick close to me. No foolish moves, is that understood?"

"Yes, sir," repeated Jam. "Sir—"

A loud screech pierced the air, and Simon winced, covering his ears. It sounded like rusty hinges, and as Jam began to descend, Simon figured they were under the city somehow. He desperately wanted to know if anyone else ever used this exit, too, but the General didn't speak up again, and Jam remained quiet.

Simon couldn't decide if the silence was awkward and tense, or if it was normal for a father and son who didn't seem to have much in common other than their Animalgam form. Either way, they said nothing until Simon heard boots splashing in water.

"Meet me at the end of the cave," said the General. "No dawdling."

"Yes, sir," came Jam's predictable response, and a splash later, it was silent.

Jam waited several seconds before he scooped Simon out of his pocket and set him down on a slippery rock that smelled like mildew. "I'll see you there," he whispered before once again shifting into a dolphin and diving into the black pool that, like the cave in the planetarium, must have led out into the ocean.

Or maybe this was where the piece was hidden, and they were panicking over nothing. Maybe this was some cave underneath the city that only the General knew about, and Orion would have no chance of attacking them inside.

Crossing his little mouse toes, Simon shifted into one of the animals Jam had suggested—a white sea bass. He was smaller than he would have liked, but once he'd wriggled into the cold water, he swam as fast as his little body could manage. In the darkness, it was almost impossible to tell where he was going, but he mustered up his courage and swam straight ahead, hoping he didn't accidentally bump into the General.

Much to his dismay, the cave brought them right to the open ocean. No guards were stationed outside the narrow entrance camouflaged by seaweed and coral, and Simon could barely make out a pair of dolphins swimming ahead. Muttering to himself, he shifted into a black rockfish like one he and Jam had seen while swimming earlier, in case the General had happened to notice the sea bass following behind them. It didn't look like anything special, with silver scales and a dark tail, but Simon hoped it would be fast enough for him to keep up, and ordinary enough for him not to be noticed.

The dolphins swam with purpose, but thankfully, Simon didn't have trouble catching them. Though he made sure to stay out of the General's line of sight, he followed them as closely as he dared—close enough, as it happened, to make out the conversation the dolphins were now having.

". . . generations," said the General. "Every General passes it down to his or her successor, and the piece is moved every decade. It is our most important job as General, protecting our piece of the Predator."

"More important than protecting our communities, sir?" said Jam dubiously.

"If our piece ever leaves our custody, there is a good chance our communities would cease to exist in the war that would inevitably follow." I cannot tell you how important it is for you to keep the location secret at all times, soldier. Never, not once in five hundred years, has anyone stolen it from us, and I will not allow them to now."

Simon sensed Jam's hesitation even from a distance. "But if it's in a safe place, why are we moving it, sir?"

"Because the position has been compromised," he said. "I made the mistake of trusting Isabel Thorn, and now she's betrayed us by revealing the location to Orion."

Simon's stomach twisted, causing a sharp pain in his abdomen, or whatever passed for it in his fish form. His mother wasn't trying to betray the other kingdoms. She was protecting them.

Jam must have been thinking along the same lines, because he said timidly, "Sir, if Isabel Thorn had betrayed the location to the bird kingdom . . . wouldn't they have found it by now?"

"It's too well protected," said the General stoutly.

"Then . . ." Jam faltered. "Sir, why are we moving it then, sir?"

"Because the bird kingdom is far too close for comfort. While it may be well protected, they may have allies we haven't anticipated."

"But sir, don't we also risk exposing it to the bird kingdom while it's in transit—"

"Which is why we are out here in the dead of night, soldier, just you and me," said the General. "Orion will never anticipate it, and even if he did, he has no way to intercept underwater. This is a risk we must take. You'll understand someday."

Simon and Jam understood now, though—maybe more than the General did. As much as Simon needed to find the piece, he needed Orion not to find it more. And if it was somewhere safe, then it would be better to keep it there than to give Orion the chance to steal it.

No matter what Jam said, however, the General remained firm. They were moving the piece, and that was that.

As they swam through the dark water, Simon felt a prickling sensation, as if someone were watching him. Several times he swam off course and shifted into another animal, only to circle back to see if anyone was following Jam and the General, but he didn't spot anyone else.

Still, his nerves only grew when they finally reached Chum Bay. Jam had been right after all—the piece was hidden inside the shipwreck. There were dozens of sharks swimming around the sunken wreckage, but rather than question the dolphins, as Simon expected, they simply watched as they swam through. He thought he heard a few murmur greetings to the General, but he remained behind the rock that he and Jam had used to hide earlier that day.

Once Jam and the General disappeared into the ship, the ocean seemed eerily quiet. Simon didn't dare surface to see if Orion and the flock were circling above—he barely moved, floating near the rock and trying to make himself as invisible as possible.

That prickling feeling returned right as the dolphins emerged from the shipwreck. Out of sight of the others, Simon shifted into a hammerhead shark—partially because he thought he might be able to help if something happened, but mostly because he'd been dying to try it since he'd first gotten in the water.

It was better than he'd ever dreamed it could be. While turning into a kingsnake had made him feel strong for the first time in his life, the sleek body of the hammerhead shark gave him physical power he'd never dreamed existed. If he wanted, he was sure he could have crushed the entire world in his jaws. His eyes were now situated far apart on his wide head, which gave him the ability to see all around him—up, down, left, right, back, front, all at once, and it was bizarre. Like being in a video game, he thought, but cooler. His sense of smell also exploded, and a deluge of scents assaulted him. Fish, sharks, seaweed, salt, bird, human—

Simon floated in the cold water for a moment, stunned into helplessness despite his newfound strength. But now wasn't the time to get distracted. Even though the number of smells overwhelmed him, he shook himself out of it and let the shark's instincts take over. Dolphins. He needed to find dolphins.

He caught the trail instantly, and before he could think about it, his streamlined body was already moving. Strong and deadly, he cut through the water effortlessly, and the few creatures he could see in the dark swam out of his way. He'd never been the biggest before, and it was intoxicating—so intoxicating, in fact, that for a moment he forgot why he was out there.

But a shrill cry pierced the air, tearing his attention away from his new form, and all of Simon's instincts—both shark and human—kicked in. He surged through the water toward the sound, his heart pounding. That could have been anything. It wasn't necessarily a dolphin calling out for help.

But as Jam and the General appeared in the dark water, Simon noticed they'd come to a complete stop a few feet above the sandy ocean floor. Though they were unharmed, the larger dolphin floated protectively over the smaller one, and Simon gulped when he realized why.

Tiger sharks, bull sharks, even a great white shark circled above the dolphins, baring their teeth and ready to strike at any moment.

Jam and the General were surrounded.

10
A SHIVER OF SHARKS

"Do you have any idea who I am?" said the General, his voice booming even through the dolphin squeaks.

"You are the General," said the great white shark. A scar ran across its side, so long and deep that Simon guessed a harpoon had caused it. "But I am the king. Give us the piece, and we let you live."

Simon's heart pounded as his body filled with adrenaline, but he kept a grip on his fear. He counted eight sharks in total—too many for him to fight on his own and win. Even if Jam and the General could take down sharks, too, they were still outnumbered.

"What piece?" said the General. "I have no idea what you're talking about."

"The piece you took from the ship." The great white

shark flicked his fin toward the direction they'd come, where the shipwreck loomed in the darkness. "We see you take it. Now you give it to us. Orion says so."

Orion. Simon's blood ran cold. So this was how his grandfather intended on stealing it—but how he'd earned the loyalty of members of another kingdom, Simon didn't know. Right now, they had bigger problems. Judging by the way the shark spoke, Simon figured he wasn't an Animalgam. That meant he had no problem eating Jam and the General—or Simon, if he gave himself away. Worse, it meant he probably couldn't be reasoned with. Not in a human way, anyway.

"I demand you leave us at once." The General's voice shook with fury. "If you do not, the entire underwater kingdom will hunt down each and every one of you, and you will be punished until you are nothing more than sea foam. Is that the fate you wish for yourself?"

Despite his fearsome tone, the General had nothing to back his threats, and he must have known it. The only option he had was to give up the piece, unless he was willing to sacrifice himself and Jam to protect it. But what then? The sharks would still have it. Sacrifice would accomplish nothing.

Simon was their only hope. How was he supposed to stop eight bloodthirsty sharks from hurting both of them?

The great white growled. "You do not give, so we take. *Attack!*"

At once the other sharks descended toward the dolphins,

and Simon felt his body begin to shift with barely a thought. He grew large—larger than the hammerhead shark, larger than a wolf or a bear or even the great white. By the time he had finished shifting into a killer whale, he was twice the size of the other sharks, and while his acute sense of smell was gone, the echolocation had returned.

The battle on the ocean floor raged as the sharks attacked the dolphins. Despite being outnumbered, both the General and Jam were shockingly quick, dodging the sharks and fighting back in a way Simon had never seen a dolphin do before. Stunned, he simply watched until a tiger shark nearly took a chunk out of Jam's tail, and only then did he pull himself out of his stupor and rush toward the action, letting out a fierce cry.

The bellow was so loud that, for a moment, everyone stopped—even the General, who had been poised to take on a bull shark by himself. Furious, Simon swam as fast as he could. Despite his size, he was surprisingly agile, and he used both to his advantage, barreling through a group of sharks like a bowling ball crashing through pins. While he was hesitant to actually bite anyone, he knew he had to. This was fight or die.

He chomped down on a bull shark first, and while he'd only grabbed a fin, the shark squealed and swam out of the fight. Two more followed before one of the tiger sharks decided to attack Simon in return, and he hissed as sharp teeth sliced through his skin.

While he may not have known how to fight as an orca, he did have instincts, and he let those take over. His agility and ability to tell where each shark was allowed him to make up for being such a large target, and he took out each of his opponents one by one. It wasn't easy, exactly, but it felt natural, and he fought with everything he had.

Out of the corner of his eye, Simon spotted the great white shark swimming toward Jam, and Simon changed course as fast as he could. "Stop!" he called in a menacing voice, but it didn't work. The great white shark opened his large jaws, angling toward Jam, and—

Out of nowhere, the General darted through the water, putting himself between Jam and the shark. The great white's teeth sank into the General's dolphin body instead, and the General let out a scream that chilled Simon to the bone.

"Dad!" cried Jam—the first sound he'd made since leaving the shipwreck. Simon thought he saw something shiny drop from Jam's mouth, but it didn't matter right now. As soon as he reached the great white shark, he bit him around the middle as hard as he could, feeling the shark's cartilage skeleton crunch between his jaws.

The great white shark's body seized up, and he released the General. The injured dolphin sank to the sand, blood pouring from his wounds, and Simon dragged the great white from the scene before hurling him into the open ocean. The shark floundered, badly wounded, and Simon was torn between following him to finish the job or sticking close to the General and Jam.

Before he could make a decision, inky blackness engulfed them. The last thing Simon saw before he was blinded was several long legs with suction cups slinking across the ocean floor.

"Jam!" he cried. "Jam, are you—"

"I'm okay," called Jam from nearby. Simon could sense him floating beside the General, while the great white and the remaining sharks used the darkness to retreat. "My dad—he's—he's—"

Simon swam toward them through the black water. He wanted to shift back into a dolphin, but it was too risky. He would have to stay a killer whale until they found help or safety. "We need to get back to the city. Do you think your father can swim?"

"I don't—he isn't conscious." Jam's voice caught, and nausea washed over Simon. All too clearly he could picture Darryl on the rooftop of Sky Tower, surrounded by a pool of blood as he took his last breath. He couldn't let that happen to Jam. He wouldn't.

"Come on," he said. Taking the injured dolphin gently in his mouth, he began to swim, but Jam let out another anguished cry.

"The piece! It's gone—Simon, the piece—it was in my mouth, and then—"

Another flash of Darryl. Simon swallowed his dread and screwed up as much courage as he could muster. "We'll find it later," he said, his words muffled around the General. "Let's go."

As they swam from the scene of the fight, the water began to clear, and Simon kept his eyes to the ground, hoping against hope to spot the crystal piece the underwater kingdom had protected for five centuries. Even if he returned once the General was safe, that would give the sharks plenty of time to search for it first.

The piece or the General's life. It wasn't really a choice at all. Beside him, he heard Jam choke on a sob, and without hesitating, Simon sped up and away from the cloud of ink. He had sworn to himself no one else would die because of his hunt for the pieces of the Predator, and with a heavy heart, he didn't look back.

In order to get the General up the slippery tunnel, Simon had to shift into a bear, and together he and Jam hoisted the injured dolphin onto his back. Once the General was situated, Jam held his father in place while Simon carefully navigated his way up to the basement of the compound.

It was a risk, but he only shifted back into his human form once they reached the elevator. As soon as they were safely inside, Jam pressed the button, and Simon knelt beside the General, searching for a heartbeat. He'd lost so much blood—too much, Simon thought. Especially for a dolphin. But while he had no idea where to check for a pulse, he did see his body move as he breathed.

"Is he . . . ?" said Jam, his voice shaking.

"He's alive," said Simon. But the movement was faint, and he silently urged the elevator to rise faster.

The doors opened on the first floor, near security. "Help!" yelled Jam as loud as he could. "Someone, *help*!"

A pair of guards came running, and as soon as they spotted the injured dolphin, they too began to shout. Before Simon knew it, a crowd of soldiers had arrived, including several with red medic armbands. While Jam watched their efforts to help his father, Simon stood beside him, trying not to think the worst. But he didn't have to know much about dolphin anatomy to know the General was in rough shape.

"Benjamin?" Rhode appeared in the crowd, her face ashen. Rather than bark at her brother, she immediately swept him up in a tight hug. Simon stepped back and stared at his feet. "What happened? The General said—he said he was taking you for a swim—"

"To move the piece of the Predator," said Jam. His eyes were red, and somewhere in the chaos, he had lost his glasses. Both his and Simon's outfits were stained with blood. "We were attacked by sharks. The General—he was hurt—"

Rhode swallowed. "He'll be okay," she said, but they all knew she couldn't promise him that. With her arm wrapped around her brother's shoulders, they all watched as the medics lifted the bleeding dolphin onto a stretcher and rushed down the corridor. Rhode and Jam began to follow them, and Simon automatically tagged along, trailing behind to give them space.

"What are you doing?" said Rhode as she stopped suddenly, her gaze fixed on Simon. "Why are you here?"

"I—" Simon faltered and took a step back, shoving his hands into his pockets. "I just—"

"He helped me get the General up here," said Jam, slipping out from his sister's embrace.

Rhode narrowed her eyes. "How did you know where they would be?"

"I didn't," said Simon, lying as smoothly as he could manage. "I was looking for Felix, and—"

"He probably saved the General's life," interrupted Jam.

Rhode stared at Simon long enough to make his insides squirm, but he refused to look away. If she sensed the slightest weakness, he had no doubt she would attack, and he'd had enough of that tonight.

At last she turned away, instead leading her brother down the hallway past a cluster of guards. "Soldiers, alert the rest of the family about what's happened. And see to it that Mr. Thorn makes it back to his room without any further side trips."

The soldiers saluted, and Simon didn't argue as one of them took his arm and guided him down the hallway. But as soon as they stepped toward the elevator, Simon dug in his heels. He could still see smears of blood on the floor. "We're taking the stairs," he insisted.

The soldier huffed, but didn't force the issue. Instead they took the long way through the mirrored corridors to the staircase, and by the time they arrived in the guest area, Malcolm was pacing back and forth in the hallway. "Simon!" he shouted, hurrying up to them and pulling Simon into a tight hug. "Where have you been? We've been looking all over for you."

"I was looking for Felix," said Simon, sticking to the lie he'd told Rhode. "The General—"

"I've already been updated. The colonel's called an emergency summit meeting." Malcolm let him go, and much to Simon's dismay, he was scowling. "You shouldn't have gone anywhere without telling me first, Simon. You know how dangerous it is down here."

"I know. I'm sorry. I couldn't sleep," he said miserably. Ariana and Winter appeared in their doorway, both looking worried. From the corner of his eye, Simon could see into his and Nolan's room. His brother leaned against the wall, his arms crossed and his face like thunder.

Malcolm crouched down, studying him and his bloodstained clothing. "You're all right?" said his uncle in a dubious voice.

Simon nodded, but that wasn't true. Now that his adrenaline was fading, he could feel the deep ache of the sharks' bites in his side and leg. His heart sank. Even without looking, he could tell the wounds would need stitches. How was he supposed to explain that?

Malcolm didn't look entirely convinced, but he must

have passed it off as shock from seeing the General injured. "Ariana and I have to go. Nolan, will you keep an eye on Simon until I get back?"

Nolan huffed. "Now he wants my help?" he said, but one look from Malcolm, and he clammed up.

"I'll keep an eye on him," said Winter, also not appearing terribly convinced Simon was all right. Malcolm cast one last look at him before hurrying a bleary-eyed Ariana down the hallway. Simon wasn't sure what time it was, but judging by her yawn as she stumbled away, it had to be nearly midnight. With any luck, the emergency summit meeting would last until dawn, giving Simon time to figure out what to do—about both the piece and his wounds.

"If you were going to look for your stupid mouse, I could have helped," muttered Nolan once their uncle was out of earshot. "You never trust me."

"I'm sorry," said Simon. "Next time, okay?"

Nolan rolled his eyes. "Yeah, sure. Next time," he said before slamming the door in Simon's face.

"Ignore him. He knows as much about what's going on as a brain-dead amoeba," said Winter coldly, glaring as if she could see him through the wall.

"Amoebas don't have brains," said Simon, though he didn't protest as she took his hand and led him into her and Ariana's room.

"Precisely."

As soon as the door was closed, he collapsed on the nearer

bed, wincing and pulling up his sweatshirt. There was a semicircle of teeth marks in his hip and abdomen, and the shirt underneath his hoodie was stained with his blood.

"What—*Simon!*" Winter grabbed the sheet and pressed it against his side, her bitterness blossoming into panic. "What *happened?*"

"You should see the other guys," he said, trying to sound lighthearted, but it was difficult when Winter looked so frightened. He wilted. There was no use not telling her. She would find out eventually. "We lost the piece on the ocean floor. Orion probably has it by now, and if he doesn't, he will soon."

"I don't care about the stupid piece. I care about the fact that you nearly got turned into sushi. What were you *thinking?*"

"A bunch of sharks attacked Jam and the General," said Simon defensively. "If I hadn't jumped in, they would have died."

Her lips thinned. "You need to see a doctor."

"Later. I need to go back in the water and find the piece before Orion does. Can you patch me up?"

Winter stared at him, stunned. "You're crazy. Insane. Out of your mind."

"I'm desperate," he corrected.

"Same thing."

He winced as she touched an especially painful spot. "I promise as soon as I get back, I'll make up a story and see a doctor. *Please*, Winter."

"But—"

"We can't wait. If Orion's convinced sharks to work for him, there's no telling who else might be, too."

She groaned. "I hate you right now," she said, digging through her bag. "I have clean socks and duct tape. That'll have to do."

Simon didn't ask why she had duct tape with her, and she didn't offer an explanation. Winter wrapped the clean socks over his wounds like bandages, securing them in place with the tape. When he undressed to look at the wound on his leg, she was all business, never once making fun of him for sitting there in his underwear while she wrapped another pair of socks around the bite mark in his thigh. It was deeper than the other, and a few of his toes had gone numb. He didn't mention that, though.

At last, once he'd gingerly pulled his jeans back on, he started toward the door. "If anyone checks on me—"

"I'll tell them you're asleep," said Winter. "Be careful, all right?"

"I will," he said, and he offered her a small smile. "Thanks, Winter."

"Don't thank me. Just don't die."

Simon didn't make any promises. Ignoring the pain, he shifted into a fly and soared through the mirrored hallways, his new vision giving him a fractured, kaleidoscope view of everything around him. This might be the only chance he had to recover the underwater kingdom's piece, and he couldn't waste it.

11
BIRD'S-EYE VIEW

As Simon buzzed through the hallways, he quickly discovered he'd chosen wisely by shifting into something small. The compound was crawling with soldiers carrying weapons, and while steering clear of them completely was impossible, Simon made a point to keep his distance.

Getting caught wasn't the only thing he had to worry about. As soon as he retraced his and Jam's steps through the basement, he saw another pair of guards stationed at the mouth of the General's secret exit into the ocean. With a sinking feeling, he buzzed as close as he dared and eyed the door. It was sealed shut around the edges. He had no way to sneak inside without someone noticing.

He flew around the corner and clung to the wall, trying

to think. What were his other options? The planetarium? It was a good idea, until he remembered Al and Floyd, the great white sharks guarding the tunnel. This late, there was a chance they wouldn't be there, but the thought of facing them without Jam acting as a buffer made a trickle of fear run through him. He was too injured to get into another skirmish and win no matter what he shifted into.

There had to be other ways out of the city. Entire armies were stationed here. There must have been some kind of hatch or door—

The submarine dock. Simon pushed off the wall and flew as fast as he could to the nearest stairwell. If there was a way out of Atlantis, it had to be near the dock.

Within minutes, Simon reached the edge of the city, where they'd arrived the day earlier. It was mostly quiet now, with half a dozen vessels docked in a tunnel beneath the glass floor as a handful of workers went about their business, but there was no clear way out. No signs, no labels, no doors—nothing.

Time to get creative, then. Landing near one of the airtight seals, he made sure no one was looking and then shifted into a tuna crab. The small red creature was impossible to miss, and as Simon scuttled across the floor, the nearest worker called out.

"Hey, how'd you get in here?" The worker crouched down and caught him. For one horrifying moment, Simon thought the worker would try to crush him, but instead he stood and headed toward a hatch in the floor that was easily the size of an elevator. "Jimmy, caught another one," he called. "I thought you said you'd cleared that exit."

"I did," came a distant reply. "Must've wandered in with some cargo."

Muttering, the first worker opened the sealed door and dropped Simon inside. He landed on his back, and by the time he'd figured out how to roll over, the worker had slammed the hatch shut, and an odd whooshing sound filled the airtight room.

Simon was on the verge of admitting that maybe this hadn't been the best idea he'd ever had when a loud siren went off, and the door on the bottom of the hatch opened. With no warning, seawater rushed into the compartment, and Simon was carried off with the current into the cold ocean.

He wasted no time celebrating. Swimming away from the city, Simon shifted into an orca as soon as he was sure nothing was close enough to spot him in the dark water. Most of the other sea creatures gave him a wide berth as he swam toward Santa Catalina Island, and he used the killer whale's echolocation to return to the area near Chum Bay where Jam had dropped the piece. Thanks to the orca's size and speed, he arrived shortly after, not even out of breath. The ink the octopus had released had mostly dissipated by now, but there was still a hint of cloudiness in the water.

Despite that, it wasn't hard to find the exact spot he was looking for. The sand where the General had been attacked was brown with blood, and Simon searched for any sign of the piece. It had dropped out of Jam's mouth here—he had seen it. But no matter how hard he looked, there was no trace of it.

The octopus must have been working with the sharks, Simon reasoned. It had saved the sharks' lives by releasing the cloud of ink, and that had also given the octopus time to snatch up the piece and bring it to Orion. Nauseated at the thought of his grandfather getting his hands on another piece of the Predator, Simon fought to stop himself from spiraling into despair. It wasn't too late. The bird army would probably still be there—Simon could steal the piece back, and he would be gone before they found out.

Though he was dizzy with exhaustion and pain from the wounds on his side and leg, Simon pushed on and swam toward the cove. Every flip of his fins felt like hot knives sinking into his torso and thigh, and in his head, he could hear his mother's voice warning him how dangerous this was. Winter's joined hers, though her choice of word was *stupid*. Simon didn't disagree with either of them, but what else was he supposed to do? This was what they had come to Atlantis for. He couldn't give up now because it was harder than he thought it'd be.

As he approached the surface, he once again checked to make sure no one was watching. It was a dark, moonless night, and if anyone could see him from the beach or the sky, he couldn't see them. Taking his chances, he shifted from an orca into a seagull and bobbed to the surface. They weren't the fastest or most impressive of birds, but they would blend in, and right now, that was what he needed.

He took flight and soared toward the beach, where the bird army was camped out. Before arriving, he'd assumed everyone would be sleeping, but to his dismay, a bonfire crackled on the sand. Worse, as he grew closer, he spotted Orion and his lieutenant, Perrin, standing above what looked like a lumpy rock.

". . . did it go?" said Orion, his voice low enough to blend in with the soft crash of waves. Simon flew closer, landing on a nearby branch.

"We don't know." The rock wasn't a rock at all, but a man hunched over on the sand as he groveled. "Our allies were intercepted—"

"By what?" said Orion. "What could possibly defeat a gang of the toughest sharks on the coast? Or did you lie to me when you told me I could trust them?"

"No, no, not at all!" said the man. "The sharks want to see the seas returned to them, and they will do whatever you say, your lordship. They trust you."

"And I trusted them, but here we are." Orion limped across the sand, pacing in front of him. "How many were there?"

"How—how many what, your lordship?"

"How many attacked the sharks?"

"I—" He hesitated. "It was the General and his son, and—"

"*How many were there?*" Orion stopped in front of the

man and, with the help of a long stick acting as a makeshift cane, knelt down so he was only a few inches away. "It's a simple question. You were there, weren't you?"

"I—yes, your lordship, but only from a distance—"

"Did someone betray me? Or was there security we did not anticipate?"

The man swallowed so hard his Adam's apple bobbed. "There was an orca, your lordship. A savage beast that chased away the sharks and inflicted grave injury on several of our comrades."

Orion straightened. "An orca just happened to be there, did it?" He glanced at Perrin before refocusing on the informant. "You're dismissed."

He didn't argue. Standing on trembling legs, the man made a beeline back for the ocean, and as he ran into the water, he shifted into something long and slithery. An eel.

As soon as he disappeared, Orion turned to Perrin. "The twins are in Atlantis with the others, aren't they?"

Perrin nodded and opened his mouth to speak, but a woman's voice interrupted him.

"Nolan is a twelve-year-old boy. Even if the General did know about his . . . talents, Malcolm would never let him serve as security like that."

Simon's heart began to race. His mother. She was in the shadows, and he quietly flew toward her, landing in a closer tree. Farther from the bonfire, he could make out her silhouette sitting on a log. Now that he was hidden in the branches and away from other members of the flock, he shifted from a seagull into a great horned owl. Instantly the darkness that came with the seagull's vision disappeared, and he could see every individual hair in his mother's braid, along with the young blond man standing beside her—Rowan, Perrin's son, who had chased Simon and his friends through Penn Station only a few months ago.

"Then how do you explain an orca intercepting the sharks?" said Orion in a low, dangerous voice.

"It could be any number of things," said his mother in a bored tone. "Maybe the General did bring security. Or maybe Celeste has friends we don't know about. Either way, you lost the piece."

Simon blinked. Orion didn't have the piece? Then where—

Crack.

Simon jumped as the loud sound cut through the night air, and only a miraculous feat of balance kept him from falling out of the tree. Despite his old age and injuries, Orion had snapped his makeshift cane in half, and he hurled one half into the ocean and the other into the trees, missing his mother by only a foot. Simon's blood boiled, but she didn't so much as flinch.

"We had everything we needed for a successful mission," said Orion in a frighteningly calm voice, though his face was twisted into a hideous mask of fury. "Our partners are fierce fighters. Our insider's information was good. We had it—we *had* it, and you're telling me an *orca* stopped a plan months in the making."

"'The best-laid schemes of mice and men often go awry,'" quoted his mother smoothly. "You may not be a mouse, but you are a man."

The air around them seemed to crackle, and for a long moment, no one moved. Orion took a wobbly step toward her and Rowan, and Simon braced himself, ready to fight if his grandfather so much as touched her.

"Was it you?" he said softly, but with no less of a threat than before. "Did you tip off the underwater kingdom?"

"I've been on the beach the whole time," she said easily, tossing her braid over her shoulder. "Unless you think I can be in two places at once, I had no opportunity."

"Someone could have sneaked past my guards—"

"Then that would be on your guards, not me." She shrugged. "Maybe *you* have a spy. Have you ever considered that?"

Orion's gaze flickered suspiciously at the members of his flock lurking in the shadows, both human and bird. But almost as quickly as she had introduced the idea, he seemed to dismiss it. "My army has been nothing but loyal to me. You, on the other hand, have been hindering us every chance you get."

"I told you where to look, didn't I? You would be scouring the coastline from here to Vancouver if it wasn't for me."

"And I've been wondering why that is." Orion took another step toward her, and Simon tensed, forming the image of a tiger in his mind. He didn't want to attack, but if Orion went after his mother, nothing in the world would stop him from tearing him to shreds. "After months of doing nothing but thwarting me, why the change of heart, Isabel?"

His mother sat up straighter. "I told you. You leave the boys alone, and I will help you."

"No, no, it's more than that." He was almost within arm's reach of Simon's mother now, and Simon saw her hands tighten into fists in her lap. She was prepared to fight, too. "You may not be willing to tell me, but I know something happened in Arizona—something that had to do with Simon. There's no other reason for you abandoning him when you could have so easily escaped."

Simon's skin prickled at the reminder of what had happened in Paradise Valley. No matter how often he told himself that his mother was doing this to protect him and Nolan, her choice still stung.

"The threat from Celeste is more than enough to keep me interested in your . . . *mission*," said his mother. "We both want the same thing—for different reasons, even if you won't admit it. But you have resources I don't. And I have information you don't. The only way either of us will ever have a chance at success is working together."

Orion let out a mirthless laugh. "Since when have you ever been interested in working together?"

"Since Celeste showed up in Arizona and nearly killed my son. Family means something to me, Father, even if it means nothing to you."

"Family means everything to me," he hissed, leaning in closer. "I don't trust you."

"The restraints make that fairly obvious." She touched the metal collar around her neck, and a chain rattled. "But I'm willing to overlook them if it means getting what I want. Accept my help or don't. Either way, if I wanted to escape, I would have by now."

Orion studied her for a long moment, and finally he straightened. "Once I've assembled the weapon, you will have no choice but to fall in line and serve me—and serve your kingdom the way you were always supposed to."

"Maybe," said his mother with a shrug. "Or maybe I'll assemble it first and destroy it before you ever get the chance. We'll have to see, won't we?"

Orion growled and turned to Rowan. "Take your men and gather as much information as you can about what happened out there. I want to know who this orca is, what it wants, and how to find it before sunrise."

"Yes, sir," said Rowan. Shifting into a peregrine falcon, he let out a shrill cry, and half the flock burst from the trees and the sand as he took off over the ocean. Simon tried to melt into the shadows in case anyone spotted him, but none of them looked back.

"Perrin—" Orion returned to the bonfire as his lieutenant stood at attention. "Gather our allies and ready them for an attack. With the General injured, we must take this opportunity to strike while they're weak and scattered. We've been disrupting their supply lines long enough to ensure their resources have been depleted, and our forces are strong enough to lay siege on Atlantis. Without the General, they won't last long."

Perrin saluted. After shifting into a hawk, he followed his son, taking another portion of the flock with him. As soon as he was gone, Orion sank down onto a piece of driftwood near the bonfire, resting his head in his hands. The beach was quieter now, and while some members of the flock remained, Simon gathered his courage and flew silently to the base of the tree, only a few hops away from his mother. With Rowan gone, she was the only person in the darkness.

"I wish we could be on the same side, Isabel," said Orion after a long moment. "You and I could do a lot of good in this world."

His mother scoffed. "The only good you'd be doing is for yourself."

"On the contrary, I would stop the wars that have plagued our kingdoms for centuries," he said. "Skirmishes over nothing that still kill thousands. I can see no better good than that."

"The current system may not be perfect, but tyranny and oppression only help those at the top," she said. "You can't create peace by turning yourself into everyone's mutual enemy."

"I'll only be an enemy if I give them reason to fight me."

"You would give them reason just by existing—by having

more power than any Animalgam ever should," said his mother. "You can't control others no matter how much you threaten them. There will always be good people who rise up against tyrants and murderers regardless of what it costs them, and you will always be their enemy."

Orion sighed. "Perhaps. Or perhaps I will usher in a new era, and I will prove you wrong."

"Perhaps," she echoed. "Or perhaps you'll tear the five kingdoms apart until there's nothing left to fight for."

A smile flickered across his scarred face. "Perhaps."

Simon's stomach churned, and not only because he didn't want to imagine a world where Orion ruled over them all as the Beast King. He knew his mother was right—that no single person should ever have the powers he and Nolan had. But they couldn't help it, and for a moment, Simon wondered if his mother felt the same about them, too.

No. His mother wasn't the enemy. She was doing this for the right reasons, and she had to say these things to Orion. That was all. While Simon didn't know how much he could trust her now, he did know that she was and always would be on their side.

An uneasy quiet settled over the beach, with only the sounds of the waves breaking against the shore interrupting the silence. Simon knew he couldn't say anything to his mother, not with Orion twenty feet away, but he had to let her know she wasn't alone. So, with his vision as sharp as it had ever been, he scratched out a shape in the sand, close enough to the log that she would see it in the daylight. He couldn't leave a message, not when a member of the flock might see it, so instead he settled on a single heart. It wasn't much, but it told her everything he needed to say. He loved her, and nothing—not even what had happened in Arizona—would ever change that.

As soon as he was finished, he hopped back into the trees and shifted into a seagull once more. He took the long way around to the far side of the beach, beyond the bonfire so Orion wouldn't see him leave. But as soon as he was out of sight, he dived back into the water and shifted into a bull shark, the salt water stinging his wounds. The flock was coming for Atlantis, and he had to warn them. But beyond that, the Bird Lord's words echoed in his mind over and over again, making him swim as hard as he could for the city.

Our insider's information was good.

There was someone in the underwater kingdom close enough to the General that they had known the piece would be moved—and that someone was spying for Orion.

12

KANGAROO COURT

By the time Simon returned to the compound, only an hour had passed, and much to his relief, no one had discovered he'd been missing. Winter fussed over him, insisting on checking her makeshift bandages to ensure blood hadn't leaked through, but Simon refused.

"We need to find the summit meeting," he said. "Orion's going to attack the city."

"And if you don't see a doctor, your wounds will get infected and you'll fall over dead before that happens," snapped Winter.

"I—fine," muttered Simon. "We tell them, and then I'll go to the infirmary, all right?"

Winter eyed him suspiciously, but after a long moment,

she caved, following him out of the room and into the corridor with minimal grumbling.

By now Simon had mostly figured out the route from the guest rooms to the stairs, and he led the way through the mirrored hallways, frantically trying to remember if Ariana had said anything about where the summit meeting might be. The same floor as the dining room? A different one altogether?

"Halt!" came a deep voice as they turned another corner. Simon froze, inches from plowing straight into a broad-shouldered soldier with several medals pinned to his jacket. "What are you two doing here?"

Simon gulped. "Malcolm, the Alpha of the mammal kingdom, is my uncle, and we need to talk to him. It's an emergency."

"I cannot permit you to leave your rooms," said the soldier, starting to usher them back down the hall. "We are on lockdown—"

"This is important," said Simon fiercely. "It's about Orion."

The soldier frowned. "How would you—"

"If you don't do exactly what we tell you to do, everyone in this giant snow globe is going to die." Winter straightened her small body until she was as tall as she could be. "Do you want that to be on your shoulders, soldier?"

"Who—"

"I need to speak to my uncle. *Now*," said Simon with as much authority as he could muster. He didn't sound as convincing as Winter, but it was the best he could do.

The soldier pursed his lips and clamped his large hands on the back of both Simon's and Winter's necks. "I will escort you there," he said as he pushed them down the corridor. "But if this is a joke or a prank, I'll throw you in the brig until dawn."

Relieved, Simon marched as fast as he could, not even objecting when they climbed into the elevator instead of using the stairs. Someone had cleaned it, and he could smell a faint trace of bleach.

At last they arrived in front of the mirrored double doors they'd entered over a day ago, when they'd first arrived in Atlantis. The General's conference room. Simon silently berated himself for not thinking of that, even though it wouldn't have made a difference.

The guards opened the doors, and the three of them stepped inside. Silence fell over the room, and everyone sitting at the long table, from Malcolm to Zia to Crocker to Ariana to others Simon didn't recognize, turned to stare at them. With a jolt, Simon spotted Jam sitting to Rhode's right, his face splotchy and his shoulders heavy with exhaustion. Of course he'd be there. If the General died, that would mean . . .

"Yes, Captain?" said Rhode crisply. Despite everything that had happened to her father, Simon couldn't spot a trace of anxiety or grief on her face.

"I apologize for the interruption, Colonel," said their captor, "but these two insist they have information to tell you."

Rhode's piercing gaze settled on Simon, and he cleared

his throat. "Orion's planning to attack Atlantis at dawn. He has a bunch of underwater animals supporting him—not just sharks, but at least one eel, and probably others, too. I don't think many of them are Animalgams," he added when Rhode opened her mouth. "I think they're normal animals who are upset the General is ruling the ocean."

"How do you know this, Simon?" said Malcolm, who sat across from Rhode. The General's seat at the head of the table was empty.

"I—" Simon hesitated. "I borrowed some scuba gear and went to the surface. I'm sorry, I know I shouldn't have, but—"

"*Scuba* gear?" Malcolm rounded on Rhode, his muscles tensed as if readying himself for a fight. "No one ever mentioned there was scuba gear available for my twelve-year-old nephews to find."

Cold fear washed over Simon. What if they didn't have scuba gear in Atlantis? How was he supposed to explain himself then? But instead of arguing, Rhode sniffed and glared at him. "There's an emergency supply in the basement. It isn't available for recreational use."

"I'm sorry," said Simon hastily, barely able to stop his relief from showing. "I know I shouldn't have, but someone had to see what was going on, and—"

"It's all right," said his uncle, though judging by his clenched jaw and sour expression, it wasn't anything close to all right. "We'll talk about that later. Right now, if you have information, you need to tell us."

Simon was pretty sure that translated into *grounded for life*, but he pressed on. "Orion's upset. Whatever it was he wanted when he attacked the General, he didn't get it."

A murmur rose from the others at the table, and Simon saw Jam's shoulders sag with relief.

"But he's going to attack the city," he continued. "As a distraction, while he looks for it. He wants to choke off the supply lines—"

"He's already tried that on land," said Rhode irritably. "And he must know our barriers are impossible to breach, so what does he think laying siege to Atlantis will accomplish?"

"If we have no way of getting out, then we'll have no choice but to face them," said the captain behind Simon and Winter. "Should I ready the troops, Colonel?"

She nodded. "Wait. Jam—which species of sharks did you say ambushed you?"

"There were a few of them," he said, his face pale. "A great white. A couple of bull sharks. Tiger sharks—"

"Then we can't trust the shark brigades at all." Her mouth formed a thin line. "That's a good third of our troops."

"But they're not the ones who attacked us."

"We don't know how many of them are sympathizers," she pointed out. "We can't take the risk. Captain, send the shark brigades to San Miguel. Make up an excuse and get them out of the way."

The captain saluted and exited the room, leaving Simon and Winter unguarded. Winter shifted uneasily, her fingers laced together so tightly that her hands had gone blotchy. Simon wanted to reach out for her, but he couldn't embarrass her like that, not in front of everyone.

"Is there anything else, Simon?" said Crocker from the foot of the table. He hadn't stopped staring at him since Simon had stepped into the room.

"I . . ." Simon paused, glancing at all the faces gathered. Was one of them a spy for Orion? Or was it someone else? He couldn't not tell them, though, and after a moment of grappling with himself, he finally blurted, "Orion said he got his information directly from someone inside the city."

Rhode furrowed her brow. "A member of our kingdom would never—"

"But someone did," said Simon. "Orion said so himself. He had no reason to lie to his lieutenants."

Another murmur rose up from the table, but Malcolm spoke above them. "It's no one in this room. We know that for a fact."

"Do we?" said Ariana suddenly. It was, as far as Simon had seen, the first time she'd spoken up. "Orion attacked Jam and the General when they were moving the piece. How did they know it was happening? And how did they know where they'd be? Not even we knew what was going on."

"Someone might have overheard," said Jam uncertainly.

"Perhaps," said Ariana's adviser slowly. The General had called him Lord Anthony, Simon recalled, and he was a thin man with little hair on his head and a nose that seemed to point directly to the ground. "Or perhaps, unlikely as it would be, it could be explained in other ways. If the flock was watching the location . . ."

"Orion said his information was good," said Simon firmly. "That has to mean it came from someone on the inside."

"He could have known you were listening," said Ariana. Simon tried to catch her eye, but she refused, staring at the papers in front of her instead. "It's the oldest trick in the book. Turn the enemy against one another, and their alliances crumble. They spend so much time suspicious of themselves that they stop paying attention to you."

"You heard Simon," said Zia, leaning back in her chair. "Orion had no reason to believe anyone else was listening."

"It could be a trap," argued Lord Anthony. "Or perhaps the boy is confused."

"Are you calling my nephew a liar?" said Malcolm in a dangerous growl.

"Of course not, but—"

"We can't know for sure—" interjected Rhode loudly, but she was drowned out as a dozen voices tried to talk over one another. Simon stood awkwardly in the midst of the commotion, unsure of what to say. Maybe Ariana was right, but he would have bet all of his postcards and his pocket watch that she wasn't.

At last Crocker raised a gnarled finger. One by one, the others fell silent. "Simon," he said quietly. "Is that all?"

Once again, Simon considered lying, but this time, he

wasn't so sure he could win without help. So, with some reluctance, he said, "They're looking for an octopus they think might have—whatever it is they want. I don't know anything more than that."

Another murmur rippled through the assembled ambassadors, and Rhode straightened in her seat. "Very well. You're dismissed. Return to your rooms and wait for further instruction."

Simon and Winter left the conference room together without argument. Simon had said all he could, and someone sitting at that table was bound to believe him. They were smart people. Even if they thought he was misguided, they would take precautions. They had to.

"I thought Orion's looking for an orca," whispered Winter as they walked down the hall.

"He is, but I think an octopus really took it. If anyone's going to find it, it needs to be a member of the underwater kingdom," said Simon quietly, turning a corner.

Winter glanced over her shoulder. "Are you sure this is the way to the infirmary?"

"No idea." Simon stopped at the door nearest the conference room. It was locked. "Hold on."

After making sure no one was coming, Simon shifted into a fly and slid underneath the door. Once inside the empty room—another conference room almost identical to the first—he shifted back and opened the door for her. "Come on, I want to know what they're planning."

Winter groaned. "You need a *doctor*—"

"This is more important," he said, and after searching the room, he found an air duct. It wasn't very big, but once they unscrewed the panel with one of Winter's barrettes, it was large enough to fit them both, as long as Simon shifted into something small.

With a pang, he once again chose a brown mouse. Simon scampered through the metal duct as Winter in her cottonmouth form slithered behind him, both remaining as quiet as possible. Considering how close they were to the General's conference room, it didn't take them long to find the right opening.

". . . out of options." Rhode's voice drifted through the air duct. Remaining behind the metal grate, Simon and the cottonmouth snake settled in to eavesdrop.

"We'd have plenty of options if you'd listen to me," said Jam. "Without the shark brigades, we don't stand a chance. We have to trust our people—"

"I trust our sisters," said Rhode coldly. "That's all."

"You want to pit them against an entire army of sharks?" said Jam. "You'll get them killed."

"If I may," said a deeper voice. Crocker. "Our most pressing problem at the moment is the location of the piece. If we don't have it, and Orion doesn't have it, then who does?"

"Simon mentioned an octopus," said Zia, and Simon could hear someone drumming their nails against the table. "How likely is that intel to be right?"

"Couldn't say," mumbled Jam. "Lots of octopuses around the coast. They could be working for Orion, too."

"What about Isabel Thorn?" said Rhode, her voice like a knife slicing through Simon. He tensed.

"What about her?" said Malcolm. "She's being held hostage. We know that."

"We also know she's helping him," said Rhode. "How else do you explain Orion knowing where to look for the reptiles' piece *and* ours? Isabel is the only person on the planet who knows where both are hidden."

"Orion could easily have multiple sources," said Malcolm. "If someone in your inner circle is leaking intelligence—"

"There may or may not be a spy in my kingdom, but we know for a fact that Isabel is feeding him information," said Rhode. "What is our goal?"

A pause. "To stop the sharks from attacking us?" said Jam uncertainly.

"No. Our goal—our ultimate goal—is to stop Orion from getting the pieces of the Predator," said Rhode. "How many does he have now?"

"We don't know for sure," said Zia. "But if you're saying what I think you're saying . . ."

"We need to protect the Animalgam world above all else," said Rhode. "There are countless lives at stake. If Orion puts the Predator together, there's a very good chance we will never be able to defeat him. Not with the entire bird kingdom on his side."

"They're not on his side," said Jam hotly. "Simon isn't, his mom isn't—"

"The flock is," murmured Crocker. "But even then, it would be next to impossible for Orion to succeed."

"He's trying," said Rhode. "And he has all the information he needs in Isabel."

"The Black Widow Queen moved our piece the instant we found out Simon's mother was kidnapped," said Ariana. "It doesn't matter if Orion gets the other pieces. He'll never find ours."

"But what if he does?" said Rhode. "Everyone trusted Isabel. Our kingdoms have put our lives and our future in her hands, and now she's working with the enemy. The smartest thing for us to do is to neutralize the threat she poses the first chance we get."

Simon stared through the metal grate, his jaw hanging open. Neutralize? Did Rhode mean—

"And how exactly do you plan on *neutralizing* her, Colonel?" said Malcolm, his eyes narrowing.

"The same way we neutralize all living threats, Alpha," said Rhode coolly. "We find Isabel Thorn, and we eliminate her."

13

A JIGGLE OF JELLYFISH

Eliminate.

Simon's blood turned to ice as the world around him seemed to grow muffled. He didn't need to be raised in the underwater kingdom to know what Rhode meant by *eliminate.*

She wanted to kill his mother.

"I'm afraid I can't let that happen," said Malcolm. He stood, towering over the rest of them. "Isabel is family. She is the mother of my nephews, and she is under the protection of my kingdom."

"Your piece is already gone, isn't it?" said Rhode evenly. "You've already failed at your job."

Through the grate, Simon saw Malcolm's mouth twitch.

"Isabel has spent her life protecting the pieces and preventing anyone from assembling them. Whatever reason she has for sharing this information with Orion, I trust her."

"I do not," said Rhode.

"You barely know her," he rumbled. "And I won't stand here and let you pass judgment on a situation you know nothing about. My kingdom will fight you every step of the way, Colonel."

"The only person I have any interest in fighting right now is Orion," she said. "But if you declare yourself our enemy in the middle of this crisis, we will remember, Alpha."

Malcolm let out a sound that was eerily similar to a wolf's growl, and his focus slid from Rhode to Jam. "My family and I are leaving. We require the immediate use of one of your submarines."

"I—" Jam began, clearly startled. But Rhode interrupted before he could get any further.

"The armies are mobilizing, which means the docks are closed," she said. "And they will remain closed until the battle is over."

Malcolm snarled, baring his teeth. "I wasn't talking to you."

"I don't care who you were talking to. Private Fluke is a child, and I am the General's second in command. There is no going over my head, Alpha. You will be granted passage on the first vessel to leave Atlantis afterward, but not a moment sooner."

Spewing curses—some of which Simon had never heard before—Malcolm banged his fist against the table. "Fine. Claim command. If this goes wrong and anything happens to my family, when the General wakes up, you'll be the one explaining why you're suddenly at war with the bird kingdom *and* the mammals."

Malcolm stormed out of the conference room, slamming the door behind him. Zia stood as well, and after shooting a reproachful look at Rhode, she followed.

A long moment passed. Resounding silence filled the air, and all Simon could hear was his own shallow breathing.

"I like Isabel," said Rhode quietly, seeming shaken despite her strength. "This is a difficult decision for all of us, make no mistake, but we *must* put the security of the Animalgam world first."

"We should be rescuing her, not killing her," said Jam, angrily pushing his replacement glasses up his nose.

"She's Orion's most valuable asset," said Rhode. "He will never let her out of the flock's sight. Even if we were to attempt a rescue mission, we simply don't have the numbers above water. The flock is too powerful."

"But—we can't," he said, his voice cracking. "She's Simon's *mom*. We can't."

"Being a leader means making tough choices," said Rhode. "And no matter how we each feel about her, we must set aside personal affection and make the right decision for our families, for our people, and for each other."

Simon felt Winter's dry, scaly tail brush his, almost as a

comforting gesture. But this couldn't be happening. Even if Rhode wanted to—to *eliminate* his mother, no one else would. They couldn't.

"The Black Widow Queen would approve," said Ariana's adviser, answering Simon's unspoken protest. "Your Highness?"

For a long moment, Ariana was quiet. When she did speak, it was so softly that Simon could barely hear her. "She would."

Right as Simon felt like he was about to be sick, Jam stood, furious. "Do *you*?" he challenged. "You can't hide behind your mother on this, Ariana. We're talking about someone's *life*—"

"I'm not hiding." Ariana remained seated, sounding exhausted. "I'm here to represent my kingdom, and the Black Widow Queen would agree with Rhode. But no one else does," she added. "So it's pointless."

"It isn't pointless," said Rhode. "If we can't retrieve our kingdom's piece of the Predator before Orion finds it, then we may have no choice. Especially with a spy in our midst."

"That, I believe, is the main issue we are facing," said Ariana's adviser.

"So *now* you think it isn't a trick?" said Jam with a huff.

"Maybe it is, maybe it isn't. But all of this planning will be ruined if it gets to Orion first," said Lord Anthony.

Rhode exhaled sharply. "We can't take that chance. I'm taking Simon Thorn and Winter Rivera into protective custody. Simon himself admitted he has a way to sneak out of the city," she added loudly enough to be heard over the others' objections. "Orion is holding Simon's mother captive. We can't ignore the possibility that he might be coercing Simon into working for him and feeding us bad information."

"And your excuse for Winter Rivera?" This came from Crocker, and though he didn't growl the way Malcolm did, there was something bone-chilling in his voice. Rhode didn't flinch.

"She was raised by Orion and could still have sympathies."

"Simon. *Simon.*" Winter poked him with her tail. "We need to go."

He blinked, as if pulling himself out of a dream. Rhode was really going to try to kill his mother. "I need to get to the surface again," he said as he hurried through the air duct and back to the empty conference room.

"I'm coming with you," said Winter as she followed, her scales dry against the metal. "I'm not waiting around for them to arrest me, thank you very much."

For once, Simon didn't argue with her. The din of voices quieted until he heard only silence, and as he shifted back into a human, he gulped. "I don't know how to get you out of the city."

"Get me to the ocean," she said, brushing dust off her skirt. "We'll find out if I can really swim."

Together they ran down the corridors, making sure to

check each corner for a soldier before turning. Thanks to the mirrors, they were nearly caught twice, but somehow, miraculously, they made it to the stairwell without anyone spotting them.

"We can't get through security at the entrance, so we'll have to come up with a way to distract the guards stationed at the tunnel in the basement," said Simon as they hurried down the steps. "And as soon as we get to the ocean, you need to swim to the surface as fast as you can. If you can't, let me know, and—"

"Argh!"

He hit something hard and flew against the wall, nearly losing his balance. A hand reached out and caught the fabric of his sweatshirt, and it was only blind luck that Simon managed to hang on to the railing to stop them both from falling.

"What—" he said, but as soon as the other figure righted himself, Simon's eyes widened. "Nolan! What are you *doing*?"

"I—" His brother floundered for a moment, looking back and forth between him and Winter. "I was trying to find your stupid mouse for you. What are *you* doing?"

After making sure no one was in the stairwell with them, Simon grabbed Nolan's arm and marched him down the steps to the basement. It was mostly the same as the upper floors, but without the mirrored hallways, and there was thankfully a distinct lack of security. Finding a storage closet full of what looked like old radio equipment, Simon pulled his brother and Winter inside, closing the door behind them and flipping on the light.

"Rhode wants to kill Mom," he blurted.

Nolan blinked, any trace of his anger earlier that night forgotten. "What?"

Speaking as fast as he could, Simon explained the whole story—or at least as much of it as he could tell Nolan, who grew paler by the second.

"But—they can't hurt Mom," he said, a note of panic in his voice. "They can't. She hasn't done anything wrong."

"She's giving Orion information," said Simon. "That's enough for Rhode."

Nolan clenched his jaw and started toward the door. "We can't let them—"

Winter stepped in front of the door, blocking his way. "What are you going to do that Malcolm hasn't already tried? With the General unconscious, Rhode is running things."

"She'll listen to us—all of us, if we tell her," said Nolan, trying to get around her. Simon grabbed his elbow.

"No, she won't. She thinks Winter and I are spying for Orion."

"But—that's crazy," said Nolan, shaking his arm loose. "You're not a spy."

The matter-of-fact way he said it shouldn't have surprised Simon, but it did. Maybe he was so used to being at odds with his brother that he simply expected Nolan to believe the worst in him. "I know that, and you know that, but they don't," said Simon. "And they're going to arrest me and Winter as soon as they find us. We aren't the spies, but someone in the city—someone close to the General and the summit—is leaking information to Orion. That's how he knew to attack the General, and where he and Jam would be."

His twin's expression darkened, and for a long moment, Nolan didn't say anything. "They can't arrest you."

"They're going to, unless Winter and I can get out of here," said Simon. "Rhode said there's scuba gear down here. We're going to borrow a few oxygen tanks and swim to the surface." Lying to Nolan made him feel like his mouth was full of sand, but he didn't know what else to do or say. Now definitely wasn't the time to tell him he wasn't the only one with the powers of the Beast King.

"Where will you go?" said his brother.

"To warn Mom and make sure no one hurts her." That, at least, wasn't a lie.

"You know where she is?"

Simon nodded. "She's with Orion and the rest of the flock. I can sneak by them."

"I want to come," he said immediately. "Maybe I can help."

Behind Nolan, Winter shook her head furiously, and any hope Simon had of getting out of that closet without a fight evaporated. She was right. Nolan couldn't come, not if Simon wanted to keep his secret, and he was positive that if Nolan found out he also had the Beast King's abilities to turn into any animal he wanted, it would be the end of their fragile relationship. Nolan was far too proud about being the only one, about being something special, and Simon couldn't steal that from him. Not unless he absolutely had to.

But what was Simon supposed to say? That it was too dangerous? That would only upset him, and they didn't have time for arguments. Helpless, he opened and shut his mouth, searching for something to say. Before he could, however, Winter spoke.

"There's a tunnel down here that leads out into the ocean. If you want to help, we need someone to distract the guards so we can escape," she said. Nolan started to object, but she cut him off. "If Simon and I don't get out of here, they're going to throw us in the brig for treason. Is that what you want?"

"I—" Nolan looked to Simon. "I want to help. *Really* help, not just run around like an idiot for a minute."

"Then—you can find the real spy," said Simon, his mind racing. At least this might make his brother feel useful, even if he doubted it would work. "Pay attention to everyone. See who's listening to something they shouldn't be, or if someone disappears a lot, or—I don't know. Anything. Ariana knows a lot about it. If you ask her, she'll help."

"I guess I can do that," grumbled Nolan, much to Simon's relief. "What am I supposed to do when I find them?"

"Tell Malcolm. But don't do anything dangerous, all right?"

He snorted. "You're the one talking about sneaking into Orion's army."

"Yeah, but I'm not you," said Simon, his voice heavy with meaning. "You're more important. So just—stay safe. Please."

Reluctantly Nolan nodded. "You, too. And sucker punch Orion in the gut for me."

"If you two are done bonding," said Winter irritably, "we need to go. If they haven't already figured out we aren't in our rooms—"

Suddenly, hasty footsteps fell in the hallway, and Winter froze. The footsteps stopped right outside the closet door, and with his heart in his throat, Simon motioned for them to hide among the boxes of old radio junk.

"Simon?" said a soft voice on the other side of the door. The supply closet door creaked open, and Simon jumped out of his hiding place in a dusty corner when he saw the familiar shock of blond hair.

"Jam? How did you know we were in here?"

Breathing heavily, Jam put a finger to his lips and slowly shut the door. Once the lock clicked into place, he flipped the light switch and cast them into darkness. "I saw the light underneath the door. I figured you'd try to leave, and I ran down here as fast as I could. Rhode thinks I'm in the bathroom." Something plastic cracked, and a large blue glow stick appeared in his hand, giving them enough light to see by. "Simon, everything she said about your mom—"

"She wants to kill her," he said darkly.

Jam winced. "I know. But she won't do it, I swear."

"No, she won't," said Nolan in a threatening voice. "If she tries—"

"She doesn't have that kind of power, not really," said Jam hastily. "If—if the General doesn't make it—" He swallowed hard. "I'll be the one in charge, not her. And even if Rhode *is* stupid enough to try, the flock's on high alert. She can't risk sending a soldier there right now, and anyway, we don't have one to spare. We need everyone to defend the city."

"How do you plan on doing that without a third of your soldiers?" said Winter, cutting Nolan off before he could drag out the argument any further. "Send a jiggle of jellyfish after them?"

"A jiggle of—what?" said Jam.

"You know. A pod of dolphins, a shiver of sharks, a jiggle of jellyfish."

"That's . . . not what a group of jellyfish is called," said Jam slowly. "It's a swarm, not—"

"Do you think I care?" snapped Winter. "What's the point in escaping if you and everyone else inside the city gets killed?"

"They won't," said Jam fiercely. "I have an idea. I read it in a book—"

"Was it a military strategy book?" said Winter.

"No," admitted Jam. "It's a fantasy novel about a prophecy and a siege on this giant city, but I think the tactics they used might work."

"Can we argue about this some other time?" said Simon. "We need to get out of here."

Together the four of them crouched near the door, and Simon cracked it open enough to check the hallways. "All clear," he whispered.

"The tunnel's down that way, left at the third corridor," said Jam quietly. "There's a door on the right that should be guarded."

"I'll go first," said Nolan bravely. "Once they see me, I'll make a run for it and give you time to escape."

One by one, they slipped out of the storage closet and crept down the hallway. Never before had Simon been more aware of the quiet hum of the air pumps that seemed to be everywhere in the compound. It was never completely silent, and Simon strained to hear any hint of a footstep that didn't belong to them.

"Keep going straight," whispered Jam, falling farther and farther behind. Puzzled, Simon hung back with him, until Winter and Nolan were nearly twenty feet ahead.

"What—" he began, but Jam caught his elbow.

"We need to find the piece first," he said in a low, rushed voice. "Before the battle, before Orion has the chance to look for it."

Simon frowned. "I don't care about the stupid piece right now."

"Yes, you do," argued Jam. "If we find the piece, Rhode's excuse for—for neutralizing your mom falls apart. The piece is my responsibility, and once she sees it, I can give it back to you. No one else will know you have it, not even Orion."

Simon floundered. Jam was right. Even though every part of him was desperate to warn his mother before anyone could hurt her, it would only be a temporary solution. And she was safest in the middle of Orion's army, at least for now. "We don't know where it is," he said lamely.

"I know where it is. So do you."

Simon frowned. "What?"

"You took a rock from the octopus garden, right?"

He reached into his pocket and pulled out the stone. "I forgot to give it to Winter."

"It's a good thing you did, because I think that might be the only chance we have at getting the piece back," said Jam as they crept down the hallway. "The octopus you saw, the one who squirted ink at us—I think it's the same one that lives there. They don't usually hang out in groups, and we were in Gordon's territory—"

"Gordon?"

"The octopus that created the garden," said Jam patiently, pushing his glasses up his nose. "He doesn't like other people touching his stuff. I wouldn't be surprised if he followed us."

Simon groaned inwardly. All of this was because of a stupid octopus? "What do we do now? Give it back to him and hope he'll hand over the piece?"

Jam shrugged. "I don't see why he wouldn't. He's reasonable."

"He squirted ink in our eyes—"

"He saved our lives," said Jam. "Without him, the sharks would have won."

Simon touched the sock taped to his side. With the adrenaline rushing through him right now, he didn't feel much pain, but Jam was right. "Do you think he's back in his—"

"Get your hands off me!"

Winter's shriek echoed down the hallway, and Jam yanked Simon around a corner, causing them to crash into each other. Whispering a hurried apology, Simon peeked into the corridor. A soldier twisted Winter's arm behind her back and held her in place, while another had Nolan by the scruff of the neck. The first spoke into his sleeve.

"We've found Simon Thorn and Winter Rivera," he rumbled. "Lower level."

Simon's pulse quickened. The soldiers thought he was Nolan—or that Nolan was him. But Winter was supposed to be safe. They weren't supposed to catch her.

"What do you think you're doing? Let—us—*go*," spat Nolan, trying to break free of the soldier's grip.

"Colonel Rhode has ordered you to be placed in protective custody," said the soldier. "If you come with us quietly, you'll make this much easier on all of us."

"I—" Nolan began to object, but in that moment, their eyes met—Simon crouching down, not completely hidden by the corner, and Nolan being manhandled by a soldier twice their size. All Nolan had to do was tell them who he was, and he would be free.

Instead, he squared his shoulders, his eyes narrowing as he turned to face the soldiers once more. "I'll only come quietly if you take your hands off us," he said with more authority than Simon had ever mustered in his life, but the soldiers wouldn't know the difference.

"If you run, I'll hog-tie you and throw you over my shoulder," warned the soldier before nodding to his partner. They released Nolan and Winter. "Now come along. We have a nice room prepared for both of you."

Simon watched, helpless, as the four of them marched toward the elevators in the opposite direction. It wouldn't be long before someone figured out Nolan wasn't him, but with any luck, this would buy him and Jam enough time to leave the compound. He didn't want to leave Winter behind, but he didn't have a choice, not anymore.

"Simon?" said Jam, trying to peek over his shoulder. "What's—"

"*There* you are."

Icy fear ran down Simon's spine, and he slowly turned around, his heart pounding.

Looming behind them, her arms crossed and her blue eyes flashing with fury, was Rhode.

14

CAN OF WORMS

"What's your excuse this time?" said Colonel Rhode. "Going to tell me you were looking for your mouse again?"

Simon opened his mouth, but nothing came out. A dozen excuses ran through his mind, each worse than the last, but it didn't matter—the best excuse in the world wouldn't change the fact that there was only one reason he and Jam would be down here together.

"What are you talking about?" said Jam without missing a beat. He stood up as if they were doing nothing suspicious at all, and cautiously Simon rose with him. "This is Nolan. Your goons just arrested Simon."

Rhode pulled out a pair of plastic zip ties from the pocket of her uniform. "If you insist on lying to a superior officer, soldier, then I'll have no choice but to arrest you, too."

"He's not lying," protested Simon. "I'm Nolan—"

"I saw you half an hour ago." In one swift motion, she caught Simon's wrists and bound them together with a zip tie. "Next time, if you're going to use the identical twin lie, at least have the sense to change your outfit."

"Rhode, you don't understand—" began Jam.

"Don't understand what?" she said, turning to her brother with the other zip tie in her hand. "Don't understand that you were colluding with a potential enemy spy in order to help him escape?"

"He's not a spy," said Jam, right as Simon blurted, "I'm not a spy!"

She looked back and forth between them. "The matter will be decided at your tribunal. Now, soldier, if you would be so kind as to come quietly, that would save us both yet another headache tonight."

Jam clenched his fists. "If you're going to restrain Simon, then you'll have to restrain me, too."

A flicker of annoyance passed over Rhode's face, and she reached for his hands. "All right, if you—"

It happened so fast that Simon barely registered what was going on. One second, she was slipping the zip tie over Jam's wrists, and the next, he lurched forward, shoving her into the wall. His torso blocked Simon's view, but Rhode cried out, and when Jam backed away, her hands were bound together, not his.

"This is treason!" she shouted, lunging toward them. *"Guards!"*

Jam stepped out of his sister's path and stuck his foot out. She tripped and fell to the floor with a loud *oomf*, and Jam promptly sat on her. "Run, Simon!" he said as his sister struggled beneath him.

Simon didn't need to be told twice. Shooting Jam a grateful look, he sprinted down the hallway. Within seconds, shouts echoed seemingly from every direction as soldiers came running toward him, and he ducked into a nearby storage room stocked with cleaning supplies. The plastic zip tie cut into his wrists, but he barely registered the pain. What was he supposed to do now? He was surrounded. Even if he did figure out a way to get through the basement exit, no doubt Rhode would search the tunnel before he could get too far, and he had no idea what might be waiting for him at the exit.

But what were his other options? Shift into a tuna crab again and hope someone on the dock noticed him? That would take too long. The only other way out he knew about was through the planetarium. This late at night, it probably wouldn't be guarded, and if he could escape the compound . . .

The thought of Al and Floyd waiting on the other side made him sick with fear, but Simon had no other choice. Maybe they wouldn't be there. Maybe they would remember him. Or maybe they wouldn't, and maybe he would become an unsatisfying midnight snack for a pair of great white sharks.

It was a risk he had to take.

Footsteps sounded against the concrete floor nearby, and Simon heard the soldiers opening doors. He had seconds to hide. Huddled among mops and bottles of bleach, Simon squeezed his eyes shut and shifted into a fly once again, hoping against hope the transformation was completed before they found him.

He made it by milliseconds. Just as the door opened, the zip tie fell from his hands, and the closet morphed into a kaleidoscope of images allowing him to see all around. The soldier stepped inside and methodically searched every corner, even underneath the low metal shelves. Simon remained perfectly still.

"All clear," announced the soldier, and as he left the closet, Simon slipped out with him, flying into the hallway toward the stairs.

The basement was swarming with soldiers now. There had to be dozens of them down there, combing through every room and crawl space. Unsure whether or not there were any insects in Atlantis, Simon flew from corner to corner, careful not to allow anyone to see him, but he did make one slight detour to the spot where Rhode had caught them.

Jam sat up against the wall, his hands bound and a small smile on his face. While Simon considered letting him know he was all right, instead he flew in the other direction. If he wanted to help Jam, the best thing he could do now was find the piece and prove their innocence.

His flight up the stairwell and through the ground level was much easier compared to the basement. Most of the guards seemed to have moved down there, leaving few stationed at the exit, and within minutes, Simon burst out of the compound and onto Pacific Way.

The streets of Atlantis were crammed with soldiers marching toward the edge of the dome. Men, women—even some teenagers who didn't look much older than Simon. The entire city was mobilizing, and fear struck Simon as he watched them grimly pass by. How many of them wouldn't be coming home?

He couldn't think like that right now. Steeling himself against the flood of regret and guilt, he flew as fast as he could toward the planetarium. Despite the thousands of people marching through the streets, it was abandoned, and Simon slipped through an opening underneath the door. As soon as he reached the edge of the water inside the sea stars' tunnel, he shifted into a dolphin and dived in. Between his lack of sleep, his injuries, and the effort of sneaking out of the city, he was exhausted, but he swam as hard as he could through the eerily still water. If he found the piece, he could return it to Jam in time to sneak out again and warn his mother before dawn. He just had to keep going.

Shortly before he burst out of the tunnel, he became aware of two shapes lurking near the mouth of the sea stars' tunnel. His pulse raced, and his insides knotted with nerves. Al and Floyd.

"Hi, guys," he said as he swam into the open ocean. "Remember me? I'm Jam's friend."

The sharks circled him, somehow seeming even bigger than they had before. "I don't remember no friend of his. You remember?" said the larger one—Al, Simon thought.

"Don't recall," said the second. He was smaller, but he had just as many teeth as the first. "Can't remember the last time we ate, either, and dolphin sounds awful good right about now."

"Injured dolphin," said Al, sniffing the water. "Not fresh, but it'll do."

"Wait," said Simon as the two sharks approached. "I'm an Animalgam. Jam—Benjamin Fluke, the General's son—I'm his friend—you can't eat me."

"He won't know where you've gone," said Al. "I won't tell. Will you, Floyd?"

"Tell what?" said the smaller shark with a sinister chuckle.

Sheer panic seized Simon, and without thinking, he darted past the great white sharks toward the surface. If he could reach the sky, he could shift into a bird and fly away, but as long as he was in the ocean, as long as he was bleeding and the sharks could smell him—

"Where d'you think you're going?" Al rammed into him, knocking his smaller dolphin body off course. Simon's side exploded in pain, and he spun around wildly until he wasn't sure which way was up.

"I know where he's going, and it isn't away from here," said Floyd, catching Simon by the tail and flinging him back toward Al. His sharp teeth dug into Simon's dolphin skin, but it was a scratch at best. They were playing with him.

All he had to do was shift into an orca, and he would chase them away. No one would ever believe them, and even if they did, Simon didn't care. If he didn't do anything, he'd become a shark snack, so his options were fairly limited.

"I'm giving you one last chance to let me go," said Simon as he formed an image of a killer whale in his mind. "If you don't—"

Stars exploded in front of him as Al's tail made contact with his head. Dizzy and disoriented, Simon floated in the water without moving, his thoughts scrambled and pain pouring through him from every direction.

"Time for dinner," said Al in a menacing voice, sounding oddly like he was far away. The edges of Simon's vision went dark, and part of him was quietly resigned to the fact that this was it. The sharks would eat him, and no one would ever discover where he went. Orion would find the pieces and put the Predator back together, but most of all, Simon would never see his family or his friends again. And they would never know how much he cared, or how sorry he was for letting this happen.

As he sank toward the waiting sharks, the last thing he thought he saw was a giant silhouette speeding through the open ocean and heading straight for him. And as his consciousness faded, he could have sworn he heard it say his name.

"Simon!"

"Simon? Simon. *Simon.*"

His head felt like someone had been hammering against his skull, and he winced, pressing his palm to his temple. Dimly it occurred to him that he must have shifted back into a human at some point without realizing it. "What . . . ?"

"He's awake," said a familiar female voice. Simon opened his eyes, but his vision was fuzzy, and the colorful blobs didn't look like anything at all, let alone someone he recognized.

"It's about time," said a ragged voice—this one male and new. "I told you to use the smelling salts, Zia."

Zia Stone. Simon's thoughts swam, and he tried to sit up. That only made his head hurt more, and he groaned.

"Don't try to move too much," she said, and he felt a hand on his shoulder. "The sharks got in a few good hits, and you'll be sore for a while. No lasting damage, though, thankfully."

"Where . . . ," he managed. Zia's face began to focus. There was a worry line between her eyes, and she was sitting on the edge of the sofa where he lay.

"You're safe, Simon, I promise. It was a close call, but we found you before those goons finished you off," she said. The lights were dim, but Simon could hear the soft splashes of water against the hull, and he slowly realized that the rocking sensation was coming from the waves, not his head.

They were on a boat.

This time, despite the hand on his shoulder, Simon sat straight up. A tidal wave of pain and dizziness hit him, but as the world swam around him, he refused to lie back down. "Mom," he gasped. "She—Rhode, she's going to—"

"She's not going to do anything to your mother." That rough voice was back, and Simon looked around. A lean man with graying hair and tanned skin sat against a wall, watching him. "We've got eyes on her, and if anyone tries anything, they won't live to see morning."

Simon sighed with relief. If it was still night, that meant Orion might not have attacked yet. But that brief respite was quickly replaced with the sudden awareness that he had no idea where he was, who that man was, or what any of them were doing here. "Who—"

"Simon!" The door burst open, and Winter flew into the room. Practically shoving Zia aside, she caught Simon in a tight hug. "Felix said you were in here, but they wouldn't let me see you."

"Felix?" Searing pain from the bite in his side shot through him, but Simon ignored it. "He's—"

"I'm right here," said a familiar squeaky voice. Grouchy as ever, Felix leaped from Winter's pocket to Simon's pillow. Too stunned to shout with happiness, he scooped him up and inspected him for any signs of injury.

"I thought you'd been eaten," said Simon, pressing him

against his cheek. Felix sputtered indignantly, but at least he didn't struggle.

"That, I'm afraid, is my fault," said the man. He straightened in his seat, his shoulders narrow underneath a battered leather jacket. "I summoned our little mouse friend."

"And Zia and Crocker got me out of Atlantis. Had scuba gear ready and everything," said Winter, though she crossed her arms and positioned herself between the man and Simon. "I thought it was a good thing until they brought me here. *He* won't tell me who he is."

"I'm no one you should fear," said the man. "I won't hurt either of you. No one on this boat will."

"Crocker's on deck," said Felix, hopping onto Simon's shoulder and straightening his whiskers. "Keeps looking at me like I'm a late-night snack."

"Don't be ridiculous," said Zia, who was still perched on the edge of the sofa. "Crocker's a vegetarian."

Simon stood as fast as his pounding head could handle, but even that was too quick. The room spun around him, and as he teetered, Zia reached out to steady him. "Where are we?" he said, more insistent this time.

"Safe," she repeated. "Though if you keep this up, you'll tear your stitches and bleed to death, so do us both a favor and don't ruin my handiwork."

Simon was fairly sure she was exaggerating, but he sat down anyway. Tugging up the hem of his shirt, he saw the fresh bandages on his side, and he could feel more on his leg. "Are you okay?" he said to Winter, who nodded.

"Just traumatized for life. You should have seen the way Zia took down those soldiers."

The man raised an eyebrow. "I apologize for the tactics my team had to employ, but it was necessary to get you to safety. We couldn't be sure Atlantis hadn't been infiltrated by Orion or Celeste."

"You—" Simon stared. There was something strangely familiar about him, but Simon was sure he'd never met him before. It was more as if the man reminded him of someone, though he couldn't put his finger on whom. "Who *are* you?"

"Thought you'd never ask." With a grim smile, he rose to his feet. "I'm Leo Thorn. Your grandfather."

15

HEIR OF THE BEAST KING

This time, the way the room spun had nothing to do with the knock Simon had taken to his head. Out of everything the man could have told him, this was the very last thing he would have ever guessed.

"My—grandfather?" he said stupidly. "But I already have one. Orion."

"You have two biological grandfathers," corrected Leo Thorn, the lines in his face betraying his faint smile. "I'm the good one. Your father, Luke, was my son."

Speechless, Simon stared. Now that he knew, he could see the resemblance between the only picture he'd ever seen of his father and the man who stood in front of him, hands in his pockets as he waited for him to say something. He could even see himself in the man—they had the same eye color, and the way the man frowned reminded him all too much of Nolan. And of himself.

"You—you're really my dad's father?" he said, and the man nodded.

"Really. No tricks." Despite his gruffness, his eyes shone, and he reached out as if he wanted to touch Simon's cheek. Instinctively Simon moved a fraction of an inch away, and Leo dropped his hand. "You have no idea how long I've waited for this, Simon. I can't tell you how glad I am to finally meet you."

"I—" Simon gaped at him, a dozen different feelings rushing through his brain at once, jumbled together until they rendered him all but senseless. A grandfather. He had another grandfather. "I thought you were dead," he blurted, although that wasn't entirely accurate. Truth be told, he'd never given much thought to his paternal grandfather. His father, Luke Thorn, had died around the time Simon and Nolan had been born, and despite a few snippets here and there, he'd never heard much about him. Simon's pocket watch had once belonged to him, but that was the only piece of his father he had. No one had ever mentioned his biological grandfather.

To his surprise, Leo nodded, satisfied. "Good. That's what everyone's supposed to think. Best that way, for reasons you might be able to guess."

Maybe on a good day, but between the pounding headache and shock of discovering he had a grandfather who probably wasn't trying to kill him, Simon didn't have the faintest clue. Winter, however, groaned. "There's another one?"

"Another what?" said Simon, and she gave him a look.

"Think. What's special about the Thorn family line?"

Oh. *Oh*. Simon refocused on Leo, searching for any sign of—he wasn't sure what. "You can, too? Like—like—"

"Like you?" said Leo kindly, with an affectionate smile. "Yes. Exactly like you."

Suddenly Simon felt sick to his stomach. He knew. Somehow, some way, Leo Thorn—and possibly everyone else on that boat—knew Simon had inherited the abilities of the Beast King.

His stark horror must have shown on his face, because Leo crouched in front of him so they were nearly eye level, though he still didn't touch him. "Don't worry," he said quietly. "We're the good guys."

"No one who ever has to say 'we're the good guys' is *ever* a good guy," said Winter. She hovered over Leo like she was ready to pounce at the slightest hint that he might attack, and Simon wasn't sure whether to be grateful for her protectiveness or terrified that he'd somehow let slip the secret he was supposed to keep hidden at all costs.

"Normally I wouldn't bother," said Leo, focused on Simon. "But given everything you've been through, I figured it would be best to make that clear from the start." From his pocket he pulled a battered and creased photograph, and he offered it to Simon. "Here. This is all the proof I have right now."

Simon took the picture. It was of Leo and his mother, both standing on a boat and smiling. Behind them was a blue sky, and his mother didn't look like she was being held hostage.

"That was taken about eight months ago, in Key West," said Leo. "I promise you, nothing's changed since. We're on the same side. We all want the same thing."

Simon's head snapped up. "What?"

"The pieces of the Predator. You didn't think your mother was working alone, did you?"

His mouth went dry, and for a long moment, he said nothing. He caught Winter's eye, and she shook her head minutely.

She was right. Leo could be bluffing. A picture didn't prove anything. Even if he and Simon's mother *were* working together, there must have been a reason she hadn't told Simon about his grandfather. And whatever that reason was, Simon couldn't trust anyone until he knew for sure.

"I don't know what you're talking about," he said, the words sticking in his mouth like peanut butter.

"It's all right if you don't want to discuss it," said Leo, and he stood. "Better that way, probably. But know that we all want the same thing—for the same reason."

"We've already proven that much to you," said Zia. "In Paradise Valley, remember?"

Simon furrowed his brow. He *had* suspected all along that Zia knew more than she was letting on. Apparently he'd been right. And Crocker—Crocker had been the reason he'd gotten away with the reptiles' piece of the Predator. He'd lied to the entire reptile council to protect Simon.

"You don't have to make any decisions about us, not now or ever," said Leo, hands in his pockets again. "But our family has been preparing for this moment for a very long time. Destroying the Predator is our only goal, and I will do whatever I can to help you succeed."

"Why me?" said Simon at last, his voice creaking. "I don't understand—why not you, or Mom, or anyone else?"

That faint smile returned. "Because after the life I've lived, I don't trust myself with the Predator, and your mother couldn't risk bringing the real pieces back to Celeste. You, though . . . your mother trusts you, and I trust your mother."

"That's it?" said Simon. "That's the reason you've been putting me through this?"

"It was your mother's decision, not mine. Though in her defense, we all thought you'd be older," he added apologetically. "All I want to do is help you any way I can."

"Then let us go," said Winter furiously. "You can't keep us here and claim you're helping us, too."

"It's not safe in Atlantis, not now that you've been arrested," said Zia, her foot bouncing up and down. Simon had never seen her nervous before, but judging by the way her face was pinched, she would have rather chewed off her own arm than see Simon and Winter return underwater. "Tribunals are no joke. If you're old enough to shift in the General's kingdom, you're old enough to be charged and convicted of a crime. And treason could get you executed."

"I'll take my chances," said Simon darkly. "I'm not the spy no matter what Rhode thinks, and I need to find—"

He stopped suddenly. They knew already, but he couldn't confirm it for them. He and Winter were already at their mercy, and they hadn't had the best of luck with the adults in their lives lately. No matter how badly Simon wanted—*needed* help, he couldn't trust anyone. Especially not someone like Leo.

"It's all right, you know," said his grandfather gently. "One day you'll believe me, but you and I've just met. I know Darryl and your mother taught you better than to trust a complete stranger."

"You—you knew Darryl?" he said, his voice catching on his uncle's name.

"We all did. He was one of us, too." He opened a creaky desk drawer and pulled out a book. From between the pages, Leo gingerly removed yet another photograph, this one older, but pristine. He offered it to Simon almost reverently, and Simon took it, careful not to smudge the glossy picture.

It took him a moment to realize what he was staring at, but when he did, it hit him like a sucker punch to the gut. His uncle, younger than he'd ever seen him and without the scar running down his cheek, had his arm slung around another young man—Luke, Simon's father. They were laughing at something Simon couldn't see, but at the edge of the picture, only his profile in view, was a younger Leo.

"It's my fault," said Leo quietly. "I should have never

trusted Celeste, but we were family. The Alpha has been protecting our line ever since the Beast King was defeated, taking in our heirs as their own, and while she and I aren't related by blood, I was raised as her brother. I loved her more than anyone in the world. I thought she was on my side, and . . ." A muscle in his jaw twitched. "I wanted her help tracking down the pieces. She listened and wrung every last bit of information out of me, and after your father was killed, instead of supporting me like I thought she would, she used that information against me. Against us. Against your mother, against your brother, against you . . ."

"It wasn't your fault," said Zia. "You didn't know she'd turn out to be about as useful as a toothless piranha."

Simon tried to echo her sentiments, but nothing came out. Winter crossed her arms and glared at Zia. "I get why Crocker's part of this, since he's on the reptile council and all, but what do you have to do with any of this?"

Zia lazily pointed a finger at Leo. "He's my dad. What do *you* have to do with any of this?"

"He's my friend," said Winter, undeterred as she jutted her finger at Simon. "And I don't care if you're related. If you want him, you're still gonna have to go through me."

Related. With a jolt, Simon put the pieces together. Zia Stone was his father's sister. His aunt. Simon's head spun yet again, and he pressed his palms to his forehead. It was too much at once—finding out yet again that there was a whole branch of his family he'd never known about, that there was another Beast King heir alive and well and looking for the pieces, and realizing that this was all far more complicated than he had ever imagined. It was more than he could process, and with his head throbbing, he didn't bother trying.

"I need to go back," he blurted. "Let me off this boat."

"Are you forgetting the part where not only were you attacked by sharks, but the entire underwater kingdom thinks you're a spy?" said Zia, moving so she was sitting beside him again. "You're safe here. If you go back—"

"Do you really think I care?" said Simon, immediately regretting the nastiness in his voice. He couldn't—wouldn't—take it back, though. "Atlantis is under attack. Orion's going to kill everyone, and if I don't—if I don't do what I have to do, then he'll get there first. That can't happen."

Silence. Normally Simon would've been embarrassed by an outburst like that, but right now, nothing was more important than getting back to the octopus garden and finding the missing piece. Not even his pride.

Zia gave Leo an insistent look, but he shook his head. "Simon has gotten more done in the past four months than our family has in four hundred years. We trust him. We give him as much protection and support as we can. And we let him do whatever he has to do, like you did in November."

She swore softly to herself, but rather than fight, she squeezed Simon's knee. "You're not allowed to get yourself eaten, all right? I can't help you underwater, and you and

Dad were both lucky there were only two sharks attacking you earlier. You have to be more careful."

He nodded tightly, not sure what else to say to that. "I need scuba gear. And someone has to go after my mom, too."

Zia glanced at Leo. "Can we get word to our eyes?"

"Not safely. Orion won't let anyone but a bird on that beach." Leo rolled his shoulders and headed toward a closet. "I'll do it. It's been a while since I've been flying anyway."

A sudden thought occurred to Simon, and he focused on Zia. "You can't . . . can you?"

She laughed unexpectedly. "No, no. Luke got that gift, not me. I'm just a fox, like our mother. She was a Stone," she added, and part of Simon wilted at hearing *was*. "Everything I told you about our family protecting Stonehaven was true."

At least that hadn't been a lie. Simon stood slowly, though his head was throbbing a little less now. "What about Winter? What'll happen to her while we're gone?"

"She can stay here with us and watch the boat," said Zia, while Winter looked like she was about to spit nails. "When you have the piece—sorry, when you've *finished your mission*, you can come back."

"You want me to sit around doing nothing while Simon's out there fighting sharks?" said Winter indignantly.

"He won't be fighting any sharks again," said Leo sharply as he dug through the closet, pulling out scuba gear.

"They're all busy right now anyway," said Zia wryly, despite the very real danger Orion and his shark supporters posed to Atlantis and everyone inside. "Besides, Winter, it'll be fun. We'll braid each other's hair and paint each other's nails and tell each other all sorts of secrets."

If Simon hadn't been so anxious and confused, he would have burst out laughing at the horror on Winter's face. As it was, he heard Zia's message loud and clear: Winter was a hostage. And if he didn't come back with the piece . . . he didn't want to think about what might happen then.

His heart sinking, he half listened as Leo went through the instructions for the scuba gear. Before pulling it on, Simon changed into a wet suit that was too big for him, keeping his own clothes dry for when he returned. Once they were finished, he trudged over to the corner where Winter was pouting, the oxygen tank heavy and awkward on his back.

"Be careful," was all he could say in front of everyone, but he stared at her for a moment longer than he normally would have, and she nodded.

"You, too," she said, her words also heavy with meaning. As Simon headed out of the cabin, he heard her say, "If I have to get my nails painted, so does Felix."

"*Excuse* me?" squeaked the mouse. "I am not a poodle."

As Simon went out on deck, he noticed Crocker leaning against the railing, cane beside him. "Simon," he said in greeting, as if nothing were unusual about them being on a small boat together off the coast of Santa Catalina while a bunch of sharks waged war on the underwater kingdom below. Lights twinkled from the shoreline, and Simon guessed they weren't more than a mile from Avalon. That meant they weren't far from the octopus garden, too.

"You have your job, and I have mine," said Leo as they approached a gap in the railing, pulling off his jacket and setting it aside. "Let's both get this right. And Simon . . ."

Silence hung between them for several seconds. Leo raised his hand as if he were about to reach for him again, but instead, with a smile that looked more like a grimace than anything, he dropped it.

"Watch your back," he said quietly. "I don't want to lose you, too."

"I'll try," said Simon, but that was all the promise he was willing to make right now. Gulping in a giant breath of the salty air, he fell backward into the dark waters below, torn between fear and determination. That feeling, he was quickly discovering, was the only way he got anything done anymore, and as he sank into the water, he saw the silhouette of a peregrine falcon take off from the railing of the boat.

Now that Simon knew what it was like to have fins and gills, swimming as a human felt more like clawing his way through the water, and it took him much longer to reach the cave than he'd anticipated. No moonlight reached inside the maze of tunnels, and Simon ran his hand over the wall, remembering to turn right at each fork. Only when he sensed the larger cavern around him did he turn on the flashlight Leo had given him.

He eyed the thousands of rocks, shells, and gemstones with grim determination. It would be impossible to search by hand, but Simon pulled out his father's pocket watch, making sure to wrap the chain around his wrist so it wouldn't get lost. Underwater, it was possible the broken watch wouldn't heat up when it got close to the piece like it did on land, but Simon had to try. It was his only chance.

He had to make several passes of the large cavern, gripping the pocket watch and scanning the cavern floor, but sure enough, the metal began to grow warm toward the center. It was like playing a game—every time the watch cooled, he knew he was on the wrong track. If it felt warm, he knew he was getting closer. At last, when the metal was almost too hot for him to hold, he knew he must have been right on top of it. He ran his hand through layer after layer of shell and stone, and at last his fingertips brushed against a rock also hot to the touch.

The piece.

He grabbed it as fast as he could, shoving it into his pocket before he could lose it. The heat was no less intense, almost burning his thigh, but he forced himself to ignore it. As hot as it felt, he knew from experience that it wouldn't do anything more than make his skin a little red.

From that same pocket, he fished out the rock he'd stolen for Winter. Removing his mouthpiece, he spoke into the water, feeling as crazy as the kids at his old school had thought he was. "I'm sorry I stole it, Gordon. I didn't mean to insult you, and I know why you took the crystal from me." He sucked in another lungful of oxygen. "But I need it. It's important—really important, so I hope you're okay with a trade."

Carefully he set down the glittering stone. Replacing his mask and taking another deep breath, he shone the flashlight across the cave. No sign of the octopus. But he hadn't seen him last time either, and Simon cautiously headed back to the cavern entrance. He wouldn't make the mistake of dropping the piece again, so if the octopus wanted it back, he would have to—

Whoosh.

Simon flew backward. His mouthpiece fell out, and he tried to reach for it, only to be yanked back by his oxygen tank a second time. In a panic, he wriggled out of the straps that held the tank to his body, and once free, Simon spun around in the water.

Behind him, staring at him with dark eyes, was a great white shark.

THE SHARK'S CAVE

Simon's heart raced, burning through precious oxygen. The great white shark was small, but it didn't matter. He still couldn't fight off those teeth.

"Give it to me," said the shark in a feminine voice. He grabbed for his mouthpiece again, but she snapped her teeth at him, and he had to pull back. "Not until you give me the piece, Simon."

He almost sucked in a mouthful of water. He knew that voice. He couldn't pinpoint exactly whose it was, but he knew without a doubt that the shark was one of Jam's sisters.

"Need—air," he tried to say, but he barely had any left in his lungs. He went for the mask a third time, and yet again, she cut him off.

"The piece," she demanded, her voice growing strangled with desperation. "Or you'll never take another breath again."

His mind whirled. He could shift into a fish to breathe, but that would mean exposing his secret to her, whichever sister she was. What were his other options, though? Drown?

Simon lurched toward the mask again, using all his strength to push off from the ground, but the shark knocked him aside as if he were a Wiffle ball. "The piece. I know you have it. I saw you, I heard you talking—*you have it.*"

What little he could see from the flashlight grew dark and fuzzy. His head swam and his lungs burned, and he knew if he didn't get any air in the next few seconds, he would pass out and drown. Resisting the urge to breathe in a lungful of water, he closed his eyes and imagined the shape of a small dark fish he'd seen swimming around earlier. Maybe he could get away and hide from her, and as soon as he had enough air, he could—

"Give it back to him."

To Simon's shock, a second great white shark appeared—this one much bigger than the first. It chomped down on the first shark's tail, and she let out a bloodcurdling shriek. Simon forgotten, she spun around and tried to bite back, but the bigger shark was too fast. They sparred in the wide beam of the flashlight, the second shark sinking its teeth into her twice more, and during those precious seconds while she wasn't paying attention, Simon used the last of his energy to propel himself toward the mouthpiece. Grasping on to it, he brought it to his lips and took the biggest breath he'd ever taken in his life.

Air filled his burning lungs, and spots appeared in front of him as his body got the oxygen it desperately needed. From a dark corner, Simon watched as the bigger shark chased the smaller one out of the cavern, his mind too cloudy from the lack of air and the earlier knock on his head to put two and two together. But as soon as Jam's sister disappeared, the remaining shark let out a whoop of joy. A very *familiar* whoop of joy.

"Nolan?" gasped Simon, pulling the mouthpiece away for a moment. The shark grinned, his teeth a little bloody. Simon's stomach turned.

"That was *awesome*. Are you okay?"

Simon nodded, taking several more deep breaths before speaking again. "What are you doing here?"

"You told me to keep an eye out and see if anyone acted funny. What are *you* doing here?"

"I—" Simon stopped, using the mouthpiece as an excuse to buy himself a few seconds. What was he supposed to tell Nolan? What excuse could he possibly come up with that would explain what he was doing in a cave before dawn?

He couldn't. There was nothing he could possibly say to his brother to explain any of this, and even if he tried, the way Nolan watched him with his dark, beady shark eyes made Simon wonder if he'd heard what the other shark had been saying. He must have, Simon figured. And his brother might have been a little self-absorbed sometimes, but he wasn't an idiot.

So, taking one more deep breath, he pulled the piece from his pocket. "I was looking for this."

Instead of more questions, like Simon expected, Nolan grinned again. "I *knew* it. I knew you didn't run off to the reptile kingdom because of Winter, and I knew you didn't want to come to California for some stupid summit. You've been putting the Predator together, haven't you?"

Simon took another breath and nodded. There was no denying it now. "I'm sorry I didn't tell you. Mom—"

"I know that's why Orion took Mom," said Nolan. "It all makes sense now."

"She sent me to find the pieces before he can," he said, slipping his arms back into the scuba harness.

Nolan considered this for a long moment, swimming in a circle around Simon. If it had been any other shark, Simon would have tried to bolt. As it was, he felt oddly safe with his brother there—and also terrified that Orion's shark army would come through the cavern entrance at any moment and find them both there.

Before Simon could blurt anything out, however, Nolan spoke. "I'm going to help."

It wasn't a question or an offer. It was a statement of fact, and Simon knew he shouldn't have expected anything less. But even now, he was hyperaware of the possibility that the shark would return and bring friends with her. Simon couldn't let that happen. No matter what, he had to protect his brother.

But could he really protect him if Nolan was following him and trying to help in ways they hadn't agreed on? Knowing his brother, that was exactly what would happen, and now that he knew, there was no use trying to put it off. So, reluctantly, Simon said, "Okay."

"Really?" said Nolan, sounding slightly bewildered.

"Really," said Simon. "Right now, if you know who the spy is, you need to find her before she can warn anyone else. And I need to—" He clutched the piece. "I need to go."

"Mom?" said Nolan, and Simon nodded tightly.

"I'll be back as soon as I can. Stay safe, okay? And stay out of the fight."

"You should see it," said Nolan, suddenly enthused. "I've never seen so many sharks in my life."

He sounded impressed, but all it did was make Simon sick with fear. He couldn't think about all of those soldiers he'd seen marching through the streets, possibly to their deaths. "I mean it, Nolan," he said. "Stay away from the battle. You're too important to risk."

With a huff, Nolan mumbled, "Fine. I will. Are you sure you don't want to look? We don't have to get close to see it."

It would be good to know what was happening and what kind of support Orion really had, Simon supposed. And maybe reality wouldn't be as bad as the fight he was imagining. "Only if you promise to stay away. You need to find the spy and stop her," he repeated. "Otherwise this gets really ugly really fast."

It was hard to tell, considering Nolan was a shark right now, but Simon could have sworn he drooped a little. "Okay. At least grab on to my fin so I can get you out of here."

Simon did exactly that, and as Nolan maneuvered through the maze of dark caves much faster than Simon ever could have, he wondered if this was the right thing to do. He'd made a promise to keep his brother safe, and this was the furthest thing from safe that he could think of. But now that Simon knew about Leo, now that he knew there was more to this than he had ever realized, he also knew he needed as much help as he could get. And while he and Nolan had had their differences, there was one thing they would always have in common: their mother.

When Atlantis came into view, Simon could barely breathe. The city glowed with eerie blue light, and surrounding the city were entire swarms of underwater Animalgams. Some of the creatures, including the whales and a few of the larger sharks, were big enough for him to make out, but from this distance, Simon couldn't tell where the armies ended and Orion's forces began.

But he could see one thing for certain: there was a ring of creatures surrounding a smaller force pinned against the dome with nowhere to go. Simon gulped. What remained of the underwater army were sitting ducks. It wouldn't take more than a few hours for the sharks to pick them off one by one.

"Come on, before you run out of oxygen," said Nolan, and with one last look at the raging battle, Simon let his brother pull him away.

Once they surfaced in the predawn light, Simon pulled off the mouthpiece and breathed in the crisp, salty air of the ocean. "They're going to die," he gasped. "All of those soldiers—"

"Jam said he had a plan," said Nolan. "He and Malcolm were talking about it when I left."

"Jam?" said Simon. "I thought Rhode arrested him."

"She did, but then once you escaped, she let him go as long as he agreed to help. They know what they're doing, all right? Don't think about that right now. Think about Mom."

Simon's head hurt, and a desperate need to do *something* filled him, but there wasn't anything he could do. Not against that many sharks. "You swear you'll follow the spy and nothing else?"

"I swear. She won't be hard to find. I can smell her blood," said Nolan as he swam in circles around him, sounding slightly awed and disgusted at the same time. "I'll come back for you. And Mom, if you can save her."

Simon bit his lip. "She wants—she wants to stay. To help throw Orion off," he admitted, his voice cracking. But if Nolan was in this, then he had to know everything, no matter how much it would hurt them both.

The shark was quiet for a moment. "Oh."

"It's not about us," he said quickly, trying to convince

himself as well as his brother. "It's just—it's too important for her to give up. I'll make sure she knows someone's trying to kill her, but she won't come back with me. Not until the Predator's destroyed."

The shark seemed to tense. "Then we have to make that happen," he said firmly, after a beat. But there was a hitch to his voice Simon recognized all too well—the hitch of helplessness hidden underneath the determination.

"You saved my life back there, you know," he said, nearly drowned out by the waves.

"And don't you ever forget it," said the shark, baring his teeth in a grin once more, though Simon thought it looked halfhearted. "I expect you to let me eat your dessert for the rest of the week."

Simon managed a smirk. "Only if it isn't cake. Go find the spy," he added. "And make sure Malcolm—make sure he isn't in that mess. I'll be back as soon as I can."

"You'll be okay?" said Nolan, and he nodded. The brothers exchanged small smiles before Simon shifted into a golden eagle, and he took off into the sky, trying not to think too hard about what was underneath those dark churning waves, and what he was sending his brother back into.

He soared toward Santa Catalina Island. In the dark, his eagle vision was poor, but he could spot light from the bobbing boat a mile off the coast. Winter was there, and Zia and Leo wouldn't let her go until Simon gave up the piece. He couldn't, though—wouldn't, not when he didn't trust either of them. But how could he possibly rescue her when they'd be up against another heir to the Beast King?

His worries were cut off by a shrill scream, however, and with a start, he zeroed in on the birds' beach. It had come from there. Simon dived toward the shore, and another scream echoed in the night.

It was his mother.

17

FISH TO FRY

Simon landed in a tree on the edge of the sand. The beach was quiet now, but he was sure that the screams had belonged to his mother. He'd heard them before—the day she'd been kidnapped, the times she'd screamed at him to run. He would have recognized them anywhere.

She wasn't on the log she'd been chained to earlier that night. Frustrated, Simon cast around. The branches that had been heavy with birds were now abandoned, and he heard no trace of the flock nearby. Throwing caution to the wind, Simon flew down onto the sand, hopping around while trying to spot her. There was a cluster of tents on the other side of the smoldering remains of the bonfire, and once he was sure she wasn't out in the open, he flew over, peeking through a small rip in the canvas of the largest one.

The lighting was dim, with only a single lantern hanging from the ceiling of the enormous tent. His mother hovered in the shadows of a nearby corner, slumped over with tears running down her cheeks. In the center, near an overturned table and a sea of papers and underwater maps, stood Orion, his hands clasped around the delicate neck of a dead peregrine falcon.

Ice filled Simon's veins. Was it Leo? From a distance, he couldn't tell.

"I told you, Isabel," said Orion, his voice shaking with rage. "I told you what would happen if he stole another piece from me, yet you *insist* on helping him anyway."

"You don't know it was Simon," she said. "The entire underwater kingdom is looking for that piece—"

"And yet your son was the one to find it. How do you think he managed that, Isabel? Do you think he scoured the entire Pacific Ocean in less than two days?"

"The Flukes knew where it was. He could have easily found out from them." She sniffed, fresh tears appearing in her eyes. "You didn't have to kill the messenger. He was a good man."

"And his blood is on your hands." Orion glanced at the dead bird he still held. "Rowan!"

Orion stalked out of the tent, taking his victim with him and leaving Simon's mother alone among the mess of maps and books. As soon as the flap closed, Simon slipped through the hole in the canvas, inching toward her. He couldn't get the image of the dead peregrine falcon out of his head, but for now, he took a small amount of comfort in the grim assurance that it hadn't been Leo.

"Mom," he whispered as loudly as he dared. "Mom, it's me."

She startled as if he'd yelled in her ear, the chains attached to her collar rattling. "Simon?" Her blond braid was messy, and up close, Simon could tell how puffy and swollen her eyes were. "Is that you?"

Simon bobbed his head and hopped closer. "I can't stay."

"You shouldn't be here. It's too dangerous."

"I know. I have to tell you—"

"Did you find it?" Her voice cracked with desperation. "Orion said you did, but—"

"I did," he said hastily. "It's okay, Mom. I have it."

She slumped back against the canvas as if a giant weight had been taken from her shoulders. It only lasted a moment, though, and then she straightened again, adjusting the heavy metal collar. "You need to get out of here. If Orion finds you—"

"I will," he promised. "But you have to know—"

Suddenly two large human hands grabbed him, pinning his wings to his sides. Instinctively Simon struggled against the grip, squawking and snapping his beak at the strong fingers around his feathered body, but there was no give. He was trapped, and worse, his captor was inadvertently pressing against the wound in his side, causing the pain to intensify to agonizing levels. Twisting his head around, Simon caught sight of Rowan's face. Even in the dim light, he looked pale.

"I was wondering when you'd drop by." Orion appeared at Rowan's side, speaking in a smooth, untroubled tone. Simon was suddenly extremely grateful he hadn't shifted into anything other than a golden eagle.

"Don't you dare touch him," growled his mother, jumping to her feet so quickly that she was a blur in the shadows. "If you do—"

"You'll what? Murder me? Darling, if you could, you already would have." Orion picked up the end of a loose chain hanging from her collar. Returning his attention to Simon, he added, "I hear you have something of mine."

"It isn't yours," spat Simon, trying to bite Rowan's fingers. Somehow, despite Simon's best efforts, he managed to artfully evade each pinch.

"It isn't yours, either, so I have no qualms taking it from you." Orion turned his attention to Rowan. "Let Simon go. He's going to shift back into a boy and hand me the underwater kingdom's piece of the Predator without any trouble."

"And why would I do that?" said Simon, feeling far braver than he had any right to feel in that moment.

"Because," said Orion, "if you don't, I'm going to kill your mother."

Any retort Simon might have been able to fling his way died on the tip of his tongue. "You . . . what—" He broke off, certain he hadn't heard Orion right. His mother, on the other hand, snorted.

"It's a bluff, Simon. He won't kill me. Not when he doesn't know where the other pieces are."

"I know more than you might think." There was a strange glint in Orion's eye, and Simon had a sinking feeling that his grandfather *did* know more than either he or his mother realized. "It would be more difficult for me to find what I need, but it wouldn't be impossible. So, I will ask you one last time—do we have a deal, young man?"

"Don't do it, Simon," said his mother. "He won't touch me, not until—"

"Do be quiet, Isabel," said Orion, tugging sharply on the chain around her neck. His mother staggered, but she didn't break eye contact with Simon.

"Don't," she whispered. "Whatever happens, Simon, *don't give him the piece.*"

Orion pulled a knife from a sheath hanging off his belt. "This will be painful," he warned, running a thumb over the serrated blade as if to test its sharpness. "It's entirely up to you, boy."

"Sir," said Rowan quickly. "There must be another way—"

"Quiet," barked Orion. "Or I'll break your wings."

Rowan fell silent, and bile rose in Simon's throat. He couldn't stop staring at that knife. The dead peregrine falcon—the countless soldiers who might be dying at that very moment to defend the city from Orion's armies—memories of Darryl lying in a pool of his own blood on the rooftop of Sky Tower morphing into images of his mother lying in a pool of her own blood inside the tent. Simon couldn't let that happen. No matter what it cost him or the Animalgam world, he couldn't lose her, too.

"Okay," he said at last with a shuddering breath. "I'll give it to you."

Orion studied him, and he nodded to Rowan. "Drop him."

Rowan set Simon on the sand with more gentleness than Simon expected. Still, as soon as his talons touched the beach, Simon morphed back into his human form, shivering in the chilly predawn air.

"Simon, no," said his mother, her voice catching. "Don't do it—"

Orion yanked on the chain again, and his mother fell to her knees, her hands flying up to the collar as if it were choking her. A hot knot of rage formed in Simon's chest, and he dug his nails into his palms.

"Stop it," he snarled. "Or the deal's off."

"Is that so?" Orion took a menacing step toward him. "You aren't the one who makes the rules, Simon, or have you forgotten?"

"And she's your family, or have *you* forgotten?" said Simon, resisting the urge to shift into something with enough teeth to give his grandfather nightmares for months.

Orion lifted the knife threateningly, tip pointed toward Simon's mother. "The piece, now, or I'll—"

His voice faltered, and a strange look passed over his face. For a moment nothing happened, as if time had frozen him in place. But then, without warning, his knees buckled, and he crumpled to the sand.

Simon stared at his body, his mouth hanging open. Orion was absolutely still.

"What—" he began, but then he spotted a shiny black spider crawling out from underneath Orion's collar. "Ariana? Is that—what are you *doing* here?"

Sure enough, the black widow waved one of her legs in greeting. "I hitched a ride to the boat with Zia and Crocker. Figured you'd check on your mom, and I wanted you to have backup." She shifted into her human form and picked up Orion's knife, focusing on Rowan. "Are you going to be a problem, too?"

Rowan shook his head, holding his hands in the air. To Simon's surprise, he also held a knife. "I wouldn't have let him do it," he said. "He wouldn't have done it—he needs Isabel—but if he'd tried, he wouldn't have gotten past me."

Simon didn't have the chance to consider whether Rowan was telling the truth. His mother knelt beside Orion, checking for a pulse. "He isn't breathing."

"You say that like it's a bad thing," said Ariana, gaze still fixed on Rowan. A block of ice formed in the pit of Simon's stomach.

"You *killed* him?" Horrified, he stared at his friend, seeing her—*really* seeing her for the first time since they'd arrived in California. The dark circles were back, but there was a haunted, savage look in her eyes, too, one that reminded him of a wild animal that had been cornered. Still, never in a million years would he have thought Ariana capable of actually killing someone, no matter how terrible they were.

"He's only a little dead," she said, gaze flickering toward Orion. "He'll be deader in a few minutes."

"No," said his mother with surprising firmness. She rolled Orion over and pressed her ear to his chest. "He can't die yet. He doesn't get to die until this is over." She started compressions on his chest. "Do you have the antidote?"

Ariana snatched the knife from Rowan. "The antidote? He was going to *kill* you. I get family loyalty and all, but—"

"He can't die yet," repeated his mother, growing breathless now. "He's the only one who knows where the bird piece is. If he dies—"

"We'll never be able to destroy the Predator," finished Simon, realization dawning on him. He looked at Ariana. "You need to save him."

She scoffed, but she sounded a little less sure of herself now. "You'll find the piece without him. Someone must have some idea—"

"I don't want to be the reason you're a killer," said Simon suddenly. His cheeks grew warm—not from embarrassment, but frustration. "I don't know what's going on with you. I don't know why you've been so secretive and quiet and scared all the time. I want to help, and I will if you let me, but whatever's going on, it isn't worth this. Killing someone—it'll change you forever. And all I want is one of my best friends back."

Ariana stilled. Simon could barely breathe, and the seconds ticked by like hours until he was sure Orion had to be dead by now, despite his mother's best efforts. But at last Ariana reached into her pocket and pulled out a syringe.

"He'll need the whole thing with the dose I gave him," she mumbled, offering it to Simon's mother. "Hope it's worth it. We'd all be better off if he wasn't here."

"He won't be forever," said his mother as she pulled the cap off the needle and stuck it in his arm. "But until that day comes, we need him, like it or not."

"I take it that means you won't be coming with us," said Ariana dryly. Simon glanced at his feet. He already knew the answer to that one, and hearing his mother say it aloud again would only reopen an old wound that had barely begun to close in the first place.

Thankfully his mother didn't bother. Instead, once she'd finished administering the antidote, she waited for a pulse. Nodding once, satisfied, she stood and brushed the sand off her pants. "It's a brave thing you did, Ariana, protecting us. Thank you."

"Yeah, well. Didn't exactly help." She glared at Orion. "He's going to come after my family next."

"Probably," said his mother. "But your kingdom has always been the strongest of us all. You'll be all right."

There was something in Ariana's expression that made

Simon think she disagreed, but before he could ask, the look was gone. "He'll have a wicked headache when he wakes up, and he'll be confused for a while. I've seen full-grown men convinced they were back in diapers while recovering."

His mother's lips quirked into a smile. "A little humiliation won't hurt him too badly."

Behind them, Rowan moved, and Simon spun around, ready to stop him from attacking. But the young man was squinting through the opening of the tent and into the lightening sky. "Sun's coming up. The flock will be back soon. You need to get out of here before they find you."

"Before we leave," said Simon, "you need to know that Rhode Fluke is sending someone to kill Mom."

"I know," said Rowan, still watching the sky. "Leo was here half an hour ago."

"Oh," he said. "Good."

"Leo was here?" said his mother.

"I sent him," confirmed Simon.

"You *sent* him?"

He nodded. "I met him—him and Zia and—" Simon stopped, putting the pieces together as he stared at Rowan. "You're Leo's spy in the flock?" he managed in a choked voice. Rowan grimaced.

"If you tell anyone in my kingdom, they'll kill me."

"I won't," said Simon hastily. "I swear."

His mother set a hand on his shoulder. "I'm glad you've met your grandfather. He'll help you as much as anyone can. But Simon—"

The cry of a falcon filled the early dawn, and whatever his mother was about to say died on her lips. Instead she caught him in a hug, and Simon wrapped his arms around her in return. He was still bitter that she'd chosen to stay with Orion over being with him and Nolan, but he understood now, as much as he ever could.

"I love you," said his mother into his hair. "Be safe."

"He'd be a whole lot safer if he didn't have to worry about Orion," said Ariana, but Simon ignored her for now. She was right, of course, but that didn't mean anything had changed. He had learned on the rooftop of Sky Tower that life was made up of difficult choices—the kind of choices that had consequences, the kind of choices that would change the course of their lives. This was one of them. Orion had to live because no matter how dangerous he was, he still had a purpose in his mother's plans—in *their* plans. And without everything and everyone right where they had to be, Simon would fail. They all would.

That understanding was also the reason that, when Simon finally let go of his mother, he smiled. "Love you, too. We both miss you."

"I miss you both, too. Tell Nolan as much as you can without putting him in more danger," she said. At Simon's guilty look, she managed a watery smile. "Ah. Of course you already have. Just . . . try to remember that you two are the reason I'm doing this—all of it. And if anything happens to either of you . . ."

"I'll protect him."

"I know you will, sweetheart," she murmured, touching his cheek. "But who will protect you?"

"Pretty sure the spider princess has already answered that question," said Rowan. "Hate to break this up, but the flock's returning. I'll only be able to hold them off for so long."

Simon's mother nodded and kissed his forehead. "I'll see you soon."

"See you soon," he echoed, and he shifted back into a golden eagle and waited for Ariana to crawl into his talon. Once she was secured, he took off and flew over the water toward the bobbing boat in the distance. The dark sky was turning pink now, and an entire army of birds soared toward the beach, no doubt with news of the battle.

Simon landed on the deck of the boat only a few feet from where Crocker stood, still surveying the ocean. "Took you long enough, boyo," said the bald man as Simon shifted back. "Birds don't look too happy."

That didn't mean everyone underwater had survived. Simon tried to keep an iron grip on his nerves, but it was a fight he was quickly losing. Instead he focused on Ariana, who shifted back into her human form and curled up on the deck, trying not to look into the water as her face turned a sickly shade of green.

"Come on, it's warmer in the cabin," said Simon, kneeling beside her, but she shook him off.

"That'll only make it worse. I'll be out here."

Reluctantly Simon left her in Crocker's care and ducked

inside. Leo paced the room, and Winter sat on the sofa, looking grumpier than he'd ever seen her while Zia plaited her hair.

"Simon!" Winter jumped up, her complicated braid falling apart. Zia groaned, but Winter ignored her, launching herself into his arms instead. "Are you okay? You look pale. Were you bitten again?"

"I'm fine," said Simon, his knees nearly buckling under her slight weight. As he set Winter down, Zia handed him his dry clothes and a towel.

"It'd be a shame for you to die of pneumonia after surviving a shark attack," she teased, but there was a hint of gravity behind it. Simon chose not to argue, and he disappeared into the bathroom to dry off and change.

As soon as he reemerged, Felix crawled up his pant leg and into his sweatshirt pocket, muttering a string of chastisements about his recklessness. Simon wisely decided not to try to defend himself against the little mouse. He probably deserved them, after all.

"Did you get the piece?" said Leo, and all of Simon's relief at seeing Winter faded.

He pulled the burning piece from his jeans pocket, silently offering it to his grandfather. "Will you let her go now?"

"Let who go?" said Winter while Leo took a hasty step back, nearly tripping over his own feet.

"You," said Simon, frowning. He glanced between her and the others. Leo was staring at Simon's outstretched hand like he was offering him a live python, and Zia looked puzzled. "Isn't that why you wanted me to get the piece? So I could give it to you in exchange for Winter?"

"You think *they* could hold me hostage?" said Winter, looking both amused and insulted at the same time.

"We'd never dream of it," said Zia, joining her father and setting a calming hand on his elbow. "Like we keep trying to tell you, we're the good guys."

"But—" Baffled, Simon dropped his hand, though he still clutched the hot crystal. "If you didn't want it, then why did you make Winter stay?"

"They didn't make me do anything," said Winter. "I could have left any time I wanted."

"And instead you stayed and let Zia braid your hair?" said Simon, his bewilderment only growing.

"No one's ever braided my hair before. It was nice," said Winter, raising her chin as if daring him to make fun of her.

Leo eyed Simon's closed fist, still keeping a good distance between them. "I don't want the pieces, Simon," he said quietly. "I thought I'd made that clear before, and I apologize for any confusion. Your friend was never a hostage. *You* were never kidnapped. All I've wanted is to keep you safe."

"But . . ." Simon looked at the piece. "You want me to keep it?"

"You're doing a pretty good job of protecting them already," said Zia. "No use trying to fix something that isn't broken."

Winter rolled her eyes. "Put it back in your pocket

already and stop looking so confused. You're smarter than that."

Simon did as told. Maybe it was the pain and exhaustion, but after months of adults trying to steal the pieces of the Predator from him, he couldn't imagine someone *not* wanting one. But Zia seemed adamant, and Leo looked downright sick at the thought of taking it. Whatever was going on, it didn't seem to be a trick.

"We need to go back to Atlantis," said Simon. "Crocker said the battle's over, and—" He couldn't say the words. Jam might have been fighting down there. And if the birds and sharks had managed to break into Atlantis, his uncle would have fought to protect Nolan with everything he had. Maybe the birds weren't happy because they hadn't found the piece. Maybe it had nothing to do with the battle, and maybe . . .

"I would much rather you stay here with us," said Leo. Simon snapped his head up.

"What?"

"We can offer you protection," said Leo. "Assistance while you seek the remaining pieces. You don't have to do this alone, Simon."

"I'm not alone," he said, glancing at Winter. "And my family's down there—the rest of my family, I mean. I can't leave them."

"We're heading back soon anyway," said Zia to her father. "We'll make sure Simon and Winter get there safely."

"And Ariana," said Simon. She gave him a sharp look,

and sheepishly he explained everything that had happened on the beach.

By the time he'd finished, Leo looked green around the gills. "I would rather the Black Widow Queen not find out I'm still alive," he said.

"I'll ask Ariana not to tell her," said Simon. Normally that would have been enough, but with the way Ariana had been acting lately, he wasn't so sure. "Can we go back now?"

"We've almost reached the dock," said Zia, poking her head through the doorway. "Looks like the submarine's already here."

"You still need to finish my braid," said Winter, hurrying after Zia. Before she stepped out onto the deck, however, she turned back to Simon, flashing him a knowing smirk. "Told you Rowan wasn't a bad guy."

Once the girls had left, Leo and Simon were alone, other than the mouse in his pocket. The pair of them stared awkwardly at each other for a long moment, until Simon finally asked a question that had been simmering in the back of his mind ever since he'd woken up on the boat. "How did you know about Felix?"

"Felix?" said Leo, sounding surprised. "I sent him to you."

He might as well have punched Simon in the gut. "You . . . he . . . you *sent him*?"

"Your mother thought it was a good idea to have someone with you—someone who wasn't your uncle," said Leo with a shrug. "We knew you'd be shifting soon, and we needed Felix there to make sure that when that happened, we would be prepared."

Simon sputtered. "The whole time—you mean—he—you and Mom—"

"Now just a minute," declared Felix, and he crawled out of Simon's pocket and onto his shoulder. "Yes, maybe I came to check on you at first. But I hung around because you're my friend. You're a decent kid. Not too stupid most of the time, and when you are, you mostly own up to it."

"But—" His mind whirled with a year's worth of memories. All the times he'd told Felix his secrets. All the times he'd trusted him. "You lied to me!"

"I never lied," said Felix, puffing up indignantly. "Omitted certain details, possibly. But everything I told you was true."

Simon scooped the mouse off his shoulder and set him down on the desk. "You're not coming back with me."

Felix squeaked so loudly that he nearly toppled over. "But—"

"I mean it," said Simon, his face burning and his vision growing watery. Out of all the things that had happened since Darryl's death, this betrayal felt like the worst. "You're not my friend if you're spying on me. That makes you no better than a—than a rat."

Felix's mouth fell open, and his tail drooped. Leo, on the other hand, grimaced. "Simon—"

"You don't get to say anything," said Simon fiercely.

"Not when it was your idea. I don't care if you did it to keep me safe. I'm sick of everyone lying to me and treating me like I'm some stupid kid who can't take care of himself. I'm done with this—with you, with Felix, with everyone."

Simon stormed out of the cabin and onto the deck, missing Ariana by inches. Refusing to look her in the eye, he wrapped his arm around her and helped her to the dock, where a submarine was waiting for them.

As they walked away from the boat, he could have sworn he heard an anguished squeak behind him, but the wind carried it away, and Simon refused to look back.

18
DROWNED RAT

Simon avoided Winter, Zia, and Crocker on the submarine back to Atlantis. They must have seen him leave the boat cabin, and he wasn't ready for their questions, nor did he want to risk Winter asking why Felix wasn't with him. Instead he sat beside Ariana, letting her clutch his hand so tightly that by the time they returned to the underwater city, he was sure she'd crushed all the bones in his fingers. He didn't try to talk to her yet, not while uncertainty and unease continued to swirl around them, but he hoped she at least understood that he was there for her. *Really* there for her, not pretending to be the way Felix had been pretending with him.

As soon as the airlock opened and they were all back inside the domed city, Simon bolted for the compound.

There was an excited buzz in the streets as soldiers roamed freely, clapping one another on the back between tending to the wounded. As Simon passed a dozen stretchers being carried toward a makeshift hospital near the planetarium, he looked at each soldier's face, desperately hoping it wasn't familiar. None of them were—and as far as he could tell, none of them were seriously injured, either. The worst he saw was a bite wound as bad as the one in his side.

Had the underwater kingdom really defeated the sharks so easily? They'd been outnumbered and surrounded only hours earlier—how could they have possibly won?

When they reached the compound, security rushed them through, apparently as relieved that they were back as Simon was to see the compound still standing. None of the guards seemed to remember the fact that Simon and Winter were supposed to be in the brig right now, and neither of them mentioned it. Zia led them through the mirrored hallways to the General's conference room on the ground floor, and as the soldiers opened the door, Simon rushed past her, bursting into the room.

Malcolm, Nolan, and Jam stood around the table, all looking exhausted. Jam was sporting a sling, and Simon could have sworn he had the start of a black eye, but he was beaming.

"Simon! Winter! Ariana!" He flew toward them and threw his good arm around each in turn. "You're all right!"

"Where on earth—" Malcolm plucked Simon from the

group as easily as if he'd been a newborn kitten, and he hugged him. "Where have you *been*?"

"Kind of a long story," he said guiltily, glancing at Nolan. His brother gave him a questioning thumbs-up, and Simon returned it. Nolan closed his eyes in silent relief.

"It's my fault," said Crocker as he hobbled into the room on his cane. "Thought things might get a bit dodgy, so we took Simon and Winter to the surface to protect them."

"Without telling me first?" said Malcolm, his voice a mixture of fury and relief. Crocker merely shrugged.

"There was no time. I assumed you would rather they be safe."

Rhode stepped toward Zia, her arms crossed and eyes narrowed. "You assaulted my soldiers."

"They were manhandling a little girl," said Zia evenly. "They deserved to be assaulted."

Rhode's frown deepened. "And you—" She turned toward Simon. "You evaded arrest."

"Because I'm not the spy," he said, too drained to have this fight again. But to his surprise, Rhode sniffed.

"Yes, I know that now. At the time, the circumstantial evidence was overwhelming, and it would have been negligent for me not to take precautions." She paused. "But I am glad you're both all right."

"Thanks." Truthfully Simon was just happy she wasn't trying to zip tie his hands together again. He turned to the others. "Is everyone okay? Did you really beat the sharks?"

"We are, and we did, with minimal casualties," said Malcolm. "Turns out Benjamin is a tactical genius. He emptied the city and hid the soldiers out of sight. When the sharks attacked, there was no one there to fight, and the dome is virtually impenetrable, so all they could do was swim around the outside. Not only that," he added, patting Jam on the back, "he also had the brilliant idea of dropping an ocean's supply of chum into the water several miles away. Nearly all of Orion's forces abandoned the fight for breakfast, and once they were gone, the troops closed in and finished off the rest."

So that had been what Simon and Nolan had witnessed outside the dome. The larger swarm pinning down the smaller force hadn't been the sharks attacking the army—it had been the other way around. "That's amazing," said Simon, stunned.

"It wasn't really my idea," admitted Jam. "I read about surrounding your enemies like that in a book."

"You're still the one who put it together and led the charge," said Malcolm. "And distracting the sharks with chum—that move saved countless lives."

Jam shrugged sheepishly. "Rhode made me think of that part."

"I did?" she said, squinting as if this were somehow an insult.

"Yeah. Don't you remember when I was seven and I cut myself on some coral while scuba diving, and you protected me from the tiger shark that showed up? You said it was instinct, that he didn't really want to eat me. He was only reacting to the smell of blood in the water."

"Oh." Rhode blinked. "I'd forgotten about that."

"I didn't," said Jam. "You're the reason I still felt safe in the ocean."

This made her cheeks go pink, but she held her head high, swiftly changing the subject. "Now that we're all here, there's still the matter of the spy to deal with—"

"It wasn't Winter, either," said Simon hastily. Rhode gave him a look.

"Of course it wasn't. Thanks to your brother, we now know who the real spy is."

"You do?" he said. Nolan smirked.

"While you were relaxing on a beach somewhere, *I* was doing the dirty work," he said proudly. Nolan knew full well Simon had been doing no such thing, but for once, Simon was glad he was keeping up the charade.

Rhode called for the guards, and two soldiers entered, with a meek-looking Pearl all but hanging between them. Her feet were dragging, and there was real fear in her eyes. Simon also saw bandages on her arms—where Nolan must have bitten her, he figured. He shot his twin a furtive look. Did Pearl know about Nolan's abilities now?

Maybe the connection between twins wasn't a myth after all, because Nolan shook his head minutely, as if he knew exactly what Simon was thinking. Still, Simon made a mental note to check with his brother later on. If Pearl knew, then Nolan's secret would get out before either of them could hope to contain it.

"Pearl Anne Fluke," said Rhode in a voice that would have made the commanding officer of an enemy brigade salute her. "You have been found guilty on the charge of treason not only against your kingdom, but against your family. Your actions directly resulted in our father, the General of the Seas, nearly dying, our kingdom losing our piece of the Predator, and the injuries of dozens of soldiers."

Pearl's lower lip trembled, and for a moment Simon almost felt sorry for her. Jam must have, too, because he spoke up. "It wasn't all her fault. I mean, Orion would have attacked us no matter what," he said when Rhode shot him a blistering look. "She helped, sure, but—I want to know why."

All eyes focused on Pearl. She hung her head. "I . . . I didn't think it was fair," she whispered.

"Didn't think what was fair?" said Jam. Not in the strict way Rhode spoke, but more like a brother talking to his sister. At his hint of warmth, Pearl glanced up. The defeat in her eyes reminded Simon all too much of the way Winter had looked after Orion had abandoned her.

"I didn't think it was fair that Rhode was doing all this work and protecting our kingdom, and you'd get to be the General instead because you're a dolphin and we're all sharks," she mumbled. "Orion—Orion promised me that Rhode could be the heir apparent, that he would make things right if I helped him. So . . . so I did."

The stern expression on Rhode's face cracked, replaced by astonishment. "You did this for me?"

Pearl nodded, staring at the floor again. "I didn't know Orion wanted the piece. He promised me no one would get hurt, that he just wanted to talk to you and the General, and . . . and by the time I found out what he really wanted . . . he told me if I didn't help him, he'd kill—he'd kill you and—"

She burst into tears. Not the kind of tears Simon had seen other kids use to get out of trouble, or the kind they cried when they were more upset they'd been caught, but real, fat, mournful tears full of guilt and grief. Simon took a step toward her.

"Orion's really good at convincing people they're doing the right thing, when all they're really doing is helping him," he said to her, and while he was quiet, he knew the others could hear him. "He'll tell you whatever you want to hear if he thinks it'll get him what he wants. My uncle died because I trusted him, and I—I know how it feels, that's all. It's not your fault. Not completely. I don't blame you for wanting to help your sister."

Pearl looked at him, astonished. "But—I tried to kill you."

Simon shrugged. "You were desperate. Besides, I don't think you really would have done it in the end." That was a lie, but Pearl looked at him with such intense hope that he was sure *she* believed she wouldn't have done it, either. Maybe that would make a difference if she ever faced that kind of choice again.

"I'm sorry," she choked out. "For all of it. I'm really, really sorry."

"Me, too," he said, and after a moment's hesitation, he dug into his pocket and pulled out the underwater kingdom's piece of the Predator. "Here," he said, handing it to Jam. "I think this belongs to your kingdom."

Jam took the piece, turning it over in his hand. "Right," he said, clearing his throat. But this had been the plan all along, and even though they'd proven he and Winter weren't the spy without it, Simon couldn't let Pearl be punished under the assumption she'd lost the kingdom their piece. He trusted Jam to give it back somehow.

"Is that the real thing?" said Rhode, peering at it. Jam nodded, showing her, though he didn't let her hold it. It was still painfully hot to the touch, as close as it was to Simon's pocket watch.

"Dad—I mean, the General, he let me carry it," he said. "I'm sure it's the real thing."

Rhode took a deep breath and released it slowly. "I owe you both an apology," she said to Simon and Winter. "I will learn from my mistakes here, and I will do better in the future."

"That's all anyone can do, Colonel," said Malcolm, though Simon detected a hint of smugness on his face. "But do remember that my memory is very, very long, and I will not tolerate this kind of circus again."

"Understood. Soldier," she added, this time looking at Jam. "Because of you, Atlantis is still under our control, and I think it is only fitting that you be the one to sentence Pearl for her crimes."

Jam blinked. "Me?" he squeaked.

"Yes, you," she said. "You were able to look beyond our regulations and traditions and see the situation in a way the rest of us couldn't. Because of that, because of your creativity, ingenuity, and bravery, you saved us." Rhode paused. "We've been doing things the same way for a long time. Maybe it wouldn't hurt to shake things up a little."

His eyes the size of clams, Jam looked between his sisters. "I—" He stopped and shook his head. "You're right. We've been doing things the same way forever, and I think it's stupid that once we've shifted, we aren't allowed to make mistakes anymore. Everyone messes up sometimes. Maybe not in a way that starts a war," he added, "but Pearl never meant for any of this to happen. She was only trying to help."

"The soldiers who were injured in the battle will carry those scars for the rest of their lives," said Rhode.

"I know. Believe me, I know," he added, glancing at Simon. "And she did a lot of bad things that could have been a lot worse, which is why I think she should be dishonorably discharged, stripped of her rank, and put into a rehabilitation program, where she has restrictions and extra duties until she's eighteen."

"That's all, soldier?" she said. "That's all the punishment she should receive for treason?"

"It's bad enough, isn't it? I mean, our whole society's built around the army. If she isn't part of it, then she'll always be left out. But . . ." Jam hesitated. "I think she should be reassigned to work with injured veterans, so she understands her actions have consequences. But I also don't think she should be punished for the rest of her life. When she's eighteen, I think she should be given a chance to reenlist, if she wants. If the General thinks it's safe, I mean."

"You want to let a traitor reenlist?" said Rhode incredulously.

"No. I want to give our sister a second chance, because she's only thirteen and she knows she made a mistake. No one died. We have the piece. And it was scary, but Pearl knows that, and in the end, she was trying to protect us. I think that should all count for something, too."

Jam finished firmly, standing as tall as he could with his head held high. For several seconds, Simon was sure Rhode would overrule him, but instead she nodded curtly.

"Very well. I will inform the General when he recovers. He will, of course, have the power to modify your sentence as he sees fit. But," she added, studying him, "I don't believe he'll have any reason to do so."

Jam beamed for a brief moment before smoothing out his expression into something more neutral. "Thank you, Colonel," he said formally. "I hope I don't disappoint."

"You haven't so far," said Rhode with a hint of wryness, and she and Jam shared a brief smile.

Malcolm cleared his throat. "As much as I hate to interrupt, I think it'd be best if we left as soon as possible. You have plenty to do here, and after everything that's happened, I think the kids deserve a real vacation."

Rhode nodded. "Of course, Alpha. I'll have a submarine prepared for you."

"We should stay," blurted Simon. Every pair of eyes in the room focused on him, and he swallowed. "I mean, not down here. But I think it'd be cool to see Avalon."

"The bird army is already retreating," said Rhode, looking to Malcolm. "I could post a handful of guards to ensure your family's safety, but I don't believe they would be a problem."

"You did promise us a Christmas on the beach," said Nolan. Malcolm sighed.

"If that's what you all want, then as long as it's safe, I won't say no."

Nolan whooped and gave Simon a high five—the first high five he had ever given him. Ariana, on the other hand, wrung her hands.

"I need to go home," she said, her gaze trained on the floor. "My mom—" She stopped. "I need to go home."

"I'll make the arrangements," promised Malcolm. "You should get some rest. We all should."

Jam escorted them to the dock later that day, once they'd all had a chance to nap. Though they made plans for Jam to visit Avalon, he still hugged Simon goodbye. As he did so, Simon felt something hot slip into the pocket where Felix usually slept.

"Thanks," said Simon, letting him go. "For everything."

"I'm just glad we made it out of this alive," said Jam, though he was smiling. It quickly faded, however, and he added, "If Orion gets the Predator, all our families are going to die, aren't they?"

"We won't let it happen," said Simon quietly. "Besides, we've already survived sharks. There's nothing Orion can throw at us that will be any worse."

Jam managed a soft snort. "Don't jinx us. We'll have to battle giant tarantulas next. But I am glad you're okay," he added. "And I'm really sorry about Al and Floyd. Don't do anything stupid while I'm down here, okay?"

"Can't make any promises," said Simon, forcing a grin. "Enjoy your sushi and kale. I'm going to have real food."

Jam laughed, and with one last wave, Simon boarded the submarine, where the others waited. Winter and Nolan were near the back, while Lord Anthony, Ariana's adviser, sat ramrod straight in his crisp suit toward the middle. A few seats down, Ariana still looked green, but also relieved to be leaving Atlantis for good, and Simon made a point of sitting next to her the whole way. She didn't say anything, but she didn't have to. Whatever she was going through, Simon would see to it that she wasn't alone.

"You're sure you're all right with me sticking around for Christmas?" said Zia from her spot next to Malcolm. "Don't get me wrong—I'd kill for a few days on the beach, but I don't want to intrude."

"The more the merrier, as far as I'm concerned," said Malcolm, who looked oddly pleased at the prospect. "Simon? Nolan? Winter? Do any of you mind?"

Simon shook his head while Winter examined her nails. "I suppose that wouldn't be terrible," she said loftily.

Nolan made a dismissive gesture. "Don't care," he called from the porthole, where he was watching Atlantis grow smaller and smaller.

"Well, after that rousing display of enthusiasm, how could I possibly say no?" teased Zia. Their eyes met, and Simon hastily averted his gaze. He wasn't sure yet whether he could trust her entirely, but she *had* proven they were in this together. So, reluctantly, he met her curious stare again and smiled.

Zia winked. For a moment, Simon wanted to laugh, until he shoved his hands in his pockets and felt the hot crystal where Felix usually slept. A hollow feeling settled over him, and he glanced around at the people surrounding him. He had the underwater piece of the Predator, but had lost one of his best friends in the process. Felix hadn't been his friend to begin with, he supposed, not really—but what else would this journey and the secrets he uncovered cost him? What other devastations would success bring?

And by the time it was over, how many of his friends and family would survive?

19

MICE AND MEN

An SUV was waiting for them when they reached Avalon. While Malcolm and Zia packed the luggage in the back, Simon lingered on the edge of the dock, where Ariana waited with her adviser. It was a cloudless day, and the blue sky seemed to stretch out for miles around them as the ocean lapped at the beach, but Ariana looked like she was going to a funeral.

"Can I stay until the boat picks her up?" he said to Malcolm.

"I can't leave you here alone," said his uncle, lugging Winter's heavy suitcase to the trunk.

"I'll stay with him," offered Zia. "You go on ahead and get the house ready."

"You're sure?" said Malcolm, and she nodded. "All right. I'll send the car back to get you."

"Take your time," said Zia. "We'll be fine."

As the SUV pulled away with Malcolm, Nolan, and Winter inside, she made a show of sticking beside Simon and Ariana, but as soon as it was out of sight, she stepped away. "The boat won't be here for another half hour, and it seems I have some Christmas shopping to do. Lord Anthony, do you mind coming with me?"

Ariana's adviser sniffed. "I would much rather—"

"I know that sounded like a question, but it actually wasn't," said Zia, hooking her arm around his.

"Go," said Ariana quietly. "I'll be fine."

Lord Anthony started to protest, but Zia cheerfully drowned him out with inane comments on the weather while half dragging him toward the nearest shop. There was an odd glimmer in her eye that made Simon think she once again knew more than she was letting on, but this time he was grateful.

Ariana sat on her suitcase at the edge of the dock, staring into the blue water with a faraway look. Simon waited nearly a full minute for her to say or do something, and when it became clear she wouldn't, he sat down on the wooden planks beside her. "We need to talk."

"No, we don't." Though her words were biting, there was no fight left in her voice.

"Yes, we do. Something's going on with you, and I'm not letting you out of my sight until you tell me what it is."

Ariana turned away. "I don't want to talk about it."

"Did I do something?" he said. "You know I'm not mad at you for what happened with Orion, right?"

"It isn't that," she mumbled. "Not everything has to do with you, Simon."

"I—" He squinted at her. "Then what's going on?"

She said nothing. After several seconds, however, her eyes watered, and her chin started to tremble. Without saying a word, Simon stood and wrapped his arm around her.

Ariana burst into tears. For several minutes, she sobbed into his shoulder, and all Simon could do was not let go. He'd never seen her cry before, not like this. Ariana was the toughest person he knew, and seeing her break down—a lump formed in his throat. She was supposed to be the strong one, the one who never let anything get to her.

Maybe that was why she'd let it build up to this point. Maybe everyone expected her to be strong, and she'd spent so long believing it that having any weakness at all made her feel like a failure. He could understand that. After all the pressure his mom and people like Leo put on him, he knew the feeling all too well. The only difference was, he knew he was allowed to be weak sometimes. Or, more accurately, most of the time. Maybe no one had ever told Ariana she could be, too.

"You can always talk to me, you know," he said once her tears had mostly stopped. He pulled out a napkin from his pocket. A few old crumbs from Felix's meals clung to it, but he brushed them off and handed it to her. She blew her nose.

"My mom's sick," she whispered. Her eyes were red and puffy, and they still leaked tears. "Really sick—not like the flu or anything. The kind she probably won't recover from."

Simon's heart plummeted. "I'm sorry." He knew all too well how empty those words must have sounded, and Ariana shook her head.

"That's why I had to go to the summit instead of her. She isn't strong enough. She's been trying to hide it, but some of the other leaders in my kingdom found out, and now they're planning to overthrow her. They can't even let her die in peace." Her voice crackled with anger and frustration. "This Christmas might be the last time I ever get to see her. I don't want to go back to school, not when she's so sick, but she insists it's safer there. At home, there are a dozen different people plotting to kill us, and my mom isn't strong enough to hold them off anymore. We can't trust anyone, not even her closest advisers. And now—" She choked up. "Now I won't even get to be there for her."

Ariana buried her face in his shoulder, the tears starting anew, and he didn't bother telling her it would be all right. It wouldn't be. If her mom didn't make it, if her kingdom erupted into war, there was nothing either of them could do to change any of it. Pretending otherwise would make them both liars.

"Can't your mom go someplace safe?" he said. "Maybe another kingdom? Malcolm would protect her."

"She—she refuses." Ariana hiccupped. "I tried to convince her. Malcolm already knows. That's why—that's why he's been so nice lately. But no matter what I say or do, she won't *listen*. She cares about the kingdom more than protecting herself, and I don't know what to do anymore."

Silence settled between them until the only sound was the splash of waves against the beach. Simon kept his arm wrapped around her, and she set her head on his shoulder, now wet from her tears. He didn't mind. Time seemed to stand still, and though a dozen different thoughts popped into Simon's head, he stayed quiet. They wouldn't help. Right now, Ariana needed someone to simply be there and listen.

At last, a loud growl sounded from Ariana's stomach. Simon pulled back enough to look at her. "When's the last time you ate?"

"Dunno. Lunch yesterday, maybe." She managed a watery smile. "Haven't really been hungry."

"Yeah, me neither," he mumbled. "Grab something at the airport, all right?"

"I will." Ariana peered at him. Her eyes were still rimmed with red, but she looked stronger now, somehow. "It's my kingdom next."

"I know." Simon pursed his lips. "You don't think your mom would just . . . give us the piece, would she?"

Ariana shook her head. "I tried asking. She thinks ours is hidden well enough that no one will ever find it."

"Do you know where it is?" he said.

"She said—she said I'd find out when she . . ." Ariana looked down at her hands. "I'm sorry."

"Don't be. We'll find it somehow." Simon tugged on a tuft of his short hair. "You know I'm always here for you if you need to talk, right? Or—not talk. We don't have to say anything."

"Thanks." She flashed him a small smile, but it quickly disappeared. "I don't know how you keep going while your mom's life is in danger. This feels like the world's ending."

"Yeah, it kind of does," mumbled Simon. He couldn't lie to her and tell her it would be okay. If he owed her anything at all right now, it was the truth. "You aren't alone, though, no matter what happens."

Ariana found his hand and squeezed it. "Thanks," she said, her voice breaking. "You, too, okay?"

Simon took a deep breath and let it out slowly. "I think right now that's the only thing I know for sure. Everything else . . ." He made a vague gesture with his free hand.

"We'll figure it out," said Ariana. "We always do."

"Until we don't," he said. She said nothing, but he didn't expect her to. Just like he'd told her the truth, her silence returned the favor. Nothing in their world was for certain anymore, and while they would have each other, they would both still need to find a way to survive it.

Avalon was exactly the kind of town Simon had thought the base for the underwater kingdom would be. The beaches were beautiful and, in December, not crowded at all. Most of the Animalgams living on the island were families with children who hadn't shifted yet, and it was a much more colorful place than Atlantis, with all kinds of things to do.

Simon spent most of the next two weeks on the beach. Though he was forbidden from going in the water while his injuries healed—injuries Malcolm now thought he'd received while running from Rhode—he read book after book while Nolan and Winter snorkeled and splashed around in the ocean on the warmer days. When the temperatures dipped, they went into town and spent hours exploring the island of Santa Catalina. The General had woken up shortly after the battle, and there was no sign of the flock anywhere near the coast, so Jam was even able to visit a few times now that he didn't have an entire kingdom to worry about.

Christmas was a bright and festive occasion full of more presents than Simon had ever expected. He and Darryl had always had a quiet holiday, with Darryl cooking lasagna while they both pretended Simon wasn't anxiously watching the front door, waiting for his mother to arrive—if she arrived at all. He regretted it now, not paying more attention to Darryl and appreciating all his uncle had done for him. And that was why, without a hint of complaint, he spent the entire day with his uncle, brother, Zia, and Winter. His mother wouldn't be showing up, and there was no front door to watch anymore.

Jam and several of his sisters joined them for dinner,

including Nixie and Coralia, who was escorted by a slightly bewildered young man who could only be her boyfriend. To Simon's surprise, Nixie brought Winter a gift.

"I'm not apologizing," she said as Winter handled the small box like it was a bomb about to go off. "Just thought you might like it."

The gift, as it turned out, was a glittering opal shell turned into a hair ornament. Winter immediately slipped it into the elaborate crown of braids around her head, and from that moment on, she and Nixie were inseparable. Simon didn't understand, but as long as Winter was happy, he supposed he didn't have to.

In the evening, after they had consumed the last of Malcolm's barbecue, they all gathered around a bonfire on the beach. "Daddy isn't entirely convinced," said Coralia, her fingers intertwined with her boyfriend's, "but he's agreed to meet him, so that's a step in the right direction."

"Coralia says her family has a thing for the ocean," said her boyfriend, pushing back his long hair. "I was practically born on a surfboard, so I'm not too worried."

As the others tried to muffle their snorts of laughter, Zia touched Simon's elbow. "Do you mind helping me with something?" she said quietly.

There was nothing Simon could think of that she could possibly need his help with, but he nodded anyway, curious. Things between them were still a little awkward, though she'd been nothing but kind to him, even cracking a few jokes that had made Malcolm turn red and insist she remember they were kids. Simon hadn't minded—he couldn't remember laughing that hard in a long time, and Zia seemed to appreciate the ice breaking between them. So, for that matter, did Simon.

He followed her down the beach, toward a cove he and Nolan had explored a few days earlier. As soon as the coast curved out of view of the others, Zia stopped, and Leo walked out of the trees with a small wrapped package tucked under his arm.

Simon froze, rooted to the sand. He hadn't seen or heard from Leo since the revelation that he had sent Felix to spy on him, but part of him had been expecting something like this. His newfound grandfather didn't seem like the type of person to let an argument go unfinished.

"I'll give you two a moment," said Zia, and she headed toward the water, putting several yards between them.

"You look stronger," said Leo after a heavy few seconds of silence. "Well rested."

"Thanks, I think," said Simon. "What are you doing here?"

"I wanted—needed to clear up a few things," said his grandfather. "Well, we both did."

Felix popped his head out from Leo's pocket. Simon immediately took a step back, any hint of forced politeness dissipating between them. "I don't want to talk to you."

"I don't want you to talk," said Felix. "I want you to listen. I'm your friend, Simon. Not a spy, not a rat—your friend."

"If this is how you treat your—"

"I wasn't finished," snapped Felix, jumping onto Leo's shoulder. "You weren't supposed to be my friend—I was supposed to keep an eye on you and watch for any signs of danger, and that was it. No part of it included getting chummy. But I did it anyway, because you did things other humans didn't. You helped injured pigeons, you nursed me back to health after I showed up half-starved—"

"You can't pretend that was real anymore," said Simon, frustrated.

"But it was. The rats took all the good food, and I wasn't about to go Dumpster diving," said Felix. "You didn't treat any of us like an enemy, no matter what kingdom we belonged to."

"I didn't know about the kingdoms then," he pointed out.

"Doesn't matter. You still do it. You meet someone and you see who they are, not what they are. You got any idea how rare that is, kid?"

Simon shrugged, caught off guard. "I—"

"I'm still not finished." Felix glared at him with his beady little eyes, and Simon quieted once more. "I get it. I hurt you. I'm sorry. Cross my heart, hope to die and all that—I never meant to, you know. Neither of us did. All we ever wanted was to keep you safe. Sometimes that meant making stupid decisions or not telling you everything, but it's all out in the open now. It doesn't have to be all secrets and lies anymore, and I don't want it to be. I want to be your friend. That's it, full stop. I won't apologize for protecting you, but I will apologize for hurting you, because you're right—that was a ratty thing to do. Friends don't hurt friends, and I won't do it to you again, not if I can help it."

Simon stared at him, and Felix tugged his tail nervously.

"That's it. You can speak now."

Anger and loneliness warred within him as the seconds ticked by. On one hand, Felix had lied to him for a year, pretending to be something and someone he wasn't. Simon had had enough of that in his life already. But on the other, he missed his best friend. He missed his biting commentary and not-so-witty jokes, and he even missed his seemingly endless stream of complaints.

He'd managed to forgive Pearl for trying to kill him. Why was it so hard to forgive Felix for lying?

Because that had hurt more, he realized. It had been personal. He'd trusted Felix, and this felt like more of a betrayal than anything Pearl could've possibly done to him. But holding on to that bitterness was eating away at Simon, and he didn't want to be mad anymore. It was too hard, too exhausting, and he had more important things to worry about. They all did.

Decision made, he stepped forward and scooped Felix off Leo's shoulder. "I'll give you one more chance, but only one. No more lies," he said sternly. "You tell me the truth, and you don't keep anything from me, or you'll be out on your own and have no choice but to beg the subway rats for scraps. Deal?"

Felix squirmed. "I'd rather eat my own tail than ask those vermin for a crumb."

"Do we have a deal or not, Felix?"

With a disgusted twitch of his whiskers, the little mouse nodded, and Simon let him crawl down his sleeve and back into his pocket, where he burrowed and rearranged himself as if moving in for the first time. "You got any idea how much lint you've collected while I've been gone?"

Simon almost smiled, but when he caught Leo's stare, any trace of happiness faded. "I don't know if I can trust you or not," he admitted.

"Good. You shouldn't, not until I've earned it." Leo tapped his foot against the sand, as if he could barely stand to be still. "Ask me why I don't want the pieces."

Simon frowned. "What?"

"You've been yanked around by the adults in your life long enough. I owe you an explanation, and I'm trying to give you one," said Leo. "Ask."

He exhaled slowly. "All right. Why don't you want the pieces?"

"Because I don't trust myself with them."

That piqued Simon's curiosity. "Why not? You already have all the powers of the Beast King."

Leo shrugged. "I wouldn't need to use them to kill in order to be dangerous. If given the chance, I fear I would use them to force the leaders of the five kingdoms into a truce."

"But—wouldn't that be a good thing?"

"In an ideal world, yes. But we don't live in an ideal world, and all the Predator has ever brought anyone is pain. If I used it, even only to threaten our world into peace, the five kingdoms would have no choice but to rise against me and start the worst war our world has seen in five hundred years. No single person should have that much power, no matter how good their intentions might be."

"You don't think I would try the same thing?" said Simon, though the thought had never crossed his mind.

"No," said Leo. "I don't think you would."

Simon nodded, not sure what to say. There was an entire history between them that he hadn't known existed up until a few days ago, and he didn't know how to breach it. They were strangers who had too much in common to name, and Simon wanted to feel connected to him. He wanted to know his grandfather. But after all they'd both been through, he had no idea how to start. "I'm sorry," he said at last. "About my dad, and about Darryl."

"Don't be," said Leo. "Neither was your fault."

"Darryl was," said Simon despondently. "He was only on the roof because of me."

"No." Leo knelt in front of him, balancing himself on the shifting sand. "Orion killed Darryl, not you. You're the one who's stopping him from killing others. Do you understand?"

He didn't, but he nodded anyway. Leo gave him another pained smile before handing him the package he'd brought with him. "Here. I thought you might want this."

Simon unwrapped the brown paper slowly. Inside was the book Leo had showed him on the boat, and tucked between the pages was the picture of his father and Darryl, with Leo's profile in view. Simon held it as tightly as he dared, afraid the breeze would carry it away. "I can't take this. It's yours."

"It's a memory for me," said Leo. "For you, it's a glimpse into a life you should have had. One my stupidity took from you."

Simon started to protest, but Leo shook his head.

"I've been atoning for my mistakes for over a decade, and I will continue to do so for the rest of my life. There's no use pretending otherwise. I owe you a debt I can never repay, and the least I can do is give you a piece of your story."

Simon examined the picture in the moonlight, studying his father's face. He was happier here than in the portrait Simon had seen hanging in the Alpha's office back in the L.A.I.R. He could almost imagine who his father had really been, could almost hear his laugh and see him move. It wasn't real, but it was more than he'd had before.

"Thank you," he finally said. "And for what it's worth, I don't blame you."

Leo smiled sadly. "Only because of loyalty I don't deserve." Standing, he patted Simon on the shoulder. "Now, go be braver than all of us. If there is ever anything you need, all you have to do is ask. Don't you forget, Simon—you're never alone."

It was as much a warning as it was a promise, a fact that didn't escape him. After a brief goodbye, his grandfather melted back into the tree line, and he joined Zia at the water with Felix tucked securely in his pocket. "Does Malcolm know who you are?" said Simon without preamble.

"He knows we share a brother," said Zia, seemingly unfazed by his bluntness. "But we never really knew each other growing up. I was several years younger than him, plus Luke was in New York with the Alpha's family, and I was in Stonehaven. I got to know Darryl through my father and your mother," she added. "But by the time Luke died, Malcolm was only eighteen or so, and Darryl didn't want him getting mixed up in this. We've been getting closer recently, though."

There was a strange cheerfulness in her voice as she said it, and Simon eyed her. "What kind of getting closer?"

Grinning, she ruffled his hair and started back toward the bonfire. "The kind you don't need to worry about. He's a good guy, your uncle. He deserves a little happiness, too."

"Yeah, but—what *kind* of happiness?"

One look at his expression, and she laughed so loudly it echoed across the dark water. Simon huffed.

"Think they're going to date?" said Nolan later that night, once the celebrating had ended and they were back in their cozy nautical-themed guest room, curled up in their individual twin beds. Apparently Simon hadn't been the only one to notice how Zia had spent the rest of the evening talking to Malcolm, who hadn't seemed to mind at all.

"She lives in Colorado, remember?" said Simon with a yawn. Felix slept soundly on his pillow, and Nolan had taken their vague excuses as to why he'd suddenly reappeared in stride. "They can't date when they're so far apart."

"You never know." Nolan was quiet for a long moment. "I wonder what Mom's doing right now."

"Probably wishing she was here with us." Now that Nolan knew she'd had a choice, Simon was all too aware of how a single wrong word could make his brother feel the resentment he'd been living with since their mother had willingly gone back to Orion in Arizona, and he never wanted Nolan to feel that way, too. He rolled over onto his side so he could see the outline of his brother in the dark. "I'm sorry I didn't tell you what I was doing earlier."

Nolan shrugged. "It's okay. I get it, I think. You and Malcolm keep trying to protect me, but I can protect myself, you know."

"I know." Simon twisted the corner of the sheets. "I need your help. I can't do this on my own anymore."

"Good, because I was going to help whether you liked it or not. When do we start?"

Simon hesitated. "You have to promise me something."

"What?" The wariness in Nolan's tone made Simon even more nervous somehow, and he picked at a loose thread. He could still see the fear on Leo's face as he'd backed away from the underwater kingdom's piece of the Predator, could still hear his voice as he explained why he didn't want it. And as much as Simon wanted to trust his brother, he knew without a doubt that Nolan thought he could use the Predator to make the world better, too.

"Let me handle the pieces," said Simon. "It's too dangerous for you to hold on to them. If Orion captures you, he would have both you *and* a piece, and that would make a bad thing even worse."

For several seconds, Nolan didn't say anything. Simon steeled himself against any protests his brother might have, but to his surprise, Nolan just shrugged again. "Makes sense."

Simon exhaled. "Really?"

"Sure. Orion won't hurt you—you're a golden eagle, like he is. You're practically the only Animalgam on the planet he wouldn't use the Predator against. So I get it. I'm special, and sometimes that means I have to make sacrifices."

He said it as if he were quoting someone else, and though Simon couldn't be sure, he thought he heard shades of their mother in those words. "Yeah. You can do the cool stuff, so let me do the dirty work."

"Only 'cause you asked so nicely."

Simon smirked into his pillow, and the two of them fell silent again. Enough time passed that Simon thought Nolan had fallen asleep, until he heard his brother whisper, "What if we can't do it? What if we lose her forever?"

It hurt to hear his boisterous, confident brother voice the very worries Simon had been grappling with since September, and his stomach ached with the fresh reminder of how bad things could get. Instead of admit it, however, he said, "I was worried about the same thing. But now that you know and we're in this together, I'm not anymore."

"Yeah?" said Nolan. Simon could practically hear him smile.

"Yeah. Now get some sleep. We're not going to be able to stop Zia and Malcolm from dating if we're too tired to think."

Nolan made a rude sound, and Simon closed his eyes, letting himself relax. Things hadn't gotten easier now that his twin knew—if anything, they'd only gotten more and more complicated. But the burden he'd been carrying by himself was lighter with Nolan helping him, and for now, that was all Simon could hope for.

20

FLOUNDERING

They returned to Atlantis one more time before their vacation ended, for what Malcolm would only describe as a *meeting*. He'd forced them to dress nicely, though, even buying Simon and Nolan ties to wear, which had both annoyed Simon and made him suspicious something else was going on.

It took every ounce of courage Simon had to head back down to the underwater city, and when they arrived, he nearly choked upon seeing Colonel Rhode greet them with an entire platoon of soldiers.

"It's purely ceremonial," said Rhode dryly. And instead of leading them to the compound, they marched toward the very center of the dome.

Simon had never been this deep inside the city before, and with every step they took, he grew more and more nervous. Had the General discovered Jam had slipped him his kingdom's piece of the Predator? Had he reviewed the evidence and decided Simon deserved to be arrested after all? But if that were the case, then why would Simon have to wear a tie? He forced himself to relax. Everything would be fine. Malcolm would never let anything happen to him.

Unless this was a trap.

Rhode ushered them through a gate in a high stone wall, and holding his breath, Simon stepped inside. Instead of the angry army he'd half expected to face, he found himself inside the strangest park he'd ever seen. A glass path branching in several directions stretched out across acres of low water, and beneath their feet was a rainbow of colorful coral.

"These are the coral gardens," said Rhode as they approached the center platform, where the General stood, leaning heavily on a cane. Jam and the rest of the Fluke family lingered around him, all dressed in full military uniform.

No, not all of them. Pearl stood off to the side in a simple blue dress, pale and withdrawn. Her gaze was fixed on the glass floor, and Simon had never felt sorrier for her.

"Alpha. Glad you could make it," said the General. Though he seemed weak from his injures, his voice boomed as loudly as ever.

"We wouldn't have missed it," said Malcolm, and as Rhode rejoined her family, he gestured for them to step toward the edge of the platform.

"What's going on?" said Simon, confused.

Malcolm shook his head. "Watch."

The General limped to the center and pulled from his pocket a small box. "I asked you all here today because this is a moment that deserves to be recognized and remembered not only by my kingdom, but by the entire Animalgam world." He studied the box for a moment, weighing it in his hand as if he didn't know exactly what was inside. "My son, Benjamin, has always been the odd man out in our family. Not simply because he is my only son and the only one of my children to inherit my Animalgam form, but also because he always saw the world differently than we do. Where we see need for order, Benjamin sees beauty in chaos. Where we see black and white, Benjamin sees color. These are typically not celebrated traits in our kingdom, and I'm sorry to say he has endured a great deal of difficulty for openly displaying such gifts."

Standing in the middle of his family, his mother on one side and Rhode on the other, Jam turned pink. Simon tried to catch his eye, but he stared resolutely at the General, his back straight and his shoulders square.

"Our kingdom is a great one, but we, like all others, have our limitations," continued the General. "We believe in tradition and doing things the way they've always been done, and had we continued to uphold those beliefs during the battle for our city, we would have surely lost. Benjamin was the one who was not only able to see possibilities we were blind to, but also had the courage to speak up and help redirect our efforts, saving thousands of lives and the autonomy of our kingdom in the process."

The General opened the box, revealing several pins shaped like sea stars. Jam's eyes widened as his father limped toward him, and the General took a pin in his shaking hands. "It is my honor to award you, Benjamin Fluke, the rank of Major of the Underwater Armies. You have made me proud, son—prouder than I could say, and we all owe our lives to you. The kingdom is lucky to call you its next General, and I am lucky to call you my son."

The General reached for Jam's lapel, but before he could, Jam took a small step back. "Sir, if I may," he said, his voice trembling nearly as much as his father's hands. "I'm the one who's honored to call you family, sir—all of you," he added, looking around at his mother and sisters, too. "And I would be honored to lead our kingdom in the future. But I don't deserve it."

The General studied him. "Of course you deserve it, Major. You're my son."

"And Colonel Rhode is your daughter, sir. She was the one to keep the kingdom together. I could never match her discipline and dedication, and it shouldn't matter that she's a shark instead of a dolphin." Jam's gaze shifted toward Pearl, who was watching with almost desperate hope in her eyes.

"That kind of discrimination only creates bitterness, and our people deserve better. They deserve her as their next General. Sir."

A few of Jam's sisters began to whisper, and the General frowned, clearly befuddled. Before anyone could say a word, however, Rhode stepped beside her father and gently took the pin from his shaking hands.

"Thank you for your kind words, Major," she said, her fingers working at Jam's lapel. "I have dedicated my life to serving our kingdom, and I will continue to do so. But I am proud to call you my brother, and when the day comes, I will be proud to call you my General. Our kingdom must move forward, and while I will always remain at your side, I have no doubt that you are the right person to guide us toward the changes that will help us reach our full potential—not only as soldiers, but as compassionate and diverse human beings, too." She stepped back, and the stars were fixed to Jam's uniform. "As our father so eloquently stated, you see in color, and we could all use a little more of that right now."

She saluted him. Jam's chin trembled, and to Simon's surprise, he threw his arms around his sister. Rhode stiffened, but after a moment, she unwound ever so slightly and offered him a hug in return.

The General cleared his throat, and Jam straightened, his face red. "Sir, my apologies, sir. It won't happen again, sir," he said, his arms glued to his sides once more. The General smiled faintly.

"I should hope it happens often, Major." And though he didn't embrace Jam, he did pat him on the shoulder. It didn't look like much, but judging by the way Jam was beaming, it was the happiest moment of his life.

"Come on," said Winter once the ceremony was over, tugging on Simon's arm. "Nixie said there's going to be a party in the compound, and somehow she convinced her mother to serve cake that doesn't taste like a sushi roll."

"I bet it still looks like one," said Simon, and he laughed at the face Winter made. No matter how many small steps forward the underwater kingdom was taking, he supposed some things—like their love of sushi—would always stay the same.

As they reached the end of vacation, Simon was sorry to leave Avalon behind. He didn't have much of a tan thanks to Zia's obsession with slathering them with sunscreen, but he did feel, at least for now, like the weight of the world wasn't resting entirely on his shoulders.

They said their goodbyes to Zia at the Los Angeles airport. Simon's goodbye was brief—a word and a wave from him, and a wink from Zia—but when Winter's turn came, Zia knelt in front of her, and they spoke quietly for a full minute out of hearing range. Once Malcolm left to walk Zia to her gate, Winter disappeared into the bathroom for nearly fifteen minutes, and when she finally reemerged, her eyes were bloodshot. It hadn't escaped Simon's notice that

Winter's hair had been braided a different way every day they'd been on the island, but he didn't dare say anything.

They landed in New York right as the sun was setting. With a day to go before the other students returned to the L.A.I.R., the school was all but abandoned as they traipsed across the moat and into the five-sided underground building. The quiet was unnerving, and Simon was grateful to climb the winding staircase in the Alpha's section and head to his bedroom. Before he could drag his suitcase inside, however, Nolan let out an angry shout from the room next to his.

Simon darted to his open door. "What's—" He stopped. Nolan's room was a mess. His sheets had been yanked off the mattress, which was ripped open. His drawers had been overturned, the contents spilled across the floor, and his books were strewn throughout the room, the pages and covers torn.

With dread looming over him, Simon sprinted back to his bedroom and threw open the door. His room had also been turned inside out, and he stared at the chaos, his heart pounding. He couldn't breathe, he couldn't think—he automatically moved to the sock drawer that had been wrenched out of its slot. His hands moved over the smooth wood of the false bottom, and his fingernails caught the edge. Mouthing a slient, desperate plea, Simon pried it apart.

The reptiles' piece of the Predator was still nestled in its corner, as safe and secure as it had been when Simon had left.

His shoulders slumped with relief, and his pulse was beginning to slow when, out of the corner of his eye, he spotted the wall above his desk. The edges of his vision faded, and his body went numb.

No. *No.*

"What's going—?" Malcolm began, but the question died on his lips when he appeared in Simon's doorway. "What the . . ."

"My room's the same," said Nolan, his expression dark. "They ripped my books."

"I'll get you new ones." Malcolm must have seen the look on Simon's face, because he stepped toward him like he would approach a wounded animal. "Simon? Is something missing?"

Simon stared at the blank wall, his head spinning. "My—my postcards. The ones my mom sent me—" His voice caught in his throat, and for a dangerous moment, he thought he might cry. "They're gone."

21

DEER IN THE HEADLIGHTS

It took Simon and Nolan hours to clean up the mess. Malcolm, Winter, and Jam all pitched in, and while Winter murmured her condolences over the loss of his mother's postcards, none of them tried to comfort Simon. It was pointless; unlike Nolan's books, Simon would never be able to replace the postcards his mother had sent him.

No other part of the school had been touched. Malcolm seemed baffled as to why anyone would bother taking a hundred and twenty-four postcards while leaving behind expensive electronics, but Simon knew the answer. Someone else had realized that those postcards were a roadmap of where his mother had been all his life, and more important, where the remaining pieces might be hidden.

Over a late dinner of pizza, which Simon mostly left

untouched, he wrote down every postcard he could remember. Some of them appeared in his mind as easily as if they were in front of him, but others he struggled to recall. Not since the weeks after Darryl had died could he remember feeling like this—like he'd lost a part of himself he could never get back. They might have been nothing more than cheap postcards to most people, but they were some of the only pieces he had left of the life he'd lived before discovering Animalgams existed, and every time he looked at the blank wall where they had hung, he felt the full impact of bitter, gut-churning loss all over again.

"I think it was Orion," said Simon quietly while Winter, Jam, and Nolan were helping him fold his clothes and put them back in the drawers. "He's broken into the school before, and—and when he was threatening to kill our mom, he said he didn't need her. That he had other ways of finding the pieces. Maybe that's what he meant."

"Maybe," said Winter doubtfully as she searched for a matching sock. "But I've been thinking—Orion still has your mom, and even if he could find the pieces without her, he'd be stupid to try."

"He'd be stupid to try to hurt her again, too," muttered Nolan, tossing an unfolded pair of pants into his pile. "I'm pretty sure these are mine."

Winter shot him an exasperated look. "Does Orion know about the postcards?" she said, refocusing on Simon.

He hesitated. "I don't know. Maybe."

"There are over a hundred of them, right?"

"A hundred and twenty-four. A hundred and twenty-six if you count the ones she's sent since she was kidnapped."

"How many of those were about insects?"

"Maybe twenty-four or twenty-five. I'm not sure."

"That's still too many for him to narrow down where to look for the next piece from your postcards alone," she said. "He would have to be desperate to use them instead of your mom, especially when all signs point to her helping him at least a little already."

"She's right," said Jam, who was folding Simon's shirts with military precision. "He isn't stupid, and he isn't desperate. Yet."

"It could be a backup in case she stops cooperating," said Simon, although he sounded unsure even to himself.

"I don't think it was about the postcards at all," said Winter. "Your room was ransacked. Nolan's, too. If all they wanted was the postcards, those were hanging in plain sight. I think they were after the pieces."

Simon's hands stilled in the process of weeding his underwear out of the pile of clothing. She was right, of course. The postcards were a consolation prize. "I don't know what to do next," he said miserably. "I don't know where to go. I don't know how to keep the pieces safe—"

"We'll help you," said Jam. "You're not alone in this."

"Sometimes it feels like it," he mumbled.

"Well, you're not," said Winter, distinctly more waspish

than Jam. "We'll figure it out, Simon. We always do. Ariana will help us, and we'll find the rest of the pieces."

"But the postcards—" began Simon.

"They weren't the ones fighting vipers and sharks. You were," she said. "So enough of this. You get to be upset for the rest of tonight, but tomorrow, once Ariana's back and everyone's distracted by the tournament, we're going to figure out our next steps together."

Jam groaned. "I forgot about the tournament."

So had Simon. But while he would still have to represent the bird kingdom in the finals, after everything that had happened in Atlantis, none of it seemed all that important anymore.

"Let someone else fight to win the stupid tournament," said Nolan. "We're fighting to save the entire Animalgam world."

And despite his grief, as Simon looked between them and saw the determination on their faces, he let himself believe that maybe, just maybe, they would win.

That night, long after Felix had started snoring, Simon sneaked into Nolan's room. His brother was fast asleep, and Simon slipped into the secret tunnel that led out into the Central Park Zoo.

It had been weeks since he'd last searched for a postcard, and he was sure whoever had raided his room would have stolen any his mother had sent him in the meantime. But he had to check anyway, and he walked through the darkness across the cobblestones of the zoo, to the spot where the two huge wolf statues sat.

As he walked past, his fingertips brushed against the wolf that was his father. He'd tucked the picture Leo had given him away in the secret drawer, all too aware that he was in desperate need of a more secure hiding spot. He'd gotten lucky this time, but his luck wouldn't last forever.

Stopping in front of Darryl's statue, he ran his hand over the wolf's muzzle as if petting the stone beast. He'd only seen his uncle in the form of a wolf a handful of times, but this was an important part of who he'd been. As the months had passed since Darryl's death, Simon had begun to see him as more than simply his uncle.

"I met Leo," he said so quietly that the darkness seemed to swallow his words whole. "He misses you. I think we all do."

He paused, his breath visible in the cold night air. He was never really sure what to say to his uncle. Sometimes he felt ridiculous, talking to his grave, but even if it was childish, he didn't care. He needed this. He needed to remember.

"I wish I'd known I had so much family growing up," he mumbled. "But I also don't want you ever thinking you weren't enough for me. You were. You and Mom, when she could come—you were great. And I miss that. I miss eating breakfast together. I miss how we used to spend Saturdays at the library. And—and no matter how bad the kids at school were, I knew I could always come home and things would be okay. I miss that, too." He swallowed thickly. "I miss you."

"How *touching*."

Simon snapped his head up. Out from the shadows emerged a gray wolf. It was smaller than his uncle had been, but there was a gleam of twisted savagery in its eyes that made it more dangerous than the entire pack combined.

"Celeste?" he said, his voice breaking.

"Hello, Simon."

He hadn't seen or heard from the former Alpha since Malcolm had chased her out of Paradise Valley, and he'd hoped she'd been scared off permanently, but of course she hadn't. Simon took a step back. "You're the one who stole my postcards."

It wasn't a question, but her low laughter gave him all the confirmation he needed. "I had no idea your mother had been so vigilant about tracking her whereabouts over the years. Thank you for keeping them safe, Simon. I promise to put them to good use."

He took another step back, nearly stumbling over the cobblestones. "What do you want?"

"The pieces, Simon," she said, moving closer and closer. "Bring them to me, and I will leave you all alone."

"You know I won't give them to you."

"Not even to protect your brother and uncle?"

"Malcolm's already proven he can take you down in a fight, and we both know you don't stand a chance against Nolan," he said, sounding braver than he felt. "So what do you really want?"

He thought he saw a flicker of a wolfish smile. "You always were the smart one, weren't you? Your mother chose wisely." She began to circle him, her movements easy despite the tension in her muscles. "We should be working together, Simon."

He snorted. "Like you were working with my mother?"

"I know secrets not even your mother knows, secrets about the Predator and Orion that could change the course of history." She stopped barely a foot away, close enough now for him to see each pointed fang as she spoke. "It's only a matter of time before you realize you need me, and by then, I might not feel so charitable."

There was something about the way she said it that made Simon believe she wasn't completely bluffing, but there was no question in his mind. "I'll take my chances, thanks."

She growled, the low sound hair-raising in the dark. "I won't offer again, Simon."

"Yeah, you will," he said. "You need me a lot more than I need you, and you know it. Else you wouldn't be here begging for my help."

Celeste snarled and snapped at him, and he barely managed to dodge her teeth. The image of a golden eagle was half-formed in his mind when from the trees came a low trilling hoot, and the wolf froze in her tracks.

In the branches above them was a white-faced owl unlike any Simon had ever seen before. Its front was dappled with brown and yellow feathers, and it stared at the wolf, saying nothing. Celeste slowly backed away from Simon, her body low and her ears flat.

"When you need me, I'll be waiting," she said to Simon before disappearing back into the shadows.

He bowed his head and took a shaky breath. That had been close—too close. He should have bolted back into the L.A.I.R., but the break-in had proven that the school wasn't safe from her, either. Nowhere was. Whatever secrets she claimed to know, whatever deals she tried to make, she would fight to the bitter end, just like Orion. And just like Simon.

Only once he'd steadied himself again did he spot the loose stone at the base of Darryl's statue. He didn't dare hope, not after Celeste had been prowling the grounds, but out of habit, he nudged the stone aside with his toe—and to his astonishment, a colorful postcard was hidden underneath.

His chest tightened. Glancing warily into the darkness where Celeste had disappeared, he knelt on the freezing ground and carefully extracted the postcard from its hiding place. On the front was a picture of a delicate web in the middle of a garden bursting with flowers. Several drops of dew were caught in the complicated pattern, and when

Simon squinted, he could see an orb spider sitting near the edge, waiting for her prey.

He flipped the card over. On the other side, in his mother's loopy handwriting, was a single line.

Actions speak louder than intentions. Trust no one.

He read her writing three times as he shivered in the winter air. There was no address—no city or state or hint of where she and Orion might have gone. His hopes evaporated. He and his friends were on their own this time.

The howl of one of the wolves patrolling the zoo cut through the silence, and he heard the soft crunch of a dead leaf nearby. Clutching his postcard, he looked around, his pulse racing. No one was there.

You're never alone.

His grandfather's words whispered in his ear as if Leo were standing over him. Simon shuddered, and this time it had nothing to do with the cold. A promise or a warning—he couldn't be sure, not anymore.

He hurried back toward the center of the zoo, listening hard for any sign of more unwanted company, but the night air seemed to come alive as a symphony of animals played around him. The call of a bird on the overhanging trellis, the buzz of an insect despite the cold, the meowing of a stray cat that must have found its way into the zoo—they were always there. Always listening, always watching.

As Simon reached the eagle statue that marked the secret tunnel to Nolan's room, the strange owl landed in a nearby tree on silent wings, only the rustle of branches alerting Simon to its presence. For a split second, their eyes met, and neither of them said a word.

Trust no one.

With one more gulp of freezing air, Simon ducked into the tunnel, leaving the foreboding winter night behind.